The Colourful Cases of Sherlock Holmes

(Volume 1)

From The Notes of
John H. Watson M.D.

Edited by

Roger Riccard

First published in 2022 by
The Irregular Special Press
for Baker Street Studios Ltd
Endeavour House
170 Woodland Road, Sawston
Cambridge, CB22 3DX, UK

ISBN: 978-1-901091-85-4

Cover Concept: Antony J. Richards

Consulting detective icon courtesy of openclipart.org, Palette icon by Daniel Bruce
courtesy of Iconscout, Boxing Glove icon courtesy of the Noun Project, Grail icon
courtesy of freesvg.org, Parrot icon created by Arthur Bauer of the Noun Project,
Gravestone icon by Iconic of the Noun Project.

Typeset in 8/11/20pt Palatino

About the Author

Roger Riccard has Scottish roots, which trace his lineage back to the Roses of Highland, Scotland. This ancestry encouraged his interest in the writings of Sir Arthur Conan Doyle. He is now the author of over fifty stories featuring the world's first consulting detective.

He lives in a suburb of Los Angeles. When not editing Watson's notes of Sherlock Holmes adventures, he is singing with a group which entertains at retirement homes, or watching baseball, crime dramas, musicals and old movies (Thank you, Turner Classics!) and British mysteries on BBC America.

Note to the Reader:

As with all the stories I put forth about the world's first consulting detective, Mr. Sherlock Holmes, I must give thanks and credit to his original chronicler, Dr. John H. Watson. While not all his notes are complete or, in some cases, orderly, those which were left to Mrs. Hudson's care and subsequently entrusted to her grandniece, my 'Grandma Ruby (*nee* Hudson)' of New York, in the days leading up to World War II, have provided the essential facts of the tales herein. I have attempted to flesh out historical and geographical details via internet research and networking with other Sherlockians and British associates. I beg the reader's indulgence for any errors and trust that the stories in this collection shall be entertaining in and of themselves.

Roger Riccard
Los Angeles, CA, USA

IN MEMORY OF MY ROSILYN,
A LOVING PARTNER IN ALL THINGS
WHO BROUGHT TRUE COLOUR TO MY LIFE
YOU ARE MISSED MORE THAN WORDS CAN SAY
YOU WILL BE LOVED AND REMEMBERED,
ALWAYS

Contents

5 Star Review by Nicholus Schroeder

The Colourful Cases of Sherlock Holmes: Volume One is a mystery/detective book by Roger Riccard. The beloved detective Sherlock Holmes takes on multiple cases in this book over different time periods. Sherlock will be taking on cases that would be impossible for the average detective to solve. In one such case, he has to locate the whereabouts of a famous painting with little to go on in terms of clues. Sherlock will have to rely on his skills and his close friend, Dr. John H. Watson, to help solve these baffling and intricate cases. Join the greatest detective of all on his quest to find the truth behind the bewildering puzzles that are his cases.

What I loved most about this book were the multiple cases presented to me instead of a single 'main' case that had to be solved for the entire book's length. The inclusion of separate unrelated cases helped keep things fresh and interesting. My personal favourite has to be *The Golden Grail* case as that one was a real head-scratcher for me to try to solve before Sherlock. The complexity of the cases was great too as it took me a while to piece everything together or to come up with a theory (playing detective is a hobby of mine) and that's what makes this a well-written detective book. A book in this genre should draw in the reader and make them put on their detective cap and *The Colourful Cases of Sherlock Holmes* did this beautifully. The character of Sherlock was well-written, as were the supporting characters. Roger Riccard was able to create some cinematic-like scenes and that's how I pictured them. This book kept me entertained and so I have no worries recommending it to fans of mystery/detective books or readers that enjoy a good puzzle.

Introduction

From the very beginning, with *A Study in Scarlet*, the stories about Sherlock Holmes written by Dr. John H. Watson have been interspersed with colourful cases such as:

The Red-Headed League
The Five Orange Pips
The Blue Carbuncle
The Copper Beeches
Silver Blaze
The Yellow Face
Black Peter
The Golden Pince-Nez
The Red Circle
The Retired Colourman

In this vein I have searched through the good Doctor's notes and found some other cases which suggested similar colourful titles.

I have attempted to verify historical facts, and other pertinent information about the Victorian and Edwardian eras with English colleagues and Sherlockian experts. At times I may have taken some literary license for which I ask the reader's indulgence.

All in all, Holmes and Watson were involved with some fascinating cases and it is my sincere hope that you will enjoy them.

Roger Riccard

The Olive Garden Painting

Introduction

In January 1900, after the case I have recorded elsewhere as *The Twain Papers*[1], I was going back over my notes and my curiosity was aroused at the detail my friend, the consulting detective Sherlock Holmes, had recounted about one of the suspects, John Clay. As readers of my writings of the adventures of the celebrated criminologist will recall, Clay was arrested in 1890 for his attempt to tunnel into the vaults of the Coburg branch of the City and Suburban Bank, using his position as a pawnbroker's clerk in the adventure of *The Red-Headed League*[2].

As I pondered my notes at my writing desk, Holmes was lounging by the fire, going over the morning papers for any possible mishap which might be of interest to him. A steady stream of smoke was arising from behind his newspaper as I stole a glance in that direction. As this was accompanied by various grunts and harumphs, I deduced nothing of interest was catching his eye. Thus, I chose to interrupt his task with questions of my own.

"I say, Holmes, I find myself most curious at the great detail of information you seem to have gathered regarding John Clay, the self-proclaimed Duke of Dartford."

[1] *Sherlock Holmes and the Case of the Twain Papers* by Roger Riccard (Baker Street Studios Limited, 2014).
[2] *The Adventure of the Red-Headed League* by Arthur Conan Doyle (*Strand Magazine*, 1891).

I confess, I knew that title would get a reaction out of my friend, for he had made it clear Clay's pretention to such a rank was invalid under the standards of British peerage. Holmes slowly lowered his paper and stared in my direction with skeptical eyes.

Setting *The Daily Telegraph* aside, he removed the pipe from his mouth and leaned on the arm of the chair. "Your attempt to goad me into responding is most transparent, Doctor. As you recall, I sympathized with Clay's plight of being unable to claim the title of his grandfather, due to his own father being born out of an illicit liaison by the Duke with Clay's gypsy grandmother. The man himself is a talented fellow, whose path was inextricably bent by Professor Moriarty. My only fault with him is that he appears unable to mend his ways. Though we shall see."

"So, you stand by your disagreement with Inspector Jones's assertion that Clay's crimes included murder?" I asked, for I found this to be the great crux of the matter regarding Clay's behaviour.

Holmes shook his head and declared, "Whenever someone eludes their pursuer for as long as Clay did Jones, the hunter has a tendency to exaggerate the skills of the hunted. After all, were the fellow not so dangerous and clever, he should have been caught long ago. I do not dispute that persons were killed because of actions attributed to Clay. But I am certain Clay himself was not the killer. His job was to 'crack the crib' as Jones implied. His skills are in his hands, which are most sensitive and artistically steady. The same talent which allows him to forge documents and works of art is also that which gives him the ability to open any combination safe or pick any lock. Every time someone was killed, it was at least a two-man job with the second person providing the 'muscle', so to speak. Even the tunnel from Wilson's pawn shop to the bank vault was largely dug by Clay's partner whom he had smuggled in behind Wilson's back. There were no callouses on his own hands. His talent lay in calculating the mathematics required to reach the vault and to carefully chisel out the proper floor tile, as one might skilfully carve a sculpture."

I nodded, then read from my notes, "You said, 'Personally, I do not believe Clay to be a violent man. His forte was forgery and counterfeiting cheques. His victims were always among the wealthy or banks, or insurance companies. His pathological need being to take from those who were of a station in life which he felt he was denied because his bloodline was tainted. I also believe his founding of the orphanage in Cornwall was an effort to help those who, like himself, were deprived a legitimate childhood'. Have I recorded that correctly?"

"Nearly word for word, Watson and I stand by them."

Holmes poured himself some coffee, apparently not realizing how much time he had spent on the morning papers. When he took a sip of the lukewarm liquid, he made a face and rang for Mrs. Hudson.

Our landlady appeared within a minute, assessed the situation with a sigh and without being asked, she took up the coffee pot. "Would you like it refilled with coffee or tea, Mr. Holmes?"

"Whatever is convenient, Mrs. Hudson," he replied with a wave of his hand.

"Either would be absolutely fine with me," I said. "In fact, let me help you and save you another trip up the stairs."

Mrs. Hudson is hale and hearty but she is somewhat older than Holmes and myself and, as a friend and a doctor, it seems only polite to relieve her of any exertion whenever possible.

Within minutes I had returned with a fresh pot of hot coffee. Holmes was beside the bookshelf, perusing a volume of his indexes. I poured him a cup, set it by his chair, then returned to my desk where I could record details of the conversation that I hoped would follow.

My friend of many years returned to his seat by the fire, index in hand, took a sip of the fresh coffee and re-charged his pipe. As he did so he commented, "Are you certain you wish to take the time to do this today? Would not the winsome Mrs. Savage be more companionable?"

I smiled at his mention of Adelaide Savage. We had come across the widow of Victor Savage[1] and her children during our investigation into Samuel Clemens's missing papers. Events had led to Mrs. Savage and I spending time together and we had fallen into an easy friendship which we had agreed to continue.

"Adelaide and Marina are spending the day shopping. She and I are dining together tonight. Thus, I am free to hear the tale of your early run-in with John Clay."

Holmes set the index upon the table, crossed his long legs and resumed sending plumes of smoke toward our discoloured ceiling. His long, thin face took on a languid look as his steel-grey eyes turned in my direction. His mood seemed to match the overcast day outside our window as he spoke.

"Very well. Since the London criminal classes have chosen to avoid the inclement weather, rather than ply their trades, I can spare the time for you. It may be just as well. Since Clay is now out and about, there is every possibility we shall run into him again and you should have all the facts."

He pointed the stem of his briarwood pipe at me and began. "I first came across John Clay in a case I was investigating shortly after you and I began to share these rooms. You may recall that I was coming and going at all hours in those days. I was starting out in my profession and could not afford to be as selective in my choice of cases. I am afraid I was not good company for you during the first few months. The thought had not yet occurred to me that a companion in my investigations could be of value."

I was tempted to respond but chose not to take the chance on distracting him from his narrative.

Noting my silence, he continued, "It was the second Tuesday in February. I was contacted by the National Gallery. By Professor Wooley, in fact, whom you may recall from the

---

[1] Victor Savage was the victim of his uncle's deceit in *The Adventure of the Dying Detective* by Sir Arthur Conan Doyle (1897 per Baring-Gould). In the Granada television version, Adelaide is his wife and George and Marina, their children. Victor's uncle, Culverton Smith, evicted them from their home once his nephew was dead.

origami case[2] later that spring. I responded to his request for my presence as soon as I had received his message early that morning. Professor Wooley was of tremendous assistance to me in those early years. Much of what I learned about art and the forging thereof, I owe to his tutelage.

"Upon my arrival I was directed to his laboratory where he greeted me with a hearty handshake ..."

---

[2] *The Origami Mystery* from *A Sherlock Holmes Alphabet of Cases, Volume 3 (K-O)* by Roger Riccard (Baker Street Studios Limited, 2019).

Giuseppe Cesari's *The Agony in the Garden (Christ on the Mount of Olives)* painted between 1597and 1598 and measuring 28 by 37.5 inches.

Chapter One

"Sherlock, my lad! How good of you to come so quickly. I'm afraid we have a bit of bad business here and I need your unique talents."

Professor Wooley greeted his student with a combination of enthusiasm and concern. The elderly art expert was looking well in his late middle age, with a full head of grey hair and a thick moustache with a medium sized beard. He was *sans* coat, but wearing a waistcoat which stretched tightly across his pudgy frame. The hand he held out to Holmes was more like a meaty paw and the fingers were calloused where paintbrushes had made their mark over the years. Holmes took it and said, "I am yours to command Professor. What has been stolen?"

Wooley tilted his head, "Now, how did you deduce that?"

Holmes deigned to explain, "If something were merely damaged, you would not need my services, as you have a number of conservators, in addition to yourself, to address it. If a person were injured or missing, you would exhibit far greater concern with no time for pleasantries. The fact that you know of my work as a consulting detective makes it highly probable then, that something has been stolen and you seek my help in its restitution."

Wooley folded his hands across his ample waistline, pursed his lips and nodded gravely. "Yes, Sherlock. A highly valuable painting has gone missing. Come with me and let me show you."

The two walked back to a section of the lab devoted to paint restoration and framing. There were three men in the area, working on paintings of various styles and sizes. When they reached one particular easel, Wooley threw back the sheet covering the work. Before he could say a word, Holmes had pulled out his magnifying lens and was examining the canvas minutely. It was a painting of Christ in His agony in the Olive Garden. In a matter of seconds he declared, "Not an original Cesari. Though it is indicative of the period. Late 16th century, I should think."

Wooley nodded, "Indeed. Your memory serves you well. Cesari was one of the last of the Italian Mannerist style before Baroque became the rage. This is supposed to be one of his works for Pope Clement VIII. As you can see by close examination, however, this is not the original. The paint is too new and the brush strokes are off. Even the colours aren't quite right."

"When was the last time this painting was on display to the public?"

"About three years ago. Then it was returned to its owner until last month when we arranged another loan for our Italian Masters Exhibition. I can get you an exact date if you wish?"

"Thank you. Who was this generous lender?"

"It was part of an arrangement we have with the Fetherstonhaugh family at Uppark in West Sussex. They are great collectors of art and have been gracious enough to share their works with the British public through our exhibitions programme."

Holmes nodded, "I presume there was no question as to its authenticity at the time. Did you discover this forgery yourself, or did someone point it out to you?"

Wooley pointed a thumb at his own chest, "I inspected it myself upon its arrival, as for insurance purposes we are obliged to carry out condition checks, to ensure that no damage has occurred in transit which could be attributed to the gallery, you understand? It was quite genuine, I assure you. Then, the other day, one of my restorers noticed that something did not seem quite right. A bright young lad from Oxford by the name of John Clay. He has been working on cleaning it for some time, as this is a service we provide for our lenders, if they so wish. He brought it to my attention late yesterday."

Holmes pondered that remark as he continued his perusal of the painting. Using his thumb, he carefully ran it across the edge of the canvas. Then he examined it with his lens and nodded to himself. Returning to the front, he asked Professor Wooley, "How long has Clay been working on this?"

Wooley rubbed his beard in thought and finally replied, "Let me think ... I believe it's been just over two weeks now."

Holmes hummed and asked, "What took him so long to realize it was a forgery?"

Wooley smiled, "He is a gifted fellow, but he is still learning his craft. His task was a gentle clean and to touch up areas with significant cracks or damage. His prior assignments have been the works of the early Italian Renaissance masters. This is his first foray into the Mannerist period."

"His curiosity became aroused when he noticed a variation in the gold tones. The whites also seemed to be inconsistent, which made them difficult to restore."

"And just where is this prodigy today?" asked the detective.

"He has a lecture to attend at Oxford this afternoon and tutorials tomorrow. He is scheduled to return on Friday to continue this assignment."

Holmes tapped the edge of the magnifying glass to his lips as he continued to stare at the painting. Finally, he requested, "Take me to the gallery's stores. I need to have a look."

Arriving at one of the sub-basements, Wooley reached for the knob with his keys, but Holmes stopped him. "A moment if you please, Professor."

Kneeling by the door handle, Holmes again employed his powerful lens and examined the lock for several seconds. Then he stood and bid Wooley to unlock the room. Before entering, he looked at the floor and stated, "Obviously several people have been here since the painting was retrieved."

The Professor replied, "Oh, yes. Well, we certainly hadn't suspected a thief had been here or more care would have been taken. We're in the middle of a changeover from our Winter to

Spring Exhibition so many works have been coming and going from the stores. There will be quite a night of festivities on the evening of March the first, when everything is ready."

He leaned toward his former pupil and spoke conspiratorially, "Frankly, Sherlock, this is why I've called for you instead of the police. I don't wish to create bad publicity when we are so close to the launch of the new season."

"Understood, Professor. Let me just make a quick examination. Where was the painting kept?"

Wooley pointed to a numbered bay with racks raised off the ground, full of framed paintings. Holmes asked, "Was the Cesari in the middle of this section or towards the front?"

The Professor opened a small cabinet of index cards and a large ledger on a desk. "The records say it was in this particular section and I can actually visualise it being in the third or fourth one back."

Holmes pulled out the first couple of frames and set them aside as he examined the base of the racking in the approximate area where the Cesari had been leaning. Satisfied after less than a minute, he returned the other works to their positions and replied to his old art mentor, "I have seen enough. Let us return to your office."

Chapter Two

Closing the door behind him, Holmes sat down opposite Wooley. The Professor's old oak desk was piled with stacks of various papers and folders. The hazards of being one of the foremost scholars in his field, everyone wanted his opinion, approval or services. He pushed an ashtray toward Holmes. This was the only space he allowed for smoking, so as not to risk damage to the precious artworks in his charge.

He offered a cigar to the detective, who took it graciously. After he lit his own, he pulled it from his lips and studied it. "A filthy habit, Sherlock. Every New Year I resolve to give it up and before January is over, I'm back at it. The noxious weed is just too powerful and comforting. I also find I tend to eat more, and more often, when without it. Lord knows," he said, patting his ample waist with his free hand, "I certainly do not need to over-indulge in my diet!"

Turning his eyes back onto Holmes he asked, "Well, what are your thoughts? Can you determine what happened and what steps may be taken to retrieve the original painting?"

Holmes leaned back in the rickety wooden chair and exhaled a long stream of grey smoke. Picking a speck of tobacco from his lip, he examined it momentarily. In a contemplative mood he replied, "Now why do you suppose this particular tobacco leaf stuck to my lip?"

Wooley looked at him as if he were into his cups, "What?"

"Forgive me, Professor. But like this speck of tobacco, I must contemplate why your thief proceeded to steal that particular painting. Was it mere convenience? Did he have a buyer already? Was he threatened? Was he hired? When did he do it? How did he substitute the forgery? How did he get the original out of the building, or is it still here, hidden somewhere until he can retrieve it safely?

"These are the things one must deal with in my line of work, Professor. I need to contemplate them all as I conduct my investigations."

Wooley nodded, "Thank you, Sherlock. I realize this is a long shot and the painting may be long gone. However, the relationships we have with our patrons in the loan programme may be irreparably damaged if it is learned we have lost a masterpiece."

Holmes stood and left his cigar in the ash tray so as not to trail smoke through the Gallery. He shook his mentor's hand and stated, "Rest assured I will do all in my power to discover the truth as discreetly as possible. In the meantime, I implore you to treat the painting you do have even more securely than you would have the original. Do not leave it in your laboratory where someone else may notice its flaws. Put it back in the storage room and lock it up tightly. In fact, place it in an area other than where it was before. When Clay returns, swear him to secrecy and reassign him to some other task. Whether I have answers or not, I shall give you a progress report by Thursday afternoon. Now tell me, what does this John Clay look like and what lecture was he going to attend?"

*****

Upon leaving the Gallery, Holmes was delayed in finding a cab due to the storm which had begun. Pedestrians were now seeking the shelter of a hansom cab or growler instead of attempting to walk through the quickly falling snow. As his brain worked through the directions his investigation must go, he was able to order his method of pursuit of clues. Thus, when he finally flagged down an empty cab, he ordered it to Baker

Street, there to wait while he threw some items into a carpet bag for an overnight trip. Then it was on to Paddington station to catch the next train to Oxford.

Chapter Three

The weather in Oxford was faring a little better than London. The fifty-mile train ride had taken the detective out from under the storm clouds over the capital. The day was cool and the ground was damp from previous storms, but the atmosphere itself was dry under blue skies with scattered clouds. A short walk from the station took him to the home of Henry Porter, an old acquaintance from university days, who let rooms out to students. The high arched windows of the three-storey structure were a distinguishing feature in this neighbourhood of mostly two-storey brick houses which appeared to blend in to one another with little to tell them apart save their numbers.

He walked in to find construction occurring on the ground floor and spotted Porter speaking with a workman over some plans. The proprietor glanced in his direction, noting his arrival, but held up a hand with index finger extended, indicating this visitor would need to wait one moment. He continued his orders to the labourer, then turned to greet this guest.

"Yes, sir. How may I ... Holmes, is that you?"

"Hello, Porter," replied the detective. "I hope I am not arriving at an inconvenient time."

Porter approached the young detective, hand outstretched. Approaching his mid-forties, the fellow had put on some weight around the middle of his otherwise lean frame. His clean-shaven face had broken into a ready smile at the sight of Holmes and he shook the former student's hand with genuine friendship.

"It's good to see you, Holmes. What brings you to Oxford? Come up for a lecture?"

"In a way," replied Holmes. "I'm sure you recall my unique talents from our little adventure together when I was a student. I have expanded upon those and am now a consulting detective in London. I'm here to do a little investigating related to a problem for a client."

"Little adventure, my eye!" cried Porter. "You saved me a month's worth of receipts and kept the bank from repossessing my property. What can I do for you? Do you need a room?"

Holmes nodded, "If you have one to spare, I may be here for two or three days."

"Say no more. If you don't mind the noise of these workers, I can put you up for a week if need be. Emily will be delighted to see you and as will our little Anna. She's turned into a real beauty. They are out shopping now, but should be home soon."

Holmes smiled at the memory of Porter's wife and daughter, "I look forward to it. I perceive you are expanding your kitchen and dining room to accept more than just your usual handful of lodgers for meals. You are opening up as a public house?"

Porter cocked his head to one side, "Not precisely. The rooms will still only be rented to students or their visiting families. But with the variety of schedules we were keeping the kitchen open for long hours to accommodate them. We decided to open to the public so we could make full use of the time. Certainly, some extra profits will be welcome as well. I have cooks lined up so we can serve lunch and dinner seven days a week once this construction is complete. Breakfast will still be limited to lodgers only."

"A sound plan," agreed Holmes. "If I may set my things in my room, I need to conduct some business over at Wadham."

Having procured his lodgings, the detective proceeded on foot to Wadham College, and from his enquiries there he ascertained where he was likely to find John Clay. Holmes found that he was in good time to obtain a seat in the relevant lecture theatre. Wooley's description of the lad was spot on. The art Professor's eye for detail made it easy for Holmes to locate the gentleman, seated in the front row off to stage left. While Clay himself appeared young, his high forehead so resembled the receding hair of middle years it was difficult to estimate his true age from his looks alone. His habits, however, were those of a typical college student just gaining his maturity and confidence. A white spot high on his forehead was his most distinguishing feature.

Holmes took up a seat on the opposite side of the room, up in the next to last row. The curvature of the tiers would allow him to appear to be watching the lecturer while keeping a peripheral view of Clay throughout. He had the foresight to bring a notebook, so as to appear to be making notes during the session. Still being in his twenties, he would not seem out of place with the other gentlemen in the room.

The theatre itself was not particularly full for this lecture. A mixture of students and other faculty still left plenty of open seats. To himself, Holmes wondered if it were the subject matter, or the presentation techniques of the speaker, which accounted for such a low turnout. At the top of the hour a gentleman walked in from stage right and set a sheaf of papers upon the lectern. He was quite tall and thin, much like Holmes himself. Of an age which the detective estimated to be about forty, he was clean-shaven, pale, and ascetic-looking. His forehead was more of a protruding dome from a well-receded, slicked down, black hairline. He had deeply sunken eyes, and shoulders which were severely rounded so, even standing, he appeared to be hunched over a desk.

A childhood memory stirred in Holmes's mind. It was not a pleasant one.

Having set up his paperwork, the guest lecturer looked out upon the room. If he were disappointed at the turnout, he did not reveal it. In fact, a smirk upon his face was almost defiant. Even as he physically looked up at his audience, he appeared to be looking down upon them for even daring to show up for a lecture which he presumed would be far above their puny understanding.

His voice belied his stature and in a forceful, yet pleasant, tenor he announced, "Gentlemen, we are here to discuss the dynamics of an asteroid. If you are here in error, please proceed to the exit now."

For the next several seconds his gaze wandered about the room, assuring himself all were agreeable participants. His eyes lingered on Holmes for a few seconds, being an unfamiliar face in the crowd. Holmes stared back, confidently and the professor moved on to take in the rest of the room. Once satisfied, he began his lecture.

Chapter Four

The Professor's speaking ability outshone his topic. He could have been an actor performing a Shakespearean soliloquy in the way he used his voice and adopted a distinctive style. It was tempting to become lost in the presentation and lose sight of the substance. Holmes, being more interested in John Clay than the topic at hand, could not help but notice the mesmerizing effect upon the audience. Indeed, it took great effort to concentrate upon the task at hand.

His study of John Clay revealed a fellow who took copious notes and kept rapt attention upon this intellectual professor. Left-handed. A disciplined mind. Great attention to detail. Ability to maintain focus. These were among the many traits which Holmes could now ascribe to young Clay.

Roughly an hour and a half after it began, the lecture came to an end. Holmes kept writing in his notebook until Clay rose from his seat. There were murmurings among the crowd as they filed out. Three older men in particular, likely visiting scientists, were excitedly debating the points the Professor had made. When Clay finally got up, he was one of the few who dared to walk over to the Professor, where a small group of students had gathered. The academic, in what seemed an oddly tender motion, placed a hand upon Clay's shoulder and said something quietly. Clay himself was disciplined enough not to react, but one of the other students stole a glance in Holmes's direction. Whether by some sixth sense or other subconscious trigger, Holmes knew he could linger no longer and he should not look further upon Clay or the Professor, lest he draw attention to himself. There was danger in the room. Though how he knew, Holmes could not ascertain. He had subconscious observations however and left the room without another glance in Clay's direction.

Returning to the sunlight, which by now was fading quickly toward dusk, Holmes could feel a palpable relief to be out from under the Professor's scrutiny. Something was amiss. He could sense it without knowing what it was. The way that handful of students gathered around was more than just appreciation for a well-delivered lecture. In fact, Holmes was sure few, if any, of those lads could even fathom the concepts brought forth. What he had witnessed was almost worshipful. Despite his years of developing a cool and logical mind, he could not suppress a shudder at the thought.

He took up a place beneath an elm tree and waited for the departure of Clay. He contemplated the relevance of Clay attending this particular lecture. It appeared incongruous that a student studying art and working as an art restorer, would have an interest in astrophysics. Having witnessed the commanding presence of the lecturer, however, he appreciated the attraction of the performance, even in the absence of interest in the subject matter.

It was several minutes later before the fellow exited the building. He was in the company of two other students who had also attended the Professor after the lecture. They walked in the opposite direction from Holmes and he casually took up a pace to follow at a distance. As he passed by the entrance to the building, however, the Professor and two more students appeared. The young men were so busy questioning their teacher that one of them failed to avoid Holmes and bumped into him severely enough to knock him off his feet. The lad helped Holmes to stand again and the Professor, uncharacteristically it seemed, offered an apology on his student's behalf.

"I am sorry, young man. I am constantly admonishing my students to be more observant. Yet the enthusiasm of youth often overrides the necessary discipline required. Are you quite all right?"

Holmes brushed himself off and noted that his quarry had disappeared from sight. "No harm done, Professor," answered the detective. Then he noticed that the lecturer had picked up his fallen notebook and was looking at it. Fortunately, he had taken a few pages of notes and made some sketches on the topic in question. His observations of Clay he had committed to memory, as was his habit.

The elder man handed the notebook back to him, "You appear to have some elementary grasp of my subject, sir. Are you a student of astrophysics?"

"I am an alumnus, just here for a visit," replied Holmes. "My interests are far and varied and I was informed you that were a fascinating lecturer. I thought I would drop in and see the attraction. It was a very interesting experience."

The Professor gazed deeply upon Holmes for a few seconds with a frown. At last, he said, "What is your name, young man?"

"Sherlock Holmes, sir."

The Professor squinted, appearing to be searching his memory. He had tutored or taught hundreds of students in his time and this fellow seemed familiar somehow[1]. Tucking the thought away for the moment he said, "Well, Sherlock Holmes, when you get a chance, you should read my book on the subject. If you still find it *interesting*, come and see me and we can speak some more. Come, gentlemen."

He turned on his heel and his entourage followed quickly, leaving Holmes to ponder, briefly, if this encounter was mere chance or a deliberate attempt to distract him from following Clay. He shook his head. Even at this early stage of his career as a detective, he had come to be very wary of coincidences.

With darkness now approaching, Holmes chose to return to Porter's house and plan out the next steps in his investigations. The moment he walked through the door he was met with a happy cry of his first name.

---

[1] Some sources suggest Moriarty was a mathematics tutor to Holmes when he was young.

Emily Porter strode over from the kitchen door and threw her long arms around him. She was a tall, thin woman with long brown hair emphasizing her considerable height. Holmes, usually reticent at such shows of affection, tolerated this display, as he was genuinely fond of the Porter family from his days at university. She, at last, backed away, still holding his shoulders as she looked him up and down. "You've hardly changed at all. Henry tells me you are a detective in London. Do you work for Scotland Yard then?"

A slight smirk crossed Holmes's face as he answered, "I am a *private* consulting detective, Mrs. Porter. Though, on occasion, I have been able to assist the Yard on a case."

Not one for the strict decorum of the Victorian age, the lady playfully slapped Holmes's shoulder and stated, "You are of an age where you may call me *Emily*, Sherlock."

Another voice called from the kitchen door, "And what may he call me, mother?" The two adults turned their heads toward the source of the question. There stood a young woman of perhaps seventeen years. Nearly as tall as her mother, Anna Porter's heart shaped face was surrounded by chestnut curls which gently brushed her shoulders. A coquettish smile played upon her lips as she tilted her head fetchingly at the young man her mother had just bestowed such affection upon.

Even Holmes's disciplined detachment against entanglements with the feminine gender could not prevent him being taken aback at what a beauty Anna had become. She had been but eight years old when last, he'd seen her. A playful, outgoing child with a keen intelligence for one so young doted upon by her parents, and even by some of the lodgers since she no doubt reminded them of their little sisters back home. They often enlisted her aid in reading examination style questions to them so that they could practice answering them, and in so doing she had gained a thirst for knowledge and began reading books at a much higher level than normal for a girl her age. As if to prove the point Holmes noted a volume of *Plato's Apology* tucked under her arm.

Noting the brief, but telling, look upon her former lodger's face, Emily Porter smiled and said, "Mr. Holmes, this is our

Anna. If you are not otherwise engaged, I'm sure her father would give you permission to call upon her any time you wish. Anna, come and say 'hello' to Sherlock Holmes."

The young lady seemed to glide across the room, so graceful was her walk. She curtsied to Holmes and held out her hand. The detective bowed over it as he took her delicate digits in his own long fingers but did not offer a kiss. He merely said, "*Enchanté* Miss Porter," and tried not to stare into her brown, doe-like eyes.

Anna, though a bit disappointed at not receiving a courtly kiss, replied, "Such a gentleman. A refreshing change from most of our boarders. I am pleased to meet you, Mr. Holmes. Will you be staying with us long?"

"I must return to London no later than Friday morning. I have hopes to conclude my business in Oxford by tomorrow afternoon."

Anna looked disappointed as she replied, "How unfortunate."

Holmes felt it necessary to curtail the direction this awkward conversation was taking before it had even taken root, let alone begun to develop green shoots, "My business requires me to travel often and keep odd hours." Turning to Mrs. Porter he added, "It also, occasionally, can be dangerous, as I am frequently confronting members of the criminal classes. So, you see, Emily, I have chosen to avoid engaging in courtships. The life I lead is not one which is conducive to a typically safe and happy household. In point of fact, I recently began sharing my rooms with a doctor, Which, I expect, may become quite convenient as my career progresses."

Emily Porter's countenance resigned itself to the fact Holmes may not be a good match for her daughter after all. As a good hostess, however, she carried on and replied, "Well then, we must take the best care of you possible while you are here. Dinner will be ready in half an hour. If you go up to your room, there's fresh hot water in the basin, get yourself settled and we'll see you shortly ... be sure to bring your appetite!"

Holmes nodded in appreciation at her understanding, bowed again to young Anna and merely said, "I see you are still engaged in obtaining a first-class education. Even if the university is not willing to encourage you and other ladies of your intelligence, I certainly do so and wish you well and God speed." Then he took quickly to the stairs. Anna frowned in disappointment and put down her book as she and Emily returned to the kitchen. To her mother she merely said, "It's all right, Mum. It would have been nice to have someone intelligent and tall like him to literally look up to mentally and physically, but he wasn't the most handsome of suitors."

Emily shook her head at her daughter, "Looks are a fine thing, but when it comes to relationships, dear, you must look to the soul. Mr. Holmes is a good fellow with a stout heart. It is a pity he has chosen bachelorhood. I hope he does not regret it in the years ahead."

As the dining room was not yet open to the public, the only persons present for dinner were Holmes, Henry Porter and four student boarders. The ladies remained in the kitchen, keeping food hot for second helpings and preparing dessert.

Once settled in and having said the blessing, Porter enquired of the detective how his day had gone. "Did you find out anything to help you, Holmes?"

Holmes, remembering how much he enjoyed Emily Porter's cooking, smiled briefly at the taste of the gravy-smothered roast, and replied, "I was able to gather some interesting information. I attended the lecture of one Professor James Moriarty. Do you know him?"

Porter shook his head, "Only by reputation. I've heard he is a difficult taskmaster, but apparently quite brilliant himself."

One of the students, Leo Daley, spoke up, "Difficult hardly describes it, sir. He is impossible to please. He expects everyone to understand his theories because he speaks so well. But, if you ask me, he's all talk. His theories are so abstract and esoteric they cannot be proved or disproved. But because he speaks of them with such conviction, everyone just assumes he is correct. Of course, you cannot win an argument with him. Certainly, no student would dare contradict him for fear of failing his course or being reprimanded for insubordination."

Holmes looked with interest upon this young man and replied, "I can certainly understand your impression. Yet, he seems to have gathered a following of students who hang upon his every word."

All the students at the table nodded. Another, Lawrence Berra, spoke up and offered, "Ah, 'The Moriarty Mob'. They're a group of fellows with whom he has some special connection, or perhaps a hold over. They will do anything he asks. In turn, he tutors them in any subject where they need assistance."

Holmes decided to expand upon that, "Normally such actions would appear equitable, even commendable, for a professor to have such a caring attitude toward his students. Yet I sense you all have some ambivalent feelings toward him. Is there something unsavoury you suspect?"

They all looked at each other as if they'd said too much. Porter decided to put them at ease, "Gentlemen, I assure you, you can trust Mr. Holmes with your thoughts. He is one of our most admirable alumni and was an outstanding student himself. Please, feel free to share. This table is always open to discussion."

With such assurance, Edward Ford chimed in, "Nobody's ever been able to prove anything, Mr. Holmes. But circumstances suggest some of his followers have been involved in thefts within the University."

Holmes tilted his head and enquired, "What sort of thefts? What was stolen?"

"Personal property, watches, jewelled rings, a bicycle, those sorts of things. Mostly from students, but once in a while a don as well."

The final member of this foursome, Francis Robinson, spoke up and added, "Don't forget about the missing examination papers and laboratory equipment!"

"Yes," agreed Ford. "Just before an important exam was going to be given, which included experimental demonstrations, all copies of the chemical laboratory test paper went missing and several vital pieces of equipment as well. Three of Moriarty's students were scheduled to sit that paper and it was postponed for a week while he took extra time to tutor them. Or so we've heard."

"I presume no one was caught for any of these crimes?" queried Holmes.

Daley spoke again, "Nary a soul. There were no witnesses. Some of the boys were questioned but they provided alibis for each other or the Professor for them."

"Funny thing though," said Robinson. "The missing laboratory equipment turned up two weeks later in a storage closet. Just reappeared out of nowhere."

The detective leaned upon the table with his elbows, hands folded under his chin as he gazed upon the students across from him. "This is most interesting, gentlemen. Tell me, are any of you acquainted with a student named John Clay?"

Berra spoke up, "I've had a class or two with that one. Odd duck he is. Acts like a lackey around the Professor, but to the public he claims to be the grandson of a duke with royal blood in his veins."

Daley added, "I've heard he's an orphan whose parents were gypsies. Ever notice the hole in his right ear? Used to wear an earring as a lad."

Robinson inserted, "I was told Moriarty adopted him after his parents died. That's how he came to be able to attend here."

Holmes nodded in satisfaction at this information and asked, "Was he ever suspected in the thefts?"

Ford laughed, "His *Royal Highness*? Not a chance! He is a painter and sculptor, that sort of thing. Not at breaking and entering. Such would be beneath him."

The detective thanked the boys for their candour, and they all returned to their excellent meal. Afterward, the young men went off in their own directions, some to their rooms to study, others off to activities about town. Holmes and Porter retreated to the parlour where they took up cigars and Porter asked about the case.

"So, Holmes, are you investigating Professor Moriarty or John Clay?" asked the landlord, as he sent a stream of smoke into the air.

Holmes crossed his right ankle over his left knee as he leaned on the arm of the overstuffed chair and replied, "Just between us, I am investigating an attempted theft of a painting from the National Gallery. John Clay was the person who reported the substituted forgery. I had no knowledge that Professor Moriarty was part of the faculty here until today."

Porter leaned forward, elbows on his knees, the lamplight reflecting off his receding forehead, "Wait, I don't understand. It sounds like Clay is merely a witness after the fact. Surely if he were the thief, he would not have reported the substitution. Why would you follow him here?"

"There is a deep game going on here," replied the detective. "Note I said, *attempted theft*. The painting has not yet left the Gallery. I am certain John Clay knows this. But the audacity of the plot to steal it requires at least one other party. It is my hope he will lead me to that person."

"And you think the Professor might be him?"

Holmes leaned back in his chair, folding his hands in his lap, contemplating before he answered. Then he said, "Unknown at this time. However, he certainly is bright enough and possesses the aptitude to convince Clay to become involved. However, he may have merely introduced the lad to someone else of means without knowing the ultimate scheme. Risking one's reputation as an academic of his standing would be an unusual action, unless there are unknown reasons making it worthwhile. No, I cannot accuse him yet. I need to learn more about him than the schoolboy tales we heard this evening. Is Professor Nichols still teaching?"

Porter shook his head, "Nichols retired last year. Inherited the family dairy farm. He occasionally comes up to give a lecture, but he's not involved in college activities. Your best option to learn more about Moriarty would be Professor Maddux."

"Maddux knows him well?" queried Holmes.

"As well as anyone here. They've a bit of a rivalry between Moriarty's astrophysics theories and Maddux's higher mathematics."

Holmes smiled, "I remember Professor Maddux and that I had some spirited discussions on equations with respect to the laws of probability with him."

Porter chuckled, "I seem to recall him failing you on a particular assignment based on mathematical probability and that you challenged him with an experiment which proved your point against the odds he had calculated."

"Well, hopefully he won't hold that against me. Are his rooms still in the same place?"

"Yes, though I don't know his teaching schedule. You might check with Ford. He is one of Maddux's students."

Chapter Five

Having Ford's confirmation of his former mathematics lecturer's schedule, Sherlock Holmes set out early the next morning to continue his investigation. His effort was rewarded when he found Professor Maddux in his rooms, the door ajar.

The mathematician was seated at his desk in his shirtsleeves. Round-rimmed eyeglasses perched on the end of his stubby nose, adding to the overall circular shape of his chubby face. He was clean-shaven and his once jet-black hair had receded high upon his crown, now being streaked through with grey.

Standing unnoticed in the doorway, Holmes gently knocked on the frame to gain the Professor's attention. Maddux looked up, squinting over the rims of his reading glasses. Seeing the tall man filling the gap in his doorway, he assumed it was a student and said, "Not now, young man. Come and see me after lectures if you still have questions." Then he returned his gaze to the papers on his desk.

Holmes smiled, "I am afraid I shall not be attending your class, Professor Maddux. As I recall, you kicked me out."

The sound of Holmes's voice triggered Maddux's memory. He felt around the papers on his desk and found his bifocals. Exchanging them for the thick lenses he was wearing, he gazed again upon the figure, who had now stepped fully into the room, closing the door behind him.

"Sherlock Holmes? Is that you, lad?"

"It's good to see you again, Professor."

Maddux stood and walked around the desk to approach his former pupil. Hands on his broad hips, the stout fellow looked Holmes up and down. "Well, you seem to have made something of yourself, young man. Though I would bet a guinea your job has nothing to do with mathematics."

Holmes nodded his head, acquiescing to the Professor's statement. "Only upon a rare occasion. As I am sure you recall, my forte was solving puzzles of a different type."

"You've made a profession of your gift?" asked Maddux, sceptically.

Holmes folded his hands in front of his lean frame and replied, "I am now working in London as a consulting detective. I solve problems for people, including Scotland Yard upon occasion."

"Well, this I must hear. Have a seat, Mr. Holmes."

Holmes moved to the chair opposite the desk from his old teacher and got right to the point. "I am currently investigating a case for the National Gallery. It may only be peripheral, but circumstances have required me to look into a student, John Clay. Do you know him?"

"Clay? Hmm, yes. Yes, he was in my class in his first year. Performed adequately."

"Do you know of any connection between him and Professor Moriarty?"

"Moriarty! That arrogant arse?" exclaimed Maddux.

"Yes," replied Holmes, calmly. "So, I've heard. I have also heard rumours of a close relationship between him and Clay. Some even say an adoption. Do you know of that?"

Maddux leaned back, his chair squeaking under his shifting weight. "Yes, yes, that's right. I do not know if there was an official adoption, but I am aware Moriarty did take the boy in after his gypsy parents were killed when their wagon overturned. There have been rumours about his being a grandson of the Duke of Dartford. His father being the result of a liaison between the Duke and his grandmother, though I've also heard suspicions of rape were raised.

"It wouldn't surprise me if Moriarty didn't take him in to gain an inside track should the boy's claim prevail in court when the present Duke dies."

"Is this the sort of man Moriarty is, then?"

Maddux casually waved his hand and cocked his head, "Oh, I know there is a rivalry of sorts between him and me. You must have heard of it, if you've been poking around. But, in all honesty, there is nothing I would put past that man. You've heard of 'Moriarty's Mob'?"

Holmes nodded, "Yes, but that was from some students, whose words I have to weigh with care. Are you confirming its existence?"

"Oh, it's a fact. Though I'm sure they have another name for themselves. They've never been caught, but trust me, the Chancellor is keeping a close watch on things. Should proof be forthcoming, that self-proclaimed genius will be dismissed, if not actually imprisoned. I have no doubt Clay is in league with them as well."

Holmes nodded, then asked, "Can you tell me which art faculty members can attest to the level of Clay's talents? I need to ascertain just how proficient an artist he is."

Maddux rubbed his jaw as he thought and then declared, "You could check with Professors Caffrey and Mundy. They would be the best judges of his talent."

The mathematician leaned forward, keeping his voice low as he glanced at the door to ensure it was closed, "Whatever you do, Mr. Holmes, if you wish to avoid Moriarty hearing of your investigation, do not speak to Senior Fellow Malachi Stoneman. He is close to Moriarty and I always have the feeling they are in league on some non-academic scheme."

"Such as the thefts about campus?" asked the detective.

"No, not those. I believe it's something on a larger scale, or perhaps an on-going enterprise."

"I shall take your words to heart, Professor," offered the detective. "Thank you for your time and opinions. You have been most helpful."

He rose and shook Maddux's proffered hand as he asked directions to the arts faculty. The half mile walk with his long legs took him a mere ten minutes and fortunately the weather was cooperating. While patches of snow lay strewn about, the paths were clear and the skies were overcast with occasional patches of blue, giving hope of warmer days ahead.

Once there however, he found both instructors had already started their classes for the day, and he had an hour before he could speak with either one of them. He decided to take advantage of this time to enjoy the breakfast that he had skipped at Porter's house in his attempt to catch Maddux before the mathematics lecturers had begun. There was a café nearby and he ducked in to partake of a light repast, as he abhorred the distraction of digesting a heavy meal when he was busy with an investigation.

As most students were in lectures at this time, the tables were sparsely populated, and he chose a spot along a side wall in a corner where he could see out of the front windows as well as have a view of the entrance. This location had become a habit since his career as a detective had progressed, as it offered him greater opportunities for observation.

Sitting quietly with his toast with jam and a pot of Darjeeling tea, he gazed about the room at its few occupants. A handful of students in a rear corner appeared to be studying together for an exam later in the day. Another lad had his nose buried in a textbook about the Roman Empire. The few remaining seemed to just be socializing and engaged in various conversations about sports or politics.

Shortly after he sat down, two fellows came in whom he recognized. They were in the group of hangers-on surrounding Moriarty the previous day. One of them looked in his direction, but it could not be certain if he was just seeking out a place for them to sit or if he was, in fact, spying out Holmes. When they sat down it was across the room and the fellow who had first looked his way had his back to the detective. This gave the other one, a much taller student, an easier line of sight towards Holmes. As he was appearing to try and avoid eye contact, just as Holmes was doing the same, his intentions were not clear. Thus, Holmes took it upon himself to act. Finishing his tea in a final gulp, he strode out of the café and back toward the arts faculty. As there were multiple windows along the ground floor, he was able to observe the reflection of what was behind him. The two young men left the café and were about fifty yards to his rear. Knowing they hadn't had time to order or eat anything, Holmes deduced they were indeed on his trail.

Upon entering the building, Holmes bypassed the reception desk where he had earlier established Caffery and Mundy's schedules. He made a dash up the stairs and found a window where he could surreptitiously observe his followers. He saw them split up, one heading off in a direction which would take him around the back of the building, the other remaining by the front door, reading a newspaper. The fact that they had not followed him inside was concerning. To him it meant they were only confirming his destination. It was likely that Moriarty had spies or informants within the building, or among the students in Clay's classes, who could attest to Holmes's activities. He needed to come up with another excuse for being there in order to allay any suspicion that he was looking into John Clay.

Since he wasn't followed inside, he took the time to explore the building, seeking out the offices of faculty members. Coming to a door which was wide open and labelled with Professor Mundy's name, he took a peek inside and noted a student seated at a small desk off to one side. He knocked and enquired, "Excuse me, I am looking for Professor Mundy?"

The student turned. He was a stout fellow, with blond hair, red cheeks and a ready smile. He replied to Holmes politely, "I'm sorry, the Professor is in a class for at least another half hour. Is there something I can help you with?"

"Forgive me for not making an appointment," said Holmes, courteously. "My plans changed, and I thought I would take a chance to see if he was in. I represent the National Gallery. I would like to speak with him regarding recommendations for students who may be talented enough to do some work for our art department."

The fellow stood and invited Holmes to come in and sit down, "I am his secretary, Forrest Burgess, you are …"

"Sherlock Holmes, at your service. We currently have a need to add to our staff regarding cleaning and restoration of some of our works. We find that students from Oxford have been taught quite well and serve our purposes admirably. Professor Mundy was referred to me as one who would be well-suited to make a recommendation or two and perhaps an introduction."

Burgess nodded, "'Well-suited to be sure. You won't find another member of the faculty who is a greater stickler for details. It takes a supremely talented artist to pass muster with the Professor. This may be a problem for you since it is rare for him to be completely satisfied with anyone's work. Oh, he'll pass them from his class for their efforts. But to meet his expectations of perfection is rare indeed. To actually obtain a recommendation, especially to the National Gallery, would be nearly impossible. Though you are certainly welcome to ask."

"We do have one fellow from here working for us already," replied Holmes. "A lad named John Clay."

"Clay isn't one of Professor Mundy's students," replied Burgess. "He was, but has transferred to Stoneman's class this year. Frankly, I don't think the Professor would have recommended him to you. A bit headstrong in his methods, you see. Couldn't seem to grasp the concept that original art must maintain its originality, not be subjected to so-called 'improvements'. The original artist's integrity must be kept intact, flaws and all, if it is to be appreciated."

"Oh, I quite agree," stated the detective. "We certainly don't want students trying to *improve* on the masterpieces they're working on. I don't believe it has been a problem, but I will mention it to Professor Wooley at the Gallery so he might keep an eye on things."

"If you don't mind waiting," continued Burgess, "You are welcome to speak with the Professor when he returns. He usually steps out for a late breakfast after this class."

"That would be splendid," replied Holmes. "I can just sit here and read my paper if you wish to continue your work."

"Thank you, sir. I am afraid I do have a schedule to keep, if you don't mind?"

"Not at all."

Holmes pulled the morning paper from his coat pocket and quietly perused its contents. Half an hour later, Professor Mundy walked in. He was a stocky fellow with long, thick, silvery hair parted down the middle and combed up and back behind his ears, giving almost a leonine effect. He was clean-shaven and the crow's feet and other wrinkles of age had begun to settle in on what was likely once a handsome face in his youth.

Spying Holmes in the guest chair, he studied him as he asked a question over his shoulder to his secretary, "Burgess, who is this fellow darkening our office? He has the eyes of an artist but the countenance of scientist."

Before Burgess could answer, Holmes stood and bowed to the elderly gentleman, "Sherlock Holmes, Professor. I am working with Professor Wooley at the National Gallery and have come to seek your opinion on some matters."

"Montgomery Wooley? That old reprobate? How is he? We miss having him around here. Always had a story or two to share."

Holmes smiled and replied, "He's still sharing them, sir. I was wondering if I might have a few minutes of your time?"

"If you don't mind walking with me over to the coffee house in Queen's Lane for a late breakfast. Always hate to eat first thing in the morning. Digestive juices need time to wake up, you know."

"I should be happy to accompany you, sir. In fact, I shall gladly buy you breakfast myself."

Mundy looked back upon his secretary, grinned and offered, "Perhaps I was wrong. Not a scientist, but a salesman?"

Holmes grinned, "Just a messenger for now, Professor Mundy. Shall we go?"

Holmes and Mundy walked out the front door of the building past the student who had followed Holmes. While within the youth's earshot, the detective steered the conversation around to Professor Wooley, to emphasize the fact he was there looking for more workers for the Gallery.

As they continued on, Holmes's former pursuer went inside, walked through the building and found his compatriot by the back door. Repeating what he had overheard, they agreed there was no more reason to follow this fellow and left to report their findings.

Chapter Six

Most students being in lectures, Holmes and Mundy had the café nearly to themselves and chose a table where they could look out upon University Parks. The blue patches of sky were getting larger as the clouds floated off and it promised to be a sunny day by noon.

Holmes stood by his story of seeking recommendations for students who may wish to work at the National Gallery for the experience it would give them. Mundy mulled this over as he ate heartily. Finally, he replied, "I've none whom I would accept personally, however, Wooley is an excellent teacher and I do have two fellows whom he might be able to inspire to acceptable standards."

Holmes wrote these names down, along with where they lived so he could contact them. Then he addressed the Professor again, "We currently have a student named John Clay working at the Gallery. May I make a discreet inquiry as to your thoughts of the young man's talent and character?"

"Ah, the heir apparent Duke of Dartford, or so he claims. Are you aware of that fact, young man?"

Holmes acknowledged he was, and the Professor continued, "Unfortunately, Clay has allowed this questionable situation to colour his character. In his efforts to overcome his disadvantages at being the son of a bastard, he has overcompensated and become an arrogant fellow with an insufferable ego who believes the world owes him. He is also constantly critical and is certain he can improve on the works of others. What is he doing for the Gallery?"

"Professor Wooley has him cleaning and touching up old paintings. Would this be of a concern to you, given his conceit?"

"Indeed, it would," regarded Mundy. "You tell Wooley to keep a close eye on him. That fellow would try to improve the Mona Lisa if he got his hands on it!"

Holmes chose to test out his theory on the Professor. After laying out what he had deduced, he asked, "Are they capable of such a plot?"

Mundy replied, "It's incredibly audacious and bold and only the most egotistical of men would attempt it. So yes, they might be. Have you mentioned this to Wooley?"

"I wanted to look into the players more closely first," replied the detective. "What I have seen and heard thus far has not dissuaded me from my theory."

"Well, I should be most interested in how it bears out, Mr. Holmes. Please, keep me apprised and let me know how your case is resolved."

They parted ways after their meal. Mundy returning for his next tutorial and Holmes electing to stop at the post office in St. Aldate's to send a telegram to Professor Wooley.

After the half mile walk, he entered the grey, three storey structure with its multiple arched windows and wrote out his form. Handing it to the telegrapher, the elderly man perused it quickly to ensure he could read Holmes's handwriting before he started transmitting, then he noticed the signature. "You are Sherlock Holmes?" he enquired.

"Yes. Why do you ask?" replied the young detective.

"Oh, no matter," replied the telegrapher. "It's just I've never heard the name Sherlock before and now I've come across it twice in one day."

"Someone mentioned my name in a telegraph?" Holmes enquired, with surprise and no little bit of concern.

"Och! I've said too much," said the fellow, realizing he had breached a confidence. "I cannot tell you any more."

Holmes thought quickly and asked, "Well, no matter. I am returning to London soon. I'm sure it will reach me there. Can you tell me, if I were to send a letter from there to Professor James Moriarty, should it be addressed to this post office?"

Warily, the clerk looked at Holmes, which told the detective volumes, as he answered, slowly, "Aye, he keeps a box here."

"Thank you," replied Holmes, tipping his hat to the gentleman and stepping out to the street. He casually looked about and noted no one suspicious in plain view. However, there was a fellow in a shop across the street, who seemed to be sending glances his way through the large front window. He decided to take a surreptitious route back to Porter's house. Ducking through various areas of Pembroke College, he was sure he had lost his watchdog and eventually approached his destination from Osney Mead.

As he entered, Henry Porter could see something was amiss and approached him. Holmes, noting the presence of workmen still working on the renovation, held a finger to his lips and motioned the landlord to follow him to his room.

As soon as the door closed behind them, Porter asked, "What's wrong, Holmes? Can I help?"

The former student waved his host to a chair. Clasping hands behind him, he paced the room, a bundle of nervous energy with a myriad of thoughts, plans and alternatives racing through his mind, competing for prominence. Finally, Porter could stand it no longer, "If I may suggest? I find whenever a situation seems beyond a quick solution, I sit down and smoke a pipe or two upon it. It relaxes me and the repetitive action of inhaling and exhaling a good tobacco tends to focus my mind."

Holmes smiled at this attempt by his old friend to assist and replied, "I'm afraid I do not have a pipe with me, Mr. Porter."

Porter clucked his tongue, "Never leave home without a pipe and tobacco in your pocket."

He reached into the inner breast pocket of his coat and produced a cigar, which he handed to Holmes, "In the absence of a pipe, a good cigar will have to do. Try this Tatiana. They come from the Caribbean and have a soothing vanilla flavour. Just what you need to calm those racing thoughts."

Holmes accepted, though more out of politeness than any theory of smoking to organize one's thoughts. Porter lit the cigar for him and then one for himself. The landlord then leaned back in his chair, crossed his legs and pointed his cigar at his young friend, "Now, from the beginning, take me through your day and leave out no detail, no matter how trivial. You would be surprised at how merely voicing the situation out loud to another person can help to coalesce everything and provide various avenues of possible solutions. I do this with Emily often and we always come up with plausible and sometimes unique, answers."

Holmes took Porter through the events of the previous day as well as his sojourn that morning. The older gentleman listened without interruption, puffing on his cigar and nodding occasionally. When the detective had finished his report, Porter withdrew the cigar from between his lips and held it aloft to one side, leaning his elbow on the arm of the chair. He rubbed his temple with his middle finger as he thought through all Holmes had told him. At last, he spoke.

"So, as I understand it, you believe Moriarty and Clay have conspired to somehow steal this Olive Garden painting, even though it is still at the Gallery. But you believe the Professor suspects you and is having you followed, probably to find out if you are onto his scheme. Do you think you are in any physical danger?"

Holmes sent a puff of cigar smoke ceiling-ward and watched it as he thought through his answer. At last, he replied, "I feel a malevolence around Moriarty. I do not know if he personally would commit a violent act. However, I've no doubt he could convince any number of his minions to do so. His hypnotic hold over them seems incredibly strong and I've always believed when mere mortals become the object of blind faith, evil is not far behind.

"The men following me have all been rather large, but it may be because he doesn't want a spy who would be intimidated by my own height. I have kept up my boxing and fencing skills. I own a revolver and am a fair shot, but I did not bring it with me."

Porter nodded, "Yes, Emily told me of your remark regarding the dangers of your profession. While I would have approved your courtship of Anna, I appreciate your honesty and the fact that you care for her safety."

Holmes coloured slightly, "I meant no insult, sir. She is beautiful and intelligent, but I am not of a mind to be distracted from my work by emotional entanglements at this early stage of my career."

Porter held up his hand, "Enough said. It seems to me you've gleaned all the information you can at this point. Why not return to London and prepare a trap?"

"There is one more piece of information I should like to obtain," replied Holmes. "But to do so under current circumstances is highly unlikely. I believe you are correct. I shall return to London on the morning train."

Chapter Seven

The next morning, Holmes enjoyed a light breakfast with the Porters and their boarders. The students were curious as to his activities of the previous two days, but he could not indulge their questions without revealing too much. "I promise you, gentlemen, should anything of interest come out of my stay here, I shall ensure that you are all informed. In the meantime, I must go, for I have to send a telegram before I catch the morning train. If you will excuse me?"

He returned to his room, took up his carpet bag and left the pleasant household, with grateful nods to Mr. and Mrs. Porter and a courteous bow to young Anna. This Thursday morning had dawned with the threat of precipitation. Grey clouds blanketed the sky above, while black ones in the distance were ominously crawling their way across the sky toward Oxford. Holmes sent a telegram from the railway station to Wooley, advising him that he had discovered two possible candidates for the Gallery's art department and would be back in London that afternoon.

By the time the train had returned him to the capital, a heavy snow was falling. The cab from the station had a difficult time navigating the streets and Holmes decided it would be best to return to Baker Street while he could, rather than get snowed in at the Gallery, where he had originally intended to go. He found a generously stoked fire at home. Watson, not yet recovered enough from his war trauma to return to work, was studying *The Lancet,* in an effort to be well-read in the latest medical news when the day finally came.

His new roommate looked upon Holmes with some surprise, "Well, hello, Holmes. I was beginning to wonder if our paths would ever cross again. May I enquire as to where you have been off to, or is that confidential due to your business?"

"My apologies, Watson. I'm afraid I've been living alone for so long I have forgotten my manners. I was on a brief trip down to Oxford conducting research for the National Gallery."

"Interesting. Is there anything I may do to assist?"

Holmes mulled his offer over for a bit, recalling the advice Porter had given him regarding voicing a problem out loud to another party. However, his course was set at this point, and he decided not to risk any danger to his new friend.

"Thank you, Doctor. I believe things are under control, but I shall keep your offer in mind for the future."

"As you wish, Holmes," replied Watson. "I'm a little restless these days and would like to feel useful. Though I'll admit, this current storm is playing havoc with my leg."

Holmes looked out of the window. The snow was falling thickly. Neither pedestrian nor cab were now in sight. In spite of being mid-day, the darkness gave Baker Street a twilight look. One expected to see the lamplighters at any moment.

"Yes, I can imagine. It is not fit for man nor beast out there at the moment. I must amend my plans. If you'll excuse me, I have preparations to make."

Holmes retreated to his bedroom, leaving Watson to pour himself another cup of tea. It was nearly time for lunch and the doctor assumed he would have his new friend's company. Perhaps some scintillating conversation would ensue. The Doctor had few friends in London and no family outside of Scotland. He recalled saying to Stamford, when the meeting with Sherlock Holmes was first proposed, "I should prefer a man of studious and quiet habits. I am not strong enough yet to stand much noise or excitement. I had enough of both in Afghanistan to last me for the remainder of my natural existence."

Now, however, he found to his own amazement, he craved some adventure. Certainly not the frenzy of war, but something which would stir the blood. He was getting a bit long in the tooth for athletics and his leg and shoulder precluded most such activities, though he believed he could still hunt and perhaps an occasional game of golf when the weather warmed again. For now, billiards, cards and an occasional trek to the racecourse were the limits of his activities, with Stamford his primary companion for those sojourns.

Holmes soon returned, interrupting Watson's reverie. He glanced out of the window again, noting "Shall we have lunch, Doctor? It appears I shall not be venturing out again any time soon."

"I would enjoy your company, Holmes," replied Watson with a nod.

The detective rang for Mrs. Hudson and requested lunch for the two of them. He walked over to the sideboard and poured himself a small drink, offering one to his companion, who declined, preferring to curtail his alcoholic intake until after eating.

Once served, the two young bachelors enjoyed their landlady's simple fare. This time it was a hearty stew, perfectly suited to stave off the effects of the inclement weather.

Breaking off a piece of bread, Watson asked his companion, "Tell me, Holmes, when you are not gallivanting about on these researches of yours, do you engage in any recreational activities?"

Holmes dipped some bread of his own into the stew before replying, "I am not sure you would consider it 'recreational', Doctor. However, there are some activities I engage in to exercise my physical abilities. I occasionally box, not only to keep my self-defence skills sharp, but also to supplement my income to help with the rent. I practice fencing and am a fair singlestick player."

Watson nodded, "Did you ever go in for any other sports? Rugby, polo, cricket, tennis or perhaps golf?"

"I was never much for the team sports," replied Holmes. "My mind tends to anticipate strategies and actions which lead me to make moves which my teammates are not ready for. I have occasionally played golf, but that was years ago." He smiled at a memory and added, "My billiard game was of great use to earn extra pocket money while at school. How about you, my friend?"

Watson smiled with a bit of pride, "My own billiard game is rather top notch. We should play sometime. At school I was on the rugby team and have occasionally indulged in a golf match. How about hunting?"

"When I was young, I went on a few hunts with my father," said his roommate. "I am quite adept with both rifle and shotgun, but I prefer archery when hunting game. I believe it is more sporting for the quarry." Then a thought occurred to him, "How are your shooting skills, Doctor?"

"I am quite proficient with firearms," replied Watson. "I appear to have a natural gift for it. My army instructor was very impressed."

Holmes nodded, "I noticed you have retained your army Webley revolver. I have a five-shot Bulldog, myself."

He looked gravely at his roommate and declared, "I pray the situation shall not arise, Watson and I do not wish to alarm you, but it may be prudent for you to keep your weapon clean and loaded. In my line of work[1] for the Gallery I am occasionally involved with valuable pieces of art and I never know who might drop in with unpleasant intentions."

"Just what do you do for the Gallery, Holmes?" asked Watson, surprised at this revelation of a threat of danger. "I was under the impression that you were a chemist."

Holmes hesitated briefly to formulate an answer, then replied, "In exchange for access to their private researches, I use my chemistry skills to assist in touching up classic paintings, or repairing ancient sculptures. Sometimes I use chemical analysis to determine authenticity of documents."

---

[1] Per Baring-Gould, Holmes would not reveal his actual profession of consulting detective to Watson until the first week of March.

"What was the experiment you were working on when first we met? Something about detecting hæmoglobin in old bloodstains?"

Holmes smiled as he recalled the excitement of that day, then replied, "Because I have occasionally detected forgeries, the police are aware of my skills and will call upon me from time to time."

"And this puts you in danger?" asked the Doctor.

"On occasion I have been threatened with vengeance when a criminal is caught. I only bring this up so you may be aware of the possibility and be prepared, Watson. I do apologize for not mentioning it sooner, but this recent situation has brought it to my mind again and I felt you should be forewarned."

"Well," replied the former army physician, "I shall take your advice to heart and clean my weapon this very afternoon."

After their meal was done, and the conversation waned, Holmes took up an experiment at his makeshift laboratory in the corner, frequently turning to observe the weather. By three o'clock the black clouds had turned to grey and the snowfall had ceased. An occasional Hansom cab or private carriage could be seen slowly trudging their way through several inches of snow on the roads. Holmes, anxious to put his plan into action, threw on his ulster and his ear-flapped traveling cap with the flaps tied down. He took up a walking stick that he rarely used – the one with a heavy, leaded handle shaped like a dog's head – and strode out the door. "I may be gone overnight again, Watson. If all goes well, I shall see you for dinner tomorrow evening."

Managing to flag down a cab, he ordered it to the National Gallery. The snow-laden streets impeded the horse's progress, and it took an hour to make the trip of less than two miles. He alighted at last at the magnificent structure. The stairs leading up to the main entrance were pristine in appearance until he trudged through snow up to his shins, leaving a trail behind. While it was opening hours, there was a gentleman at the door who had to unlock it to let him in.

Holmes enquired, "Is there something amiss? Why are the doors locked at this time of day?"

"Standard procedure sir," answered the docent. "When the weather turns cold the beggars seek shelter. We can't have them inside. There are too many valuable pieces of art to risk any damage they might cause. Generally, they are allowed to stay outside under the portico where it is dry."

Holmes frowned but did not comment. Instead, he enquired, "Is Professor Wooley in?"

"Yes, sir," replied the young man. "He arrived before the storm this morning."

"Thank you," said the detective and strode off without waiting for an escort. Holmes located Herbert Franks, a regular attendant in the gallery adjacent to the staff areas, who admitted him to the conservation workshops.

The Professor was examining a painting with his magnifying lens and, being so engrossed in his work, he did not hear Holmes's approach. Not wishing to unduly startle the elderly man, the detective backed off after he went unnoticed and knocked on the open door, calling out Wooley's name as he did so.

"Professor Wooley, it's Sherlock Holmes."

Wooley turned at the sound and called out to his former student, "Sherlock, come take a look at this."

Holding out the magnifying glass to Holmes, he stepped back and let the younger man conduct an examination. Holmes indulged him and stepped up close to the painting where a bright light and powerful lens enabled an inspection in minute detail. The work was roughly twenty-five by thirty inches and depicted a young woman standing at a virginal with a gentleman looking on.

Noting the signature, nearly hidden in the frame of a painting within the painting, he commented, "This is Vermeer's *Music Lesson*? How did it come to be here?"

"It was sent over from the Palace.[2]" replied Wooley. "They were concerned over the effects of aging and asked for our opinion on what could be done to better preserve it."

"Well, at least this one is an original worth preserving. I have been experimenting with some chemical compounds which may be of assistance to you, Professor. Though we should experiment with something less valuable first."

"Perhaps the fake *Olive Garden*?" offered Wooley, with some trace of bitterness. "Were your researches of any help at all in finding out what happened to the original, Sherlock?"

"Did you keep it locked up and less conspicuous as I advised?" asked the young detective.

"Certainly, though I cannot imagine your reasoning."

"Let us go and take a look, Professor."

They went to the storage room where Wooley began to use his key to open the door. Holmes stopped him, momentarily and handed him his own magnifying lens to observe the lock. Wooley frowned but took the instrument and bent his portly frame toward the doorknob. He gasped at what he saw and started to question his former student, but Holmes held up his hand. "Wait," he said. "There is more."

Once inside, Wooley weaved through the antiquities to an out of the way stack of minor works of art leaning against a wall. *The Olive Garden* was tucked between two larger paintings. Holmes retrieved it and set it upon a table upside down.

"Here, Professor," he said, once again handing him the powerful lens. "Take a look at the back of the canvas."

Wooley again bent over and closely peered through the glass. He moved along to several places, nodding as he went. Finally, he straightened up and said, "It appears whoever did this found a canvas of the same period. It is definitely quite old."

[2] *The Music Lesson* or *A Lady at the Virginals with a Gentleman* by Dutch master, Johannes Vermeer was painted between 1662 and 1665. It was purchased by King George III in 1762 and spent time alternately at Windsor Castle and Buckingham Palace. A Virginal is a keyboard instrument of the harpsichord family.

"Indeed, as it should be," replied the detective. "Now watch"

Holmes removed the painting from its frame, turned it right side up and invited the Professor to examine the edges. His mentor threw a sceptical look in his direction but bent over again. In a matter of seconds, he jerked his head up and shot a look at Holmes who merely smiled and nodded for him to proceed checking some more. Wooley went around all four sides shaking his head as he went. At last, he straightened up and enquired, "Does this mean what I think it does, Sherlock?"

Instead of replying, Holmes stepped forward and demonstrated exactly what it meant. Wooley was flabbergasted. "Who? How? When?" he blurted in quick succession.

"Clay is obviously involved," answered Holmes. "I believe at least one, perhaps two of his tutors at Oxford may be in on it."

"What do we do? Have him arrested?"

"Not yet. I should like to see how far this scheme goes. Let me explain what I have in mind."

Chapter Eight

When John Clay returned to the Gallery the next day, Wooley assigned him to new duties, while praising him for his astuteness in discovering the forgery. Clay, nodded in satisfaction at this appreciation and enquired, "What will happen to the painting, Professor? Surely the Fetherstonhaugh family will not desire this forgery to sit amongst their fine collection of genuine masters?"

Wooley looked troubled, "They are demanding an investigation to determine when the substitution took place, for they are insistent they owned the original. As to the forgery, I have advised them that we have discreet ways of disposing of such items, so as not to bring any embarrassment upon either them or the Gallery."

Clay started to walk toward his new assignment, then turned back toward the elderly academic, "If I may be so bold, Professor, I believe my tutor at Oxford would be able to put such an item to use as a teaching aid for his art students."

Wooley stroked his grey beard as he pondered the suggestion, "Perhaps such an arrangement would be suitable. I shall mention it to the family to see if they are amenable once this investigation has concluded. You are referring to the fellow I send your evaluation reports to, I presume, Dr. Stoneman?"

"Yes, sir. Shall I tell him to expect to hear from you?

Wooley blanched at this suggestion, "Oh, no, no, no! Not yet. We must keep this unpleasant business quiet until the investigation is complete. Too many reputations are at stake. I will keep you apprised. I imagine it shouldn't be more than a few days."

Clay could not hide a small pout, but quickly recovered and replied, "Very good, sir. I'll just get to work then."

Over the next few days, Holmes, acting as go-between for Professor Wooley and the Fetherstonhaugh family, proceeded with the plan he had hatched with his mentor's consent. After an appropriate amount of time, a contract was finally given to Clay to convey to his tutor, including the following language:

> *In return for the sum of thirty pounds sterling, I, Frances Fetherstonhaugh, agree to sell the canvas painting copy of Giuseppe Cesari's 'Agony in the Garden - Christ on the Mount of Olives', now in possession of the National Gallery, to Dr. Malachi Stoneman of Oxford University. I hereby appoint Professor Montgomery Wooley and/or his agent to conduct the transfer of ownership and act as my representatives in receiving the purchase price in cash.*

Appropriate signatures and dates were affixed. The transaction was carried out at the National Gallery on Friday the 25th of February 1881. John Clay, acting with written authorization from Malachi Stoneman, handed over three ten-pound notes. In return, Professor Wooley took him to an open crate where Sherlock Holmes pulled back the padding from the centre of the artwork so Clay could see the painting was within. With a nod of approval from the student, Holmes recovered the painting, nailed the lid on the crate and turned it over to the lad.

After evening lectures, Clay and Stoneman were joined by Professor Moriarty at Stoneman's flat. The crate was laid upon the dining room table where the student dutifully pried it open for his tutors. As Clay carried the top aside, Stoneman threw back the padded blanket which had protected the painting in transit. He smiled at the work of his young protégé in copying the painting just well enough to make it look like a clever forgery. Moriarty, however, frowned and asked, "Tell me boy, is that the frame the painting was received in?"

Clay, having returned to the table grew fearful, "No," he gulped in reply. Then the realization hit him, "No, no, no, no, no!"

He lifted the painting out of the crate and turned it over. The golden colour of the frame was correct, but the filigree pattern was all wrong. Furiously he pulled a knife from his pocket and began removing the wooden blocks which acted as fasteners. When he was able to pry up the edge, he breathed slightly more easily. The double canvas was still there. His forgery remained fastened to the other canvas.

Moriarty remained unsatisfied. His eyebrows revealed his scepticism and he grumbled, "Pull it off and let us see what our ten pence on the pound has purchased."[1]

Carefully Clay removed all the wooden blocks and at last was able to access the top canvas. Instead of the original Cesari, there sat an old, water-stained canvas, nearly blank. The only marking upon it was an inscription in charcoal:

> *Dear Messrs. Clay, Stoneman and any others concerned,*
>
> *You have received exactly what you paid for, the forged copy of Cesari's painting. We have retained the original you attempted to conceal under it.*
>
> *Mr. Clay, while physical evidence does not absolutely prove you are behind this blatant attempt at thievery, circumstantial evidence is sufficient that I hereby dismiss you from our restoration program.*

---

[1] The genuine Cesari would have been worth approximately £300 in 1881.

Be advised, a close watch will be kept upon you, Dr. Stoneman and any other associates involved in this scheme, for future suspicious activity.

Beware the company you keep, sir, lest your talents be corrupted. Do not let the evil streak inherited from your grandfather dictate the course of your life.

It was signed and dated by Professor Wooley, but Moriarty scowled and said, "Gentlemen, we have aroused an irritating little itch. We may have to deal with it at the proper time."

"Wooley?" asked Clay, with a scowl, the knife trembling in his hands as he gripped it tighter.

The Professor looked sternly upon the student as if he were an imbecile, rather than the grandson of a duke, pursed his lips, shook his head slowly in a reptilian oscillation and replied in a quiet, yet menacing tone, "Sherlock Holmes."

The Black Irish Pug

Chapter One

It was February 1908, shortly after the detective Sherlock Holmes and I had taken steps in the case I have recorded elsewhere as *The Student Olympian*[1]. There was little to do in relation to that case at the moment, other than wait until the Olympic Games started in April.

I had just finished breakfast and was preparing to retreat to my consulting room to await my first patient of the day. My wife had taken up her sewing in the parlour by a warm fire when the quiet morning was interrupted by a ring of the doorbell. It was too early for patients and soon our maid came in, handed me a card and announced, "A gentleman to see you, sir. He does not have an appointment, but he says it is in regards to Mr. Holmes. Shall I show him in?"

I looked at the card which bore an impressive title and a well-known name:

> Bartholomew 'Bat' Masterson
> United States Marshal
> New York, Southern District

---

[1] *A Sherlock Holmes Alphabet of Cases, Volume Four (P-T)* by Roger Riccard (Baker Street Studios Limited, 2020).

I tapped the card on the desk and informed the maid to bring him in. I admit I had only seen illustrations of him in the so-called American 'dime novels' which occasionally found their way to our shores. Thus, I was expecting a lean gentleman in a dark suit and derby hat with short black hair and a large, black moustache. Of course, those images were based upon his wilder western years in Dodge City and Denver where he served as a lawman, among other professions. I should have realized that over a period of two decades would certainly change a man. I now looked very little like the early depictions by Sidney Paget who had illustrated my Sherlock Holmes stories for *The Strand Magazine*.

When Masterson walked into the room each of us was surprised not to be facing the well-known version of the man each was expecting. Tilting his head to one side, as if confused, he asked, "Dr. John Watson?"

The man who entered my consulting room was about my height and age, but the only thing in common with my image of him was the silver-knobbed cane he carried. In all other respects he could have been any stranger off the street. He was stocky of build, grey of hair and clean shaven. His eyes had the bags of age beneath them, which gave him a drowsy look. His face was rounder, though not jowly. He was wearing a light grey suit and holding a matching fedora in his hand.

I answered his query as I stood and walked up to him, holding out my hand, "I am, though I am sure you are as surprised by my appearance as I am by yours. Our public images generally depict us in our prime. I presume you are the well-known American peace officer?"

He shook my hand and smiled, "Yes, of course. You are correct, Doctor. The years do take their toll." He looked down upon his own body and continued, "I'm sure my Dodge City version of myself would not recognize this New Yorker."

I waved him to a seat and returned to behind my desk. Picking up his card I said, "I was not aware you were still a lawman. Do you require assistance on a case?"

He pursed his lips and replied, "I was appointed a federal marshal by President Roosevelt, in recognition of my years in law enforcement. However, I still consider my main profession to be a sports reporter and columnist with *The Morning Telegraph.*"

I nodded, "I do seem to recall reading that you were also a boxing promoter and occasional referee," I replied, setting the card back upon the desk

"Yes, and it is actually in that capacity that I wished to consult with you and Mr. Holmes. I confess, I thought my Marshal's identity might be of more interest in gaining an audience."

I smiled and replied, "I assure you, Mr. Holmes is not the least impressed by titles. It is the character of the problem brought forth which attracts his attention. I've seen him turn down a royal head of Europe, offering exorbitant fees, in favour of an orphan from London's East End."

He nodded and continued, "Well, I hope then, that I can offer something of interest. Do you know where I can find him? I've been to Baker Street, but no one was at home. I spoke to a constable and he informed me that Holmes had retired to the countryside, but gave me your address, believing that you would know how to reach him."

I folded my hands together as I leaned forward, "Sherlock Holmes has retired to take up beekeeping in Sussex. Though he still will take on an occasional case of interest, or in response to a request from the British government. If you could tell me a little more about your situation, I might be able to advise you better."

He crossed one leg over the other and sat, his cane leaning against his right hip with one hand resting on top. "I believe I should give you a bit of my own background before arriving at the crux of the matter. It may surprise you to know I am Canadian by birth. A little town called Henryville about twenty miles north of Lake Champlain. My father's ancestors were Irish and my mother was a McGurk from County Tyrone in Northern Ireland. As you can imagine, with staunch Irish parents, my feelings for the English run rather thin. If you will forgive me, sir."

I smiled, "I was born in Scotland. I understand."

71

The Marshal nodded and continued, "When I was young my father moved us several times to various farms in New York, Illinois, Missouri and finally, Wichita, Kansas. In my late teen-aged years my brothers and I took up buffalo hunting. There came a time when our employer tried to skip out on us without paying. We caught up with him in Dodge City and forced him to turn over our pay, to the roar of a cheering crowd. I went on to scout for the army for a few years and then returned to Dodge where I became an under-sheriff. My career has been well-documented, as well as my associations with Buffalo Bill Cody, Luke Short and Wyatt Earp. Like them, my reputation has been overblown. It has been reported that I killed 28 men. In truth, I have only killed three and all in self-defence. Not counting my battles in the Indian Wars of course.

"In the '80s I took up an interest in prize fighting, betting, promoting and refereeing. I've known the best of the best. John L. Sullivan, Gentleman Jim Corbett, Jack Dempsey and Jack Johnson. Which brings me to my reason for seeking Holmes's assistance.

"I've been working for the paper since 1902 and promoting prize fighters on the side. I've come across an amateur fellow destined to be the heavyweight champion of the world, Black Jack O'Neill, the Black Irish Pug. He's undefeated but cannot break into professional ranks due to prejudice amongst the white promoters. No professional white boxer in America will take him on. He's the grandson of a former slave and descended from an Irish plantation owner. But if he can fight in the Olympics he could walk away with the Gold medal and they'll have to allow him a shot at the World Title."

"What makes you think he could beat all the other Olympians?" I asked, intrigued by the man's story.

"He's six foot nine inches tall and weighs two hundred and seventy-five pounds," answered the former lawman.

"My word!" was all I could say.

He went on to tell me his tale and the need to hire my celebrated friend. I believed the unique aspect of his problem would be of interest to Holmes and agreed to contact him. I asked him where I could get in touch with him and, like many visiting Americans, he named the Langham Hotel. This was another point in his favour, as the Langham is only about a mile from Baker Street and both Holmes and I were well-acquainted with the staff, due to the many clients who had stayed there.

We parted with the promise that I would be in touch. After he left, my wife walked in and enquired as to the nature of his visit. I repeated a shorter version of his story and she, who is so well-suited to my own personality, repeated my reaction, "My word!"

Chapter Two

"How does one lose a human being of such remarkable appearance in London?"

This was the first question out of Holmes's mouth after introductions had been completed and the case stated that Black Jack O'Neill had disappeared.

We were sitting in 221B Baker Street, where Holmes still retained our old rooms as his city dwelling whenever he was in town. He had wisely invested some of his larger fees and rewards and his current income was much more comfortable than in our early days when we had to share these rooms to pay the rent. It felt odd to see the makeshift laboratory in the corner now covered with a heavily fringed deep red tablecloth and a curious piece of taxidermy beneath a glass dome which reminded me of one of our earlier cases. There were some more unfamiliar items in the room. A green dressing gown I hadn't seen before was thrown on the back of the sofa. The desk held some writing paper and envelopes and a compact microscope of the latest design. The bookshelves were bare apart from a small collection of what appeared to be newer gazetteers, maps and directories and one or two books, including a title on beekeeping. It was an impersonal space, uncharacteristically tidy and reminded me of my own consulting room, which I strove to keep separate from my personal life with my wife. The familiar Persian slipper, hanging from the mantel and holding his favourite shag tobacco, was the only evidence of his former occupancy.

My telegram to Sussex had aroused Holmes's curiosity, as had the identity of our client. There are certain personalities which fascinate Holmes. Buffalo Bill Cody was a contemporary of Masterson who had also been in these rooms as a client, along with Chief Red Shirt of the Lakota Sioux Nation.[1]

He sat there, awaiting an explanation from Masterson. The Marshal frowned and explained as best he could.

"We had only been in town for three days. Naturally, wherever we went, we drew the curious stares of onlookers. You must understand that Jack is the essence of civility. He is not some backwoods brawler, or an ignorant man who never had the chance to go to school. He is a well-educated gentleman. He studied engineering at Howard University for two years. He realized that he had greater financial opportunity in the boxing ring while he is still in his prime and feels he can use his education after his boxing career is over."

"I am somewhat familiar with the upcoming Olympics program," said the detective, "I do not recall the Americans listed among the nations scheduled for the boxing events. What has brought you to England?"

Masterson nodded, "My understanding is that most of the American boxers, including all those medal winners in 1904, have declined to participate due to the length of the games. The opening ceremonies are in April but the boxing events aren't scheduled until October. They can't afford to stay here that long, nor do they wish to make two trips. These are mostly amateurs who have regular jobs, in addition to their pugilistic endeavours. I believe there is also concern that, with the host country providing all the judges, they will not get a fair shake, especially since most of them are of Irish descent.

"Be that as it may, I could not convince any of them to come. Not even Jack Johnson, the Black Heavyweight Champ, who is a contender for the world heavyweight championship."

He took a sip of the tea that Mrs. Hudson had provided and continued. "It is my hope that an Olympic medal for O'Neill will give him the legitimacy he needs to force a match with

---

[1] *Buffalo Bill and the Red Shirt Menace* in *A Sherlock Holmes Alphabet of Cases, Volume One (A-E)* by Roger Riccard (Baker Street Studios Limited, 2017).

Johnson and claim the Black Boxing Title in America. That would set him up to take on Tommy Burns from Canada for a World Heavyweight bout."

I stopped him to ask a question, "If America isn't sending a boxing team, how does he hope to compete?"

He leaned back on the sofa in a relaxed fashion as he answered, "I have been in meetings with both the International and British Olympic organizations," answered Masterson. "I am trying to negotiate a status where he can fight either as an independent athlete, or as an Irishman, being of Irish descent."

"What progress have you made?" asked Holmes, with scepticism in his voice.

"The International Olympic Committee has taken my request under advisement, so at least they are willing to listen. The British will only accept athletes who will represent Great Britain, which includes Ireland and Scotland. So, to compete under his Irish heritage, Jack would have to fight under British colours. Personally, I'm torn by that prospect. I want the man to have his chance. But, as he is an American of Irish heritage, two peoples who have rebelled against British rule, it galls me to think that his victory would be counted among the British medals."

Holmes puffed on his pipe and nodded, "I can certainly understand that. While I am English, there is a branch of the Holmes clan in Ireland. Watson has distant kinfolk in Scotland. National or ethnic prejudices can run deep and for countless generations. Have you encountered any prejudice in America regarding having a Negro represent the United States?"

"Only a handful of people knew our plans, but no one was sworn to secrecy, so the news may have spread. Are you suggesting he was kidnapped to keep him from competing?"

"I am suggesting that we need more evidence. I can think of several other reasons for his disappearance."

"For example?"

"Off the top of my head, perhaps a ransom, or a circus seeking a new attraction, or Shanghaied by an unscrupulous shipmaster. I trust you have informed the police?"

"Yes, they assigned a Scotland Yard Inspector, Stanley Hopkins, to the case. So far, he has found nothing."

"Hopkins is one of their better men. However, I propose we visit O'Neill's room and have a look for ourselves."

The desk clerk bid a familiar 'hello' to both Holmes and I as we accompanied Masterson to obtain both his and O'Neill's keys.

Once in the boxer's room, Holmes bid us to remain in the hall while he carried out a quick examination. Masterson replied, "The maids have cleaned room since his disappearance. They did so before Inspector Hopkins arrived to stop them."

"So I see," replied Holmes. "Nevertheless ..."

I had witnessed this ritual countless times as my friend scoured the room. The carpets had been swept, so there were no tracks to indicate visitors. Yet still he checked all the furniture for any tell-tale marks, he looked under the bed and in all the drawers. At last he opened the wardrobe and called us in.

"Mr. Masterson, are you familiar enough with O'Neill's clothing to ascertain what is missing?"

The American ran his fingers along the line of clothes which hung there, finally answering, "Everything seems to be here except for what he was wearing the last night I saw him."

"And you had been out to dinner and the theatre at the Criterion, correct?"

"Yes, we felt a need to stretch our legs, so to speak."

"Were you accompanied by anyone? Some female companionship, perhaps?"

Masterson folded his arms and replied, "We were not, Mr. Holmes. We are trying to maintain a low profile so as to gain a good reputation and so get favour from those who have the power to approve Jack's participation."

"Were you approached by anyone while you were out?" Asked the detective.

"There were the usual gawkers but the only people to actually approach us were three women while we waited for a cab after the show. Two of them came up to each side of Jack, while a third took me by the arm and asked if I'd like some company for the evening.

"I admit, this took me aback. It was a more common occurrence when I was a dashing young man, but at my age I hardly expect such offers. I thanked the lady but politely declined her attentions. I was able to hail a cab and hustled Jack back here."

"How did Jack feel about that?"

"He picked one lady up in each arm, kissed each of them on the cheek and apologized that he could not accommodate them. Then he joined me in the cab."

"How did the ladies react to being turned down?"

"The one who had accosted me seemed to pout, then shrugged her shoulders and walked toward another potential client. The two who had surrounded Jack merely rolled their shoulders, smiled and blew kisses as we pulled away."

"Can you describe these women?" asked Holmes.

Masterson rubbed the back of his neck with his left hand as he thought back. Finally, he looked up and replied, "The women who tried to latch on to Jack were young. Early twenties I should say. One was a thin redhead in a green evening gown with a fox fur cape. The other was blonde with very short, wavy hair. She was dressed in a midnight blue gown. She was fuller of figure."

Holmes nodded, then pulled O'Neill's trunk from the wardrobe and opened it up. It held the usual extra clothing for a long trip. The only oddities I noticed were a pair of boxing gloves and what I assumed to be his boxing outfit: trunks and ankle boots, with thick socks.

"Anything missing from here?" ask Holmes.

Masterson looked over Holmes's shoulder and confirmed the contents. Holmes closed the trunk and slid it back into the wardrobe. He stood and put his hands on his hips. "Very well. It appears your friend left willingly. There is no sign of a struggle. He had not changed for bed. His overcoat and hat are gone. This is not conducive to an abduction. I suggest he may have decided to take a turn about the town without you as a chaperone. Perhaps an assignation with the ladies from the theatre. They may have slipped an address to him while you were distracted. Is he married, or does he have a fiancée?"

"There is no steady woman in his life at present," answered Masterson.

Holmes nodded in such a way that seemed to confirm his hypothesis. "Let us speak to the hotel staff and then off to glean what we can from Hopkins's enquiries."

The desk clerk on duty informed us that the night clerk on the day O'Neill disappeared had not seen him leave, but then, at that time of night they usually sit in an alcove behind the desk and wait for someone to come to the counter, rather than stay on their feet all night when their services were unlikely to be needed.

The doorman also told us that his night time counterpart had seen nothing untoward and suggested that perhaps the 'gentleman' had left via a service entrance. His tone indicated that he did not care for Mr. O'Neill's presence in their establishment. He was a bulky fellow of about six feet in height and could have passed for a boxer himself. Holmes, leaner, but taller, stepped closer to him and said in a menacingly quiet voice, "Did *you* have anything to do with *Mister* O'Neill's disappearance?"

The doorman stared up at Holmes, not backing down, and replied, "I did not, Mr. Holmes. But, should it have become necessary, I would have been happy to assist in his eviction."

Holmes glared at the fellow, while I held Masterson back, as he had stepped forward in temper, raising his cane. Finally, Holmes waved us on ahead and I ushered our client by. I overheard the detective's parting words to the doorman. "Your feelings are noted, if misplaced. But your honesty is appreciated nonetheless. Good day!"

Chapter Three

Once in a cab *en route* to Scotland Yard, Masterson spoke. "I was not aware you had the same racial prejudices in England as we have in America, you having ended slavery so much sooner. Is this common or was that buffoon an exception?"

"Feelings vary among the classes," answered Holmes. "Class prejudice is far more common than racism. An African tribal leader will be treated with greater deference than a white costermonger on the streets of London. England has so many dark-skinned people among its colonies that they are not an unusual sight here in the capital. However, I have noted, that in more difficult economic times, racial tensions grow higher as jobs become scarcer. That does not excuse the doorman's behaviour and I shall speak to the manager about him later."

At Scotland Yard, the three of us settled into Hopkins's small office, having borrowed an extra chair from across the hall. The Inspector welcomed us, as he has always been more appreciative of Holmes's assistance than some of his colleagues.

"It's good to see you again, Mr. Holmes, Dr. Watson. I'm glad that Marshal Masterson has called you in on this case, for I was about to do so myself."

Hopkins leaned his thin frame across his desk, rubbed his moustache and picked up some papers, which I noted were filled with his hurried, and often unreadable, handwriting. He gave us a rundown on what he had discovered so far.

Like Holmes, he had concluded that O'Neill left of his own accord. While he did not discount an exit by way of a service entrance, he was also unconvinced that the night doorman was being honest when he reported seeing nothing.

"The lifts are in plain sight of the reception and the front entrance," continued Hopkins. "Unless he happened to be outside assisting a patron, it is inconceivable that he would not notice O'Neill getting off at the ground floor. The only other option is the fire escape stairwell. That leads to a side hallway from where O'Neill could have left by the rear door. As you are aware, those doors are locked from the outside to keep out intruders, but are operable from the inside in case of fire."

"Whatever method of egress he took," replied Holmes, "he must have had a reason to go out and a destination in mind."

"Our only lead for motive," observed Hopkins, "appears to be the ladies who approached him at the theatre."

"There are other considerations, Inspector, but that is one alternative we should explore," said Holmes, who went on to propose a plan of action. The four of us discussed the details and agreed to meet later on to enact it.

That evening I was with Masterson in an enclosed carriage at the crossroads in front of the Criterion theatre. We were waiting for the evening crowd to depart from the last show. As we watched, Stanley Hopkins, in formal attire which belied his occupation as a Scotland Yard inspector, came out, walked to the left side of the statue of Eros in front of the theatre, pulled a cigarette from a gold case and lit it. Another gentleman with a thin moustache and sharp goatee, went to the opposite side of Eros. He was also in formal attire, which included an opera cape and gold handled cane. As he stood there, he reached inside his breast pocket to retrieve a bright silver flask.

It did not take long for both these gentlemen to be approached by 'ladies of the evening'. Using opera glasses to obtain a closer look, Masterson noted that one of the women who approached Hopkins was the redhead he had seen with O'Neill. By pre-arranged signal using the carriage lamps, Hopkins continued to engage them in conversation. I left the carriage and walked across the street. I approached the

Inspector with a cigar in hand and asked if he had a match. This allowed me to indicate to him, with a nod of my head, that the redhead was the one we wanted. To assist him, I engaged the other lady, a petite brunette, in conversation and steered her away from Hopkins.

As we rounded the statue, the goateed gentleman freed himself from a tall blonde woman and approached me in a rather unsteady fashion. Slurring his words and waving his flask about, he pointed his cane at me as if it were a sword. "Hamish!" he cried out, "You think you could hide from me? Prepare to defend yourself, you cad!"

He came at me, swinging his cane wildly and I raised my own walking stick into a defensive position. His attack was ineffectual and I was easily able to block any swings which came anywhere near my person. His blonde and my brunette stayed back out of the way, debating if they should wait for the winner of this confrontation. Hopkins and his redhead had come around to see the commotion and joined in with the small crowd that had gathered to laugh at the spectacle of this drunken fool. It did not take long for a constable to come along and subdue the fellow and handcuff him. He insisted on my coming along to file charges and we left with him in the direction of the carriage where Masterson waited.

Once out of sight behind the carriage, we quickly entered it. The drunkard removed his facial hair and became Sherlock Holmes. Masterson was keeping his eye on Hopkins, who was now being led down the street by his would-be paramour. Our driver, a constable in plain-clothes, brought the carriage around and followed slowly. Holmes, in the meantime, changed his garments for more suitable attire. Soon the redhead hailed a cab. She and Hopkins boarded and we followed, keeping in pace with the traffic. They headed west into Mayfair. Finally, the cab stopped, letting Hopkins and the woman out. Before entering the establishment, Hopkins took the woman into his arms and engaged in a long lingering kiss. This provided us enough time for Holmes and me to approach quietly. When Hopkins detected our presence, he pulled his head back and held his hand over the redhead's mouth so that she would not scream. The three of us bundled the woman into our carriage. Seeing a uniformed officer, she physically shrank back, though her words were defiant, "What is this? I haven't done anything! You have no right to hold me!"

Holmes held out the flask to her and said, "We are only seeking information, Miss. Take a drink and calm yourself."

As she hesitantly reached for the flask, Hopkins spoke up, "It's all right, Molly. I am Inspector Hopkins from Scotland Yard and this is Sherlock Holmes. We are after much bigger fish than you and you will soon be free to go, with no charges, if you answer our questions truthfully."

She sniffed the mouth of the flask and, deciding it was good, she took a tentative sip. She licked her lips, then took a deep full drink. Handing it back to Holmes, she asked, "What sort of questions? What do you think I know?"

Masterson spoke up at this point, "Do you remember me from the other night? You were taking an interest in my partner, the large black gentleman."

At the mention of O'Neill, she pulled her fur tightly around her neck, "I don't recall you, sir. But, if you were there, you saw the big fellow say goodbye and drive away."

Holmes spoke up, "We have reason to believe that is not the last time you saw him. If you wish to remain above the fray in this matter, your full cooperation will be required. Now, did you see Mr. O'Neill later that night?"

With five pairs of eyes upon her, and sandwiched between Hopkins and Masterson, she tried, even more, to bury her head in her stole. "I can't. They'll come after me if I say anything."

"Who will come after you, Molly?" asked Hopkins. "You must tell us what happened to O'Neill and where he is."

She handed the flask back to Holmes and asked, "Are you really Sherlock Holmes, the detective?"

Holmes tucked the container into his pocket and answered, "I am. I can assure you that we can protect you, but we must know who to protect you from, and how we can retrieve Mr. O'Neill."

She cleared her throat and began to dab her eyes with the edge of her stole. I handed her a handkerchief and said, "Here,

Molly. Take your time and give us all the details you can. Every little thing could be important."

It felt odd for me to hear myself make the statement I had heard Holmes make a hundred times over. I glanced at him and he gave me one of those instantaneous smiles that pass by in a flash. Finally, with my handkerchief wadded up in her fist, she answered.

"The, black gentleman, the one you call O'Neill, came here later that evening. I had slipped my address into his coat pocket when we were outside the theatre."

She went on to explain the events of that night. She led O'Neill into the parlour and offered him a glass of wine which, unbeknownst to him, was laced with a sleeping draught. She then stepped out into the hallway and gave a signal. Four men came from another room and bundled him off to a motorized van, which drove away into the wee small hours of the morning. When pressed for details, she could not say where the van was going. However, she did give up the name of the ringleader and where he lived.

"Sean O'Connor. He's the one who paid me to get the man here. He gave me the sleeping draught to put in the drink."

"One other thing," asked Hopkins. "This neighbourhood seems beyond the financial means of someone in your ... position. Who owns this house?"

The girl sat up a little straighter, "A certain gentleman who appreciates me. Whose name you do not need to know as he had no knowledge of any of this, nothing to do with the kidnapping."

Chapter Four

For now, Hopkins let the matter drop. He could always check the land registry later. We sent Molly off to Scotland Yard with the two constables until we could arrange for her safety. The constables were ordered to arm themselves and join us at the address she had provided, as soon as they dropped her off. The rest of us hailed a four-wheeler and made our way to Limehouse. With little traffic in the East End at that time of night, we made the journey in under an hour.

Holmes had the cabbie stop several houses short of the actual address so that we could approach more stealthily on foot. The man we sought was Sean O'Connor. We knew there were at least four men, and possibly more.

Holmes decided that he should reconnoitre the house first, so that we could decide the best approach to take. The fact of the matter was, we couldn't even be sure that O'Neill was still with them or even at this location.

It was well past midnight and extremely cold. Therefore Hopkins, Masterson and I took turns standing in the shadows further up the street. While two of us remained in the relative warmth of the cab, the other would be close enough that he could hear if Holmes needed our assistance. I took the first watch and was comforted by the feel of my army Webley revolver in my coat pocket. I also knew that Holmes was carrying his Bulldog gun. The structure was a two-storey brick affair, set back about fifteen feet from the kerb. There was a light on the ground floor and another, dimmer, in a back corner upstairs room.

Holmes recounted his actions later on. He approached the building from the dark side and made his way across to where the light shone. He saw one man sitting in an armchair with a gun on the table next to him as he read a newspaper. The detective backed off and slipped down the side of the house until he reached the back garden. A ladder to the roof where some repairs were underway was tempting, but he decided to forgo that action for the time being. There was a cellar door that attracted his attention. It was barred from the outside with a padlock. Using a pocket torch, he examined it thoroughly. He also examined the ground around it. Convinced by the evidence before him, he returned to us at the cab.

He explained his observations to us as we awaited reinforcements. "There is one man on guard downstairs, armed with a gun. There are no others in sight on the ground floor. The soles of his boots, which were stretched out toward the window, indicate that he walks with a limp. Therefore, it is unlikely that he was among the four who carried O'Neill out to the van. He probably remained here to guard the house. Footprints around the cellar door indicate that there were only four men who took the unconscious body of our victim downstairs.

"I also believe that, were there more able-bodied men available, they would have been called upon to assist. That does not preclude the fact that other men could have joined this little band since the night of the kidnap. Therefore, we must not assume there are only five men inside."

"You're sure he's in the cellar, Mr. Holmes?" asked Masterson.

"That would certainly be the most logical place to put him. Carrying him upstairs would have been extremely difficult and I doubt that any normal door, even if locked, could hold him once he awoke," answered my friend. "There is every indication that he is still there, as there are no tracks indicating anyone leaving by that door, and it is unlikely they would have walked him out via the front door where he could be seen.

Also, there are fresh cracks in bar across the door. From their appearance and location, I would surmise that your boxer has been attempting to use his brute strength to try and break through."

At this point, a police van pulled up behind us and the two constables, armed with guns, joined our rescue party. It was agreed that they, and Inspector Hopkins, would take up posts where they could capture anyone coming out the front door. Holmes, Masterson and I would attempt to gain entrance through the cellar.

We followed Holmes around to the rear of the building and I held the pocket torch so that he could pick the lock, which held the crossbar in place. Knowing that O'Neill would only recognize Masterson's voice, we let the Marshal go first. To my surprise, he produced a short-barrelled Colt .45 from a holster behind his back. When Holmes and I each pulled the double doors slowly open, Masterson shone the pocket torch into the dark recesses of the cellar and softly called out, "Jack, are you down here? It's me, Bat Masterson."

There was silence so the Marshal slowly descended into the gloom and called out again in an exaggerated whisper, "Jack! Are you here?"

Holmes followed him while I stood guard above, my old war wound not spry enough to move efficiently on steps in the chill of this night. From my position I could see a flicker of movement just beyond the edge of the light beam. My grip on my revolver tightened as I prepared for a confrontation.

To my relief the hulking figure of a man came into the light. From the sheer mass of him it could only be Black Jack O'Neill. His hands and feet were chained together, but otherwise he was not restricted and had free movement of the cellar. Masterson spoke quickly to him, advising him of our presence and the situation. Holmes's picks made quick work of the locks on the chains and the three of them soon emerged from the cellar. I had never seen a man of such stature before and was awed by the sight of him. His skin was not the dark tone of a native African, but a much lighter shade of brown. His hair was a wavy black, as was the stubble of beard that had grown during his captivity. His captors had taken his shoes and left him barefoot. He had grabbed a blanket from his makeshift bed, but his bare feet on the freezing ground still made him shiver. Masterson and I quickly took him back to the relative warmth of our cab while Holmes closed and re-locked the cellar doors.

Masterson began to question his boxer as to his health, but Hopkins interrupted, "How many men are inside?"

O'Neill turned his gaze upon the Inspector and hesitated as he thought back over his days of captivity. "I don't know for certain. I've only seen two men who brought me meals. Sometimes I could hear others talking in the background when the door was opened to set my meal tray down, so there must be at least three. But there could be more."

"No matter," said Holmes. "If we do this properly, we can round them all up with as little violence as possible."

With the two constables remaining out the front, Holmes insisted I stay with O'Neill and perform what medical assistance I could. He, Masterson and Hopkins entered the house through the back. Holmes had retrieved a small metal drum from the back yard. The back door had opened into the kitchen where Holmes set the drum quietly near the door leading toward the front room where the guard was. Throwing some towels into it, he set it alight and soon the smoke began to billow up. He and Hopkins took up positions on either side of the door while Masterson used another towel to wave the smoke in that direction.

When Holmes heard the guard get up and start toward the kitchen, he motioned for the Marshal to take cover. As soon as the guard came to the doorway and saw the drum, he realized some intruder must be in the house. Instead of rushing to put out the fire, he kept his head and brought his gun up into a ready position. Taking his first step through the door he looked to his left, immediately seeing Hopkins. Before he could fire, Holmes on the other side of the door, brought the butt of his relvolver down on the man's skull, knocking him unconscious to the ground. Hopkins put handcuffs on him and gagged him after pulling him out of sight of the doorway.

He told Masterson to wait in the doorway to ensure that the fellow didn't try to run for it if he came to. Then the Inspector and Holmes each took a side of the drum and silently carried it to a position where the draft would take the smoke upstairs. Holmes also fed more logs into the fireplace and closed the chimney damper. As smoke filled the room and wafted its way upstairs, he called out in an Irish brogue, "Fire! Wake up lads! Fire!"

Soon three men came bursting out onto the landing. In various stages of pulling clothes and shoes on. When they were about halfway down the stairs, too vulnerable to turn back, Holmes and Hopkins stepped out into the open with guns drawn and ordered them to put their hands up. Seeing their position as untenable, the three complied and walked down the steps. Hopkins opened the front door and ordered them out to where the other constables could take charge. At this point, Masterson brought out the guard who had come to and pushed him forward to join the other three. Then he turned toward Holmes who was re-opening the damper to clear the air. He started to say something, but all at once, his eyes caught movement at the top of the smoky stairs. Faster than Holmes could raise his revolver, the Marshal's hand was filled with his own Colt and firing. The man at the top of the landing was thrown back against the wall, his gun discharging as it hit the floor. He fell where he had stood. He made no more sound, nor movement.

Holmes and Masterson, keeping their revolvers at the ready, cautiously made their way up the stairs. Hopkins had rushed back in at the sound of gunfire, but Holmes waved him to stand guard. Too many men on those narrow stairs would only get in each other's way.

Holmes checked the gunman's pulse while Masterson kept an eye on the rooms on that landing. The Marshal's shot had been true and this kidnapper was dead. Together they cleared the bedrooms and found no other occupants.

I had stepped out of the cab at the sound of gunfire and drew my own weapon, but I had to keep O'Neill from rushing to his promoter's aid. His shivering had stopped, but he was still weak. He informed me that they had only fed him two meals a day and, while they were adequate for a normal person, they were a mere snack for a fellow his size. I watched helplessly as Hopkins rushed back into the house. The minutes clicked by interminably until, at last, the Inspector, the Marshal and the detective exited, all apparently in one piece. O'Neill and I both exhaled the breath we had been subconsciously holding.

Hopkins rode with his constables as the police van with his prisoners made its way to Scotland Yard. Holmes and I, along our two clients, took the cab back to the Langham where O'Neill could bathe and change his clothes. Fortunately, Holmes had found his shoes, for I imagined their size would have made them difficult to replace in a timely manner. I was able to obtain some food for him from the kitchen staff, who were just changing shift to begin preparing for the breakfast patrons.

Once fortified, O'Neill was anxious to go to Scotland Yard to identify his captors and tell his story. He had given us a brief account of what happened, but for the sake of my readers, I shall now report what the boxer reported to Hopkins at the Yard.

After identifying two of the four kidnappers in their cells, we all went back to an interview room where we could sit and take down O'Neill's statement. In his deep *basso profundo* voice he recalled:

"After the show, Bat and I were approached by these women, obviously ladies of the evening, but of a higher class than I usually encounter. When Bat insisted that we needed to get back to the hotel, the redhead, Molly, slipped a card into my pocket and whispered that she would be waiting for me.

"Well, I went back to the hotel. But I waited until I thought Bat would be asleep. Then I went down the stairs and out the back door. I circled around to the street and hailed a cab. When I got to the address, I was welcomed by Molly with open arms. We enjoyed each other's company you understand, and the last thing I remember is drinking some wine. The next thing I know, I'm chained up in that cellar where you found me, getting two meagre meals a day with no conversation. None of them would tell me what they wanted. I thought maybe I was being held for ransom. I tried breaking through the doors where you came in. I thought I was making progress, as they seemed to give a little more each day.

"I was getting weaker by the day, however. I had almost made up my mind to jump the next person to leave my food tray at the top of the stairs. Then you all showed up. Do you know why they were holding me?"

"We are about to find that out," replied Hopkins. "Mr. Masterson, if you will wait here with Mr. O'Neill, the three of us shall question the men we captured."

Chapter Five

Holmes and Masterson discussed the kidnappers a little more, especially one of the prisoners in particular. Finally, the Inspector led the way back to the cells where Hopkins whispered to my companion, "Anyone we should take first, Mr. Holmes?"

Holmes walked the corridor, looking into each cell which held one of this night's captives. At last he pointed to one, "I believe this gentleman would be a good place to start."

Hopkins had a guard unlock the cell and handcuff the prisoner. We took him to a room used for interrogations. This was a sturdily built fellow, about five foot ten. Muscles bulged under his sleeves. His square jaw jutted out in defiance and eyes burned with contempt.

Hopkins sat him down in a rough wooden chair at a small table and hooked his handcuffs to a ring bolted through the wood. He then sat on a bench opposite the fellow while Holmes and I flanked him.

"Let's start with your name. Who are you and where are you from?"

"Téigh go hIfreann, a mhadra Béarla!" came the vehement reply.

My knowledge of Scots Gaelic was limited and there are differences between the Irish and Scots versions, but I knew enough to recognize an insult that roughly referred to Hopkins as an English dog.

To the prisoner's surprise, Holmes answered back, "Tá a fhios againn go labhraíonn tú Béarla." *(We know you speak English)*

The man, caught off guard by this turn of events, replied in English, "So, a clever Englishman, or are you a traitor to your Irish roots?"

"My name is Sherlock Holmes," stated my companion as he walked around the table and stood next to the prisoner. "You may have heard of me, thanks to my friend, Dr. Watson, here. But, if not, know that I am a detective who takes on clients of all nationalities. In this particular case I was engaged by an Irish Canadian to find his Irish American colleague whom you kidnapped."

Suddenly Holmes reached out and yanked up the left sleeve of the man, revealing an ornate tattoo. "And you are Sean O'Connor, a member of Sinn Féin[1]."

O'Connor pulled his arm away what little distance his restraints would allow. "What of it?" he said.

Hopkins picked up the questioning in his official capacity, "Mr. O'Connor, your fate may be determined by the answers to our questions. So, I advise you to answer very carefully. Were you acting on your own when you kidnapped Jack O'Neill, or were you under orders from someone else?"

O'Connor looked down at the tabletop and shook his head. Finally, he looked up at the Inspector and replied in his thick Irish brogue, "My mates and I did it ourselves. No one told us to do anything."

I looked up at Holmes who, imperceptibly, shook his head, confirming that this was a lie. I'm sure Hopkins noted it as well, but he continued on. "Then that leaves us with the question, why? What was your purpose in taking O'Neill?"

The prisoner smirked, "Just look at him. A lad that size should be worth a bit of money to someone. A circus, manual labour, a bodyguard, a deck hand on a ship. I put feelers out and was waiting for the best offer."

---

[1] Sinn Féin is an Irish republican political party dedicated to the end of British jurisdiction in Ireland.

"You did not consider the value of a ransom?" asked Hopkins.

"I did not believe his master had the wherewithal to come up with a satisfactory amount."

That comment rankled me and I spoke up for the first time, "His companion was *not* his master! O'Neill is a free man travelling with United States Marshal, Bat Masterson for the purpose of participating in the Olympic Games."

The mention of Masterson being a U.S. Marshal seemed to give O'Connor pause. But he recovered and bulled his way forward. "All the more reason not to expect a sufficient ransom."

Hopkins leaned back and folded his arms across his chest, "So, you claim full responsibility. You were not acting on orders from Sinn Féin or any other person?"

"That's right. It was all my own doing. I enlisted my mates just so we could carry the big fellow once he was unconscious."

"Very well. That will be all for now," said Hopkins. The guards will take you back to your cell."

Holmes suggested which prisoner to bring next and the guards took O'Connor back and retrieved the next kidnapper.

While we waited, I asked my friend, "How did you know that was O'Connor and that he had a tattoo on his arm?"

Holmes leaned his back against the wall and replied, "I saw the tattoo at the house as he was coming down the stairs putting on his shirt in response to our cry of 'fire'. As to his being the leader, all the other men looked to him as we were preparing to take them out to the police van."

Hopkins asked, "Do you believe he acted on his own, without orders?"

Holmes shook his head, "I doubt it, but I'll reserve judgement on that until we've talked to the others. I am aware that many Sinn Féin cells are given *carte blanche* to act on their own, as long as they inform their superiors so that they don't interfere with each other, or upset a larger plan."

Holmes made a suggestion to Hopkins who agreed and we awaited the next prisoner. This was the man who had been on guard on the ground floor of the house. The man limped into the room, escorted by a guard who again, chained the fellow to the table.

Hopkins consulted a pad of paper where he had been taking notes. "You are Michael McGurk, of Donamore." He looked up from his notes and squinted at the fellow, "I looked it up. That's in County Tyrone is it not?"

McGurk kept his head down and merely mumbled his assent. Then Hopkins nodded to Holmes who started the questioning.

"You fellows picked a particularly unusual person to kidnap," stated Holmes. "Mr. O'Connor tells us he never would have risked such an attempt on so formidable a human being, had he not been ordered to do so. Did you ever question why? Mr. O'Neill is not English, merely a visiting American. An Irish-American, in fact."

"I did nothing but drive," mumbled McGurk, still looking down. "O'Connor pays me to take people or cargo from one place to another, that's all."

"So," continued Holmes, "you were not aware that his business on that night was the kidnapping of the travelling companion of a fellow McGurk?"

Our prisoner's head shot up at that. Now that I could see him more clearly, I observed that he was only about thirty years of age. His clothes were rumpled but clean. His face was in want of a shave. But the shape of it and his features were reminiscent of photographs I'd seen of a young Bat Masterson. His black hair was unkempt and curled over his ears and collar. His clear blue eyes were in sharp contrast to his otherwise dark features.

"What be ye talkin' about?" he demanded. "That big black was travelling with that Masterson fella."

Holmes folded his arms and leaned against the wall, "United States Marshal, Bat Masterson's mother is a McGurk from County Tyrone, who emigrated to Canada before he was born."

Holmes let that statement settle. McGurk's eyes shifted back and forth as he digested this statement. Holmes let him stew on that for half a minute, then continued, "Masterson brought

O'Neill, the grandson of an Irish-American slaveholder, to England because that is where the Olympic Games are being held. O'Neill wanted a chance to beat the English boxing champions on their own soil. Did O'Connor tell you that?"

McGurk finally looked up at Holmes with defiance on his face. "I don't believe you! Let me talk to Masterson!"

Holmes shifted his hands to his trouser pockets and dropped his chin to his chest as he pursed his lips in thought and slowly paced around the table. I knew there was no real thought involved. He and Masterson had already discussed this when they discovered McGurk's identity. I'd seen him use this supposed act of indecision many times over our years working together. It was a ploy to make a suspect or prisoner feel as if they'd won a point when he finally agrees. This act of hesitation gives his opponent a false sense of confidence. Finally, he looked at Hopkins as if seeking approval and replied.

"If the Inspector has no objection, we can arrange that. Masterson is still in the building, is he not?"

This last was addressed directly at Hopkins who played along by nodding, "Yes, we've asked him and O'Neill to write up their statements. They won't be allowed to leave until I am informed."

Holmes turned to me, "Dr. Watson, would you be so good as to retrieve the Marshal?"

I knew that Holmes didn't want to leave McGurk at this critical juncture and, of course, Hopkins needed to remain with his prisoner. Holmes would continue to subtly intimidate McGurk. Small physical actions and conversation with Hopkins about him, as if he wasn't even in the room. Just enough to steer him toward the truth of the matter. Holmes had written a monograph on the subject of interrogation and was using the techniques best suited to a minion like McGurk.

I returned with Masterson and Inspector Hopkins vacated his seat so the Marshal could sit and look the prisoner in the eye. McGurk could not hide a reaction of startlement as he caught sight of his purported relative. As the Marshal sat, he also was eyeing McGurk. Each man tilted his head this way and that to examine the other's features. Just as the Marshal began to speak, McGurk asked a question, "'Bat's' not an Irish name, what did your father name ye?"

Masterson shifted in his seat, having never been comfortable with his birth name, finally he answered, "Bartholomew William Barclay Masterson."

I suppressed a smile as I recalled an old army comrade who had also hated the biblical appellation of Bartholomew. He went by Bart, except during official roll calls. He also engaged in fisticuffs when someone called him by his full name in an attempt at amusement or insult. My brief reverie was brought back to the present by the next question.

"What be your mother's maiden name?"

"Catherine McGurk," replied the Marshal.

The Irishman tilted his head, as if wrestling with a decision he did not wish to acknowledge, then asked another question, "Who were her brothers and sisters?"

Now it was Masterson's turn to search his memory, "She occasionally mentioned her sisters, Roisin and Cara. I forgot how many brothers she had. I seem to recall her Bible listed Colm, Ronan, Patrick and one or two others."

McGurk leaned back in his chair, left arm crossing his chest, right elbow resting on it as his hand came up to his mouth, thumb rubbing the stubble under his chin. After a few seconds of letting him absorb this information, Masterson asked a question of his own.

"So, which of those men was your grandfather?"

The fist at McGurk's chin dropped toward his left shoulder as he inhaled a sharp breath and slowly exhaled it. At last, he folded his hands on the table as he leaned forward. "My grandfather was Ronan McGurk, God rest his soul. Ye look enough like him to be his brother. So, apparently, ye be a distant cousin."

Holmes interrupted, "We realize you were not aware of that fact, McGurk, but you know what happens to men who are convicted of being Sinn Féin."

McGurk's eyes widened at that, "I am **not** Sinn Féin. I just drive, from one place to another, whenever O'Connor calls me.

He's never done anything violent. He hired me when I was having a hard time getting work. My limp limits a lot of manual labour and I've no temperament for office work. But it doesn't affect my ability to drive and he pays me enough to live on."

"So, you are not aware of who O'Connor gets his orders from?" asked Hopkins.

McGurk shook his head, "No, I always thought he was the boss and we were doing jobs for clients of his."

"What did you think when your latest cargo was a man?" enquired the Inspector.

McGurk shifted in his seat, "Occasionally we pick up someone who owes a client a lot of money, or has stolen something."

The Inspector looked at Holmes who shook his head and flicked his fingers in dismissal. Hopkins had the guard return McGurk to the cells with instructions to keep him far away from the others so they could not communicate.

Chapter Six

When we were alone again, Holmes asked the Marshal a question, "Had you considered the feelings of the Irish in this matter of O'Neill fighting in the Olympics?"

"What do you mean?"

"Have you heard of the Sinn Féin movement in Ireland?"

"No," answered Masterson. "What is that?"

Holmes replied, "Literally it means 'we, ourselves'. It is an Irish independence movement. Anti-British sentiment is running high in Ireland, as it always has, yet more so recently. Already several of Ireland's top athletes have refused to participate in this year's Olympics. After 1904 they decided to no longer be used by the British to boost their medal count."

"Are you saying that this band of Irishmen kidnapped Jack to keep him from fighting?"

"It is the most probable deduction. Certainly it is more palatable than the reasons O'Connor stated."

"So, what happens now?"

Hopkins replied to that, "We speak with the other prisoners and get their statements. Then, we use that information to further investigate and see what other crimes we can charge them with and possibly find a link to leaders higher up the chain. For now, the kidnapping charges will hold them for trial."

The rest of the interrogations bore out Holmes's suspicions. While none admitted to being Sinn Féin, their attitudes and reactions certainly did not dismiss the probability.

On our way home from the Yard, Holmes's expression was thoughtful as he stared out of the cab window. I knew the scenery was merely a background to the considerations swirling in his head. Arriving at the home we had shared so long, Mrs. Hudson provided us with afternoon tea, though Holmes took no notice of the excellent biscuits and merely drank half the cup of steaming Earl Grey. At last he disappeared into his bedroom. I waited patiently, contemplating whether I should leave or send a message to my wife that I would not be home for dinner.

Finally, he emerged in worn tweeds that had seen better days, a dusty old bowler hat and a reddish/brown wig with long sideboards. A tattered overcoat, stained scarf and fingerless wool gloves completed the outfit. He also sported a belly that appeared to add a good twenty pounds to his frame, enhanced by a slight stoop to his posture.

"Watson, I apologize for making you wait. I have been debating whether or not your presence is essential to this evening's task. I have decided it is better if I go by myself."

"But, if I can be of assistance, Holmes ..."

"No, I must do this alone. You go home to your wife. Please meet me back here tomorrow morning at nine o'clock. If I am not here or if I have not sent a message, give this to Inspector Hopkins. It is the location I am going to tonight where I expect to meet other members of Sinn Féin."

"Holmes!" I cried as I took the paper that he handed me. "It's too dangerous for you to step into the lion's den alone!"

"On the contrary, too many strangers would raise suspicion. I have an established, albeit not recent, identity as an Irish workman named Patrick O'Toole."

Here he switched to a thick Irish brogue, "He's a bit of a rogue who skirts the fringes of the law now and again. I'm just going to poke me nose about and see what I can learn."

Knowing better than to argue, I bid him good afternoon and returned home, hoping that the morrow would bring about the success he desired. Over dinner I discussed the events of the case with my wife. While she has admiration for Holmes and his work and has been supportive of my efforts to assist him when needed, she is always looking out for my safety. Naturally, she was in agreement with Holmes's decision to leave me behind. She has been widowed once and does not wish to repeat the experience.

"I'm sure Mr. Holmes will be quite all right, John. After all these years honing his craft and expertise, he is certainly up to the task."

"No doubt," I agreed. "But there is always the random chance that something could go wrong. An unanticipated event or person who can tip the scales in an unexpected fashion."

She finished her last bite and sat back, her long fingers running around the rim of her wine glass as she stared down into it, as if she could read the future in the swirling Muscat. Finally, she looked across at me with those intelligent and loving hazel eyes.

"You want to go to that address tonight, don't you?"

Of course, there was no denying the obvious fact that I was worried about my friend. In over twenty-five years of association with him, covering hundreds of cases, I could count the times he was physically overcome on one hand, more or less. At least, the ones I was aware of. Yet, still, I knew he played a dangerous game and that this particular case was irksome to him. The indignation he felt at O'Neill's treatment might draw him into taking a higher than normal risk.

I nodded as I set my own wineglass on the table. "I should at least like to go and assess the lie of the land. Make sure that things are peaceable."

I gazed at her with a combination of imploring and determination. She set her own glass down. "Then we shall go together."

"Oh, no, no," I replied softly but firmly, shaking my head. But she was already up and heading out to the entrance hall cupboard to retrieve her winter coat. I caught up to her, insisting that it was too dangerous.

She looked at me as she flipped her long blonde tresses over her collar. "John, I've read the notes on your stories where Mary played a role in solving the case. I'm certainly no less courageous than your previous wife, God rest her soul. I promise I will stay out of the way, but, if there comes an opportunity where I may assist, I should be proud to do so. Now, put on your hat and coat, dear, and bring your revolver."

Forty-five minutes later our cab pulled up around the corner from the address Holmes had given me. The driver was a cabbie I knew named Charlie, who often patrolled our neighbourhood seeking fares. Therefore, I had felt comfortable discussing the case with my wife *en route*. The building we observed was a public house. A two-storey wooden frame structure, painted a dark green with cream-colored accents around the doors and windows. That same cream colour declared its name in Gaelic font above the main double doors as The Stout Heart. The windows on either side of the door displayed a Celtic harp with 'Guinness Stout' on one and the 'Jameson Whiskey' logo on the other, with its red shield featuring a gold 'X' topped by a sailing ship and the family *Sine Metu* motto on the ribbon beneath.

At the moment I wished I could invoke that feeling of 'without fear'. But, imagining Holmes in this obvious den of Irishmen, seeking out knowledge about Sinn Féin without coming under suspicion and possible violence if they discovered his identity, was anything but comforting. The added burden of having my wife along and worrying about her safety made the task even less so.

The lights within were bright and there seemed to be a rousing crowd, judging by the sounds emitted whenever the doors opened to a wide variety of men going in and out. Most seemed to be labourers, but there were also quite a few who appeared to be dressed as merchants or clerks. No one in formal attire, but an occasional gentleman. I thought I even saw a Member of Parliament enter, though with his collar pulled up around his face it was hard to be sure.

It seemed everything was as it should be. No violent sounds emitted. Charlie got down off his seat and checked the horse's harness, then stepped up to the kerb and back to my window, which was on the kerbside of the cab. I having assisted my wife into the seat first. "Doctor," he said in a low voice. "I daresay we not wait here too long. There's a lookout on the corner and he'll get suspicious if I just sit here. He can see the missus from where his is, so he knows I'm not empty, waitin' for a fare."

Just then, my wife whispered, "Look, is that Mr. Holmes?"

I leaned forward a bit and saw that it was, indeed, my disguised friend. He had walked out of the pub, stopped to light a cigarette, the orange glow of the tip burning brightly as he inhaled. He began to walk in the direction of the lookout, but had not taken two steps when another fellow stepped out and began to follow.

"I don't like the look of that," I said.

Before I could move, my wife had opened her door and sprung out into the street. Walking swiftly across, she waved her hand and called out, "Patrick!"

Holmes, in character, but obviously surprised to hear a woman call out his name, turned and cocked his head at the sight of her. He stepped off the pavement and met her before she had to navigate the gutter.

She stopped in front of him, holding a hand to her breastbone and another on his sleeve, as if holding on and out of breath. "Patrick, I've been looking all over for you! James has taken a turn for the worse and is calling for you. He's delirious, seeing enemies all around him. You must come at once!"

"Are you certain, Adelaide?" he said, playing along. "This has happened before when he's in his cups."

"Oh, he's running a terrible fever. This is more than drink. You must come!" she cried, throwing her arms about him. As she did so she whispered into his shoulder. "You are being followed and the man at the corner is a lookout."

He pushed her gently out to arm's length and looked up and down the street as if checking for traffic. The man who had been following had stopped to light his pipe. The lookout was looking in the other direction and taking a sip from a flask.

Holmes looked at my wife steadily and asked, "Is that your cab?"

"Yes, Patrick. Please, come!"

"Very well," he replied, still in his Irish brogue. "Fortunately, I've finished me business for the evening. Let's be going." He took her by the arm and escorted her back to the cab. Seeing that I was inside, he made sure to stand in such a way that no one could see around him as he opened the door and passed my wife in. Once the three of us were settled, Charlie whipped up his horse and made to gallop away.

"Well, Watson, still the adventure seeker, I see. And you, Mrs. Watson, you played your part admirably, but I assure you, it was not necessary. I had a plan to lose anyone who trailed after me, and my five-shot Bulldog was handy, should I have become outnumbered."

Suitably chastised I started to offer an explanation, but he held up his hand, "A moment, Doctor." He poked his head out the window, "Charlie, please ensure we are not followed and take us back to the Watson's."

"As you please, Mr. Holmes," answered our cabbie.

By the time we had reached our home in Marylebone, Holmes had removed his wig and padded waist and looked more like his normal self, save the casual clothing. He insisted on paying off Charlie and sent the cabbie on his way. Once inside, we sat in the dining room. Over steaming cups of Darjeeling, we asked Holmes to tell us what he had achieved.

With a gesture of asking permission of my wife to smoke his pipe, he lit it with her nodded assent. The smooth aroma wafted toward the ceiling as he sat back to weave his tale.

"I entered The Stout Heart, knowing that it is a common gathering place for Irishmen in London. I know of several suspected members of Sinn Féin who frequent that particular hostelry. My intention was to put out feelers for any significant persons recently arrived in London, who might be in a position to have given orders to O'Connor regarding the abduction of O'Neill. Within five minutes I knew such inquisitiveness would be unnecessary.

"Off in a corner, convenient to the rear exit, there sat a gentleman alone with his back to the wall. I judged him to be in his middle fifties, broad of shoulder but lean of build. He had long white hair that fell in waves over his collar and kept incessantly erupting from being tucked behind his ears to give him a wild look. He was clean shaven with leather-like skin that bespoke of an outdoor occupation in his youth. His pale blue eyes took in everything around the room. One might suspect him of being a gentleman of means. He was well-dressed in a dark three-piece suit of above average quality and he ate with his right hand only, his left remaining below the tabletop. Presumably it was in his lap as good manners dictate, however, having occasion to bend over and pick up a pack of matches that I had dropped, I was able to spy out that his hand was actually tucked into his coat where he likely had weapon to draw.

"He was approached by one fellow who came hat in hand. I could not hear their brief conversation. However, as he bent down to speak softly to his fellow Irishman, I observed that he used his hat to hide the fact that he was slipping an envelope next to the fellow's plate.

"I also noted, upon his approach, two fellows nearby who tensed visibly. Each reaching inside their coats, ostensibly ready to draw weapons."

He stopped and took a hearty swallow of tea. Setting his cup back down, he continued.

"My Irish brogue had confirmed by *bona fides* with the barman as a fellow countryman when I had ordered a small bowl of stew with bread after finishing my initial beer. I took a seat about twenty feet away from the gentleman at the table. Two more fellows came by. One a docker, judging by his scarred hands, and trouser knees, merely came and gave a verbal report. He was sent off with some coins, a nod and a wave. The next fellow was well-dressed and I recognized him as a manager at the Fenchurch Street branch of the Seamen and Merchants Bank. (A fact that I will impart to brother Mycroft at his government offices.) He merely gave our fellow a small notebook. Possibly an accounting book from the fact that it was given a mere glance and the manager was rewarded with a smile.

"I gave the fellow some time to finish his meal. Then I approached. Being a complete stranger brought his two guards each a step closer. He, himself, however, greeted me with a look of curiosity, while he kept his left hand beneath the table.

"'What can I do for you, my good man?' he asked, attempting to remain nonchalant.

"Hat in a hand I pointed toward him, stating softly, 'I do not know your name, sir. But I consider meself a good judge of character. I know an important man when I see one. Especially a leader such as yourself. I've a bit of news that might be of interest to ye.'

"He looked me up and down and finally said, 'And what would this bit of information cost me?'

"'Not a farthing, sir,' I replied, hand on my heart. 'I just thought you might be a man who would like to know the whereabouts of a certain Sean O'Connor.'

"He sat back in his chair, now with both thumbs hitched into his waistcoat pockets. In answer he gave his head a slight shake, the long white hairs again falling out from behind his ears. 'I don't know the fellow, but if you care to give me your information I can spread the word to see who might be interested.'"

I set down the cup of tea I had been holding, "Sounds pretty cagey to me, Holmes. Did you believe him?"

"It did not matter, Doctor. He either put O'Connor up to O'Neill's kidnapping or can get word to whoever did."

"So, you told him?"

"I did indeed," answered the detective with a smile. "Try as he might, he could not hide the disappointment that O'Connor was in jail for kidnapping."

"What did he do, Holmes?" asked my wife, who had been listening in rapt attention.

"He said that he would share the information among his acquaintances, then he fished out a half crown from his pocket and tossed it my way. That gave me the opening I wanted. I set the coin down on the table and spoke again.

"I said, 'No pay, sir. My loyalties are my own and need not be bought. I have one more piece of information for you to pass along, if you please. The gentleman who was kidnapped, Jack O'Neill, would like to meet with whoever gave the order. Says if he understands the reason, then maybe a compromise can be reached to everyone's satisfaction.'

"He stood up and faced me with an appraising look, then held out his hand. I took it with an appropriate amount of deference. As he shook my hand, he said, 'Flanagan, Brady Flanagan. A pleasure to meet you, Mister ...'

"'Patrick O'Toole, at your service, sir.'

"'Well, now, Patrick. You give me two days and I'll see what can be done to find the people he wants to meet. Can you have him come by here the day after tomorrow at seven in the evening?'

"'As you say, sir, I'll pass that along.'

"With a loud guffaw and a slap on my shoulder he said, 'Fair enough. Good evening to you, sir!'"

Finished with his story, I asked Holmes, "Will you have O'Neill meet him or whoever shows up?"

"Oh, Flanagan is behind it. No doubt about it."

"How can you be sure?" Came the question from my wife's side of the table.

My friend smiled, "Because, he never asked who O'Neill was."

Chapter Seven

Two days later, the streets around The Stout Heart bore an unusual amount of traffic and parked vehicles. Some had been there since noon, in an effort to throw off suspicion of having arrived just around the time of the meeting. Others appeared to be in their normal nightly positions. Holmes and Hopkins had prepared for the worst.

According to my friend, as he, Masterson, O'Neill and I approached in an enclosed carriage just before seven o'clock, several of the vehicles we passed held Flanagan's men, ready for action should this prove to be a trap for him.

"I would say our resources are just about evenly matched," he remarked. "I trust that we can keep this meeting peaceable. It is certainly in Flanagan's interest to do so."

"Won't Hopkins be arresting Flanagan for kidnapping?" Masterson asked.

"I assure you, Flanagan won't admit to any such thing. He tipped his hand the other night when he said he would 'spread the word'. He'll pretend that he is negotiating on behalf of another. That way he avoids guilt and any association with Sinn Féin."

Holmes was dressed as himself this evening and led the way in. I followed and noted a few heads turned our way. Behind me was O'Neill, and once he stepped across the threshold every eye in the place snapped to and was riveted at the sight. I doubt anyone even noticed Masterson bringing up the rear.

Flanagan was at the same table with the same two bodyguards close at hand that Holmes had described. Even this elderly Irishman was surprised at the sheer mass of humanity represented by O'Neill's presence. Unlike his usual practice of remaining seated when approached, he stood. His bodyguards stepped forward and flanked him, but he held his arms out to wave them back.

"You must be the gentlemen invited by Patrick O'Toole," he began, arms crossed across his waistcoat and, I noted, his left hand inside his jacket.

He locked eyes with Holmes and each took their measure of the other. At last, he held out his hand and introduced himself. "Brady Flanagan. I'm here to represent the interest of a certain party who has a concern about Black Jack O'Neill, whom I assume is this gentleman."

Holmes shook his hand and introduced us. "I am Sherlock Holmes. O'Toole occasionally runs messages for me. This is Dr. John Watson. Of course, this is indeed, Jack O'Neill and this is his manager, United States Marshal, Bat Masterson."

Flanagan hesitated at Masterson's title, but shook each of our hands in turn, saving O'Neill for last. While he had long fingers, his hand was no match for the giant grip of the boxer. He was clearly uncomfortable at not being able to exude his personality through his handshake.

"Please, be seated gentlemen," said the Irish leader.

My part in this affair was strictly observation, though I was armed with my army revolver in case of trouble. Therefore, I sat at the next table over, close enough to hear and see what was happening and react if things turned ugly.

Holmes deferred to Masterson and his protégé. The Marshal leaned back, thumbs hitched into his belt. I knew he had his own weapon secreted in a holster in the small of his back. "Mr. Flanagan, as the son of Irish parents, I appeal to you to negotiate in good faith on behalf of your ... acquaintance. Jack here is also of Irish descent and is concerned that men of his mother country should treat him in such a fashion as to kidnap him, lock him up and give him barely enough to eat to survive."

Flanagan took this in, pursed his lips, shook his head and responded, "I am sure my acquaintance was not aware of such harsh treatment. He implied to me that O'Connor was merely to detain Mr. O'Neill until he could arrive from Dublin. His desire was to appeal to him not to be incentivised by English greed to fight in the Olympics as a British athlete. My acquaintance is aware that all Irish-American boxers have boycotted these games, as have all the athletes of Ireland. With this sort of pressure, his only choice would have been to fight under British colours. We were determined that this should not happen."

I watched Holmes's face at the slip of the word 'we'. He obviously noted it, but it really didn't matter. The detective was already convinced that Flanagan was speaking for himself.

Masterson turned to O'Neill, "I think you should speak for yourself, Jack. Tell Mr. Flanagan the situation."

Even sitting down, O'Neill towered over everyone at the table, including Holmes, who is over six feet himself. He folded his huge hands on the table as he leaned forward. In his deep bass voice, the vibrato shaking our eardrums, he told his tale.

"I believe I can be the world heavyweight champion, Mr. Flanagan. The Olympics would give me the publicity I need to demand a bout with Jack Johnson. Once I beat him, then Tommy Burns[1] would have to grant me a shot at his title."

Flanagan sat back, looked at O'Neill and replied, "Burns just defended his title against Jack Palmer over at Wonderland in Whitechapel for his 38th win and 21st knockout. Are you sure you can take him?"

Masterson spoke up at that, "I've been following boxing for over twenty years, Mr. Flanagan. Have you seen Burns?"

Flanagan shook his head, "I did not arrive in time for his recent bout."

---

[1] Canadian-born Tommy Burns had famously insisted, "I will defend my title against all comers, none barred. By this I mean white, black, Mexican, Indian, or any other nationality. I propose to be the champion of the world, not the white, or the Canadian, or the American. If I am not the world's best man in the heavyweight division, I don't want the title."

"The man is five foot seven and one hundred and seventy-five pounds. He's a fierce fighter and can take a punch. That is how he's beaten so many men much larger than he. But his footwork is sloppy and his reach is only seventy-three inches. That is long for his height, but no match for Jack here. Could I borrow one of these gentlemen, Mr. Flanagan? This fellow here is about the right size." He said, pointing to one of the bodyguards.

Flanagan looked over his shoulder and cocked his head for the fellow to walk over to where Masterson was now standing up. The Marshal looked the fellow over and asked, "How tall are you, son?"

"Five foot, eight," he answered.

"Close enough. Now you just stand right there. Jack, if you would please stand up?"

Jack O'Neill rose out of his chair, sprouting like the beanstalk in the nursery rhyme. When he finally reached his full height, he looked down on the guard. "Now Jack, please put your arm out. That's fine. Now, you, sir. Walk up to his fist and hold your arm out toward him."

When the guard's chest reached Jack's fist, his own hand fell a good seven inches short of O'Neill.

"As you can see, Mr. Flanagan, Burns would be lucky to even lay a finger on Jack. He's a foot shorter and would certainly never land a knockout punch. Let alone the fact that Jack has one hundred pounds on him. Can you believe what one punch from this fist would do to Burns?"

He patted Jack's fist which seemed the size of a large grapefruit.

Flanagan waved his man back to his position. Masterson and Jack sat back down and the Marshal continued, "I do not know if you are aware, sir, but Jack fights under the nickname 'The Black Irish Pug'. He has never had any intention of denying either his Irish roots or his race. If the British insist otherwise, he will not acquiesce to them. But it would be a shame not to allow him his full measure of opportunity."

Flanagan leaned forward, his elbows on the table, his long, white hair shifting forward to cover his ears. "Burns is scheduled to be in Dublin on St. Patrick's Day to defend his title against Jem Roche. If you can be in Dublin at that time, I should be able to arrange a meeting with Burns's manager. Perhaps we can get you on his schedule while he's in Europe. I hear he's going to Paris after Dublin."

Masterson drummed his fingers on the table, looked at Jack who nodded, and replied, "If you can pull that off, Mr. Flanagan, we would be indebted to you."

Flanagan smiled, his look alternated between the Marshal and the boxer, "Roche beat the former British heavyweight champion last October. That was satisfying to all Ireland. If he can beat Burns, so much the better. It will make the Olympic bouts pale by comparison because the real title will be ours. If he doesn't beat Burns, I can think of no better person to bring the title to Ireland than you, Mr. O'Neill. Are we in agreement?"

O'Neill looked to Masterson, who merely nodded and said, "Up to you, Jack. I'll support whatever decision you make."

The boxer nodded back, then reached his long arm across the table to shake Flanagan's hand, "You have a deal, Mr. Flanagan." But before he let go, he continued to hold the elder man's hand tightly, "Just one other point. If Roche beats Burns, I want a shot at Roche. The title still stays among the Irish, no matter which of us wins so I trust that won't be a problem?"

Flanagan frowned slightly, "While I have some pull in Irish boxing circles, I cannot speak for Roche without getting his consent. If he's agreeable, I'll make it happen."

O'Neill gave a final shake and sat back. The rest of the meeting was spent discussing particulars of the trip to Dublin. Flanagan also stated that he would ensure the kidnappers were 'dealt with' should they escape British justice.

Walking back outside, Holmes stopped in the light of the entrance and lit a cigar. This was the signal for Hopkins and his men to stand down.

Hopkins joined us and we returned to my home in Queen Anne Street.

We all sat around the dining table drinking brandy and smoking cigars. My wife had joined us, insisting on hearing all

117

the details as we relayed them to Hopkins. When at last, Holmes had given his full account, Hopkins asked, "So was it the Sinn Féin or not?"

Holmes swirled the last of his brandy around his snifter, appearing to contemplate his answer in the amber liquid. Then he answered, "I have no doubt that many of the men in that establishment are members, and that Brady Flanagan holds a leadership position. However, I do not have proof, which is why we are here and not escorting him to the cells at Scotland Yard."

Hopkins sighed, "Well, at least we have the kidnappers and that's an open and shut case. Mr. O'Neill, you'll need to keep in touch with us so we can inform you when the trial will be so we can call you as a witness."

Masterson spoke up at that, "We'll need a few days' notice on that, Inspector. We'll be leaving for Dublin soon and will likely be there until sometime beyond the 17th of March"

"As long as a telegram can reach you, that shouldn't be a problem."

"Actually, I'm looking forward to it. St. Patrick's Day in my ancestral home. How many Irish-Americans get to do that? It will be good for Jack to see the land of his ancestors as well."

The big boxer nodded, "I recognize that I've had opportunities that many of my race are denied. The more I learn, the more I can share with those less fortunate than I. Perhaps I can help lead my people to more equal recognition by proving we can get college degrees and compete among the best athletes in the world. While you all have treated me as equal, it's obvious from the remarks of my kidnappers that there is still a long way to go to reach all people's hearts and minds. If my athletic ability gains me a platform to speak out, then I have an obligation to do so."

"Well said, sir" remarked Holmes. "I wish you the best of luck."

"Hear, hear!" I declared, raising my glass in a toast. "To the next Heavyweight Champion of the World!"

Thus ended the case of the Black Irish Pug. But that's not the end of the story. As I write these words, many years after the facts, the story of racial inequality goes on. The last I heard, O'Neill had retired from his job as a civil engineer in New York City and was now the Reverend Black Jack O'Neill, a civil rights activist and preacher of some notoriety.

The Rest Of The Story

On St. Patrick's Day 1908, Jem Roche fought Tommy Burns for the world heavyweight title at the Theatre Royal, Dublin, with a purse of £1,500 (split 80:20). He was knocked out after 88 seconds.

Unfortunately, while Burns was willing to take on O'Neill, his schedule was booked for the rest of the year. He had two fights set for Paris in April and June, then on to Australia for bouts in August, September and December. It was O'Neill's bad luck that the fight in December was against the black heavyweight champ, Jack Johnson. Johnson beat Burns on points in 14 rounds to take the title.

Once he was the world's heavyweight champ, Johnson did not fight a black opponent for the first five years of his reign. Blacks were not given a chance at the title allegedly because Johnson felt that he could make more money fighting white boxers who were always billed as 'The Great White Hope' in their attempt to bring the title back to the white race.

Meanwhile, at the 1908 Olympics, several Irish champions refused to compete rather than be used again by the British. Helplessly watching the latest British suppression of Irish nationalism put the Irish Americans at a fever pitch.

On the 13th July, King Edward VII declared the Fourth Olympiad opened. The stadium displayed the flags of all the competing nations, except that of the United States. Where was the American flag? The British said that they had been unable

121

to find one. Equally insulting, the American team was assigned a marching position just in front of the British colonies, who, in turn, were followed by the United Kingdom. The symbolism could not have been lost on anyone present.

As the music of the Grenadier Guards filled the stadium, King Edward VII settled into the royal box with Queen Alexandra and Princess Victoria at his side. At the bugler's signal, the gate leading to the athletes' quarters was flung open and the parade of national teams began. One by one, they marched and dipped their flags to the King of England. It was a glorious moment for the host nation. Even the hard rain that had drenched the stadium earlier in the day had stopped. God seemed to be smiling on the British empire.

Then came the Americans, including the world-record hammer thrower and New York City cop, Matthew J. McGrath. When they approached the royal box, the County Tipperary, Irish-born, McGrath, a six-foot two-inch, 245-pound human bull of a man, stepped beside the team's flag bearer who had finally procured a proper flag and is rumoured to have said, "Dip that banner and you're in hospital tonight." Old Glory went unbowed past the King of England.

The British were left in shock. London newspapers lashed the Americans with the severest criticism they could muster and called for an apology. Veteran Olympian and world-record discus thrower Martin J. Sheridan, another New York City Irish cop, spoke for 'Mighty Matt' McGrath and the other American team members when he answered by pointing to the flag and saying, "This flag dips to no earthly king." The precedent had been set. To this day the United States does not dip its flag at Olympic ceremonies.

The Golden Grail

Editor's Note

From the notes gleaned on this case, it appears that Sherlock Holmes attempted to have Watson include textbook-like instructions on how a detective should proceed to follow a case. Something he often felt lacking in the Doctor's 'romanticized' stories. I have attempted to include the detective's observations as they were attached.

Chapter One

My notes indicate that it was the latter part of December in 1888, the week before Christmas, in fact, when an exalted person requested an audience with my companion, the consulting detective, Sherlock Holmes. This request came by way of a letter delivered by the early afternoon post and brought upstairs by our landlady, Mrs. Hudson.

Having just finished lunch, Holmes was preoccupied with a chemical experiment, therefore, I accepted the envelope from her at the doorway to our sitting room. Glancing at the addressee and seeing that it was for my friend, I carried it over and set it on the arm of his favourite chair by the fireplace, there being no safe space on his laboratory table.

I stirred the fire and added more logs on this chilly afternoon. Then I sat in my usual seat on the sofa across the way. I had just opened the afternoon paper when Holmes spoke without looking up, "Who is it from, Watson?"

I looked over the top of my paper toward him and replied, "Someone named Arthur Campbell, Baron of Bellrose."

That seemed to catch his attention. Holmes was never impressed by titles, but the fact that a Scottish baron was contacting him suggested the possibility of a case and Holmes was anxious for a new problem to solve. Inaction was the bane of his existence. More than once I had heard him cry in exasperation, "Give me data, give me problems, give me the most abstract of puzzles to solve. My brain craves exercise!"

He removed his goggles and gloves and came over to sit in his chair. He picked up the envelope and began an examination which was quite familiar to me. This time, however, he requested me to make notes of his actions.

"Watson, I am tempted to have you record my processes for future use as an instruction manual for Scotland Yard," said he, as he picked up the envelope. "Please take this down."

I retrieved pencil and paper from the writing desk.

Holmes proceeded to speak as follows:

"1. When receiving a written request, determine how it was delivered. Did it come by post? Was it hand-delivered and by whom – the potential client, or a confederate, or servant of such client, or a messenger service? Was it in the form of a telegram? If hand delivered by messenger, make a thorough examination of the outside of the envelope for any possible contaminants which may indicate a poisonous substance within.

2. If delivered by an agency, determine from whence it came by examining the postmark or telegraph office address. This will also tell you when it was sent and may give you a hint as to its urgency. This particular letter is postmarked two days ago in Ayrshire, Scotland.

3. Also note the return address and the sender's name. Is the full name used or a shortened version? Is there a title? Is it pre-printed stationery or hand-written? This can give you insights into the sender's character and status. It may determine a level of wealth, which may vary in spite of titles. As I recall, you once received a letter from a moderately wealthy friend, who handwrote 'Alex' in the return address, instead of the more formal 'Alexander'. This indicated someone who did not stand upon his station but was more informal in his manner. Here, we have a pre-printed, high-quality envelope noting the name and title: Arthur Campbell, Baron of Bellrose, Bellrose Castle, Ayrshire, Scotland.

4. Next, examine the outside of the envelope itself for quality of paper and any telltale marks such as a thumb impression, makeup, tear stains and the like. This can give you an idea of

the person's wealth, the presence of a woman, or the emotional state of the sender.

5. At this point you should feel the envelope thoroughly. Use your middle finger, as it is more sensitive to touch and more likely to discover any small enclosure. I have received, coins, locks of hair and all sorts of items people perceived as clues.

6. Now open the envelope carefully. In this case, the envelope has been sealed with wax and the clan seal has been used to impress it. Therefore, we shall preserve the seal by carefully slitting the envelope along the top."

Holmes did so with his penknife and carefully removed the sheet of paper within.

"7. The paper matches the envelope in age and quality and also includes the clan crest. Had it not been a good match, then one must be on the lookout for a possible forgery by someone who was able to steal an envelope.

8. Again, you check for any identifying features, tear stains and the like. Do not forget to look for any telltale scent such as perfume or other odour, which may help identify the sender or where it was sent from. Now you examine the handwriting."

He looked over the top of the page at me and said, "I've mentioned my monograph to you on the interpretation of handwriting, Watson. It should be noted as a separate reference tool. This particular message was written by an elderly, right-handed gentleman, suffering from arthritis. There are several hesitation points throughout, which could be due to his condition or a pause to gather his thoughts. However, the signature is quite bold and exudes pride."

I should make note to the reader of this tale that the actions described above are so natural to Holmes, that his analysis can be conducted within a minute. I asked him to read the note, for by now I was overcome by curiosity. His eyes shifted back and forth across the page for several seconds until I said in exasperation, "Out loud, if you please, Holmes!"

Holmes smirked, his impish sense of humour apparently brought forth by what he had read. He handed me the piece of paper and then retrieved one of his index volumes from the shelves.

Meanwhile, I read as follows:

> Dear Mr. Holmes,
>
> Greetings and felicitations of the Season. Allow me to introduce myself. I am Arthur Campbell, Baron of Bellrose and titular head of my branch of the Campbell Clan at Bellrose Castle.
>
> To get straight to the matter, I have been the victim of a theft. Such that, it is not merely against myself, but against my family, now and for generations to come.
>
> The local police are befuddled. In desperation, I wrote to the police in Edinburgh, hoping they might have more formidable resources. In reply, you were recommended to me by an official named Ewan Gibson.
>
> The item stolen is a golden Grail. Family tradition says it is the actual Holy Grail, entrusted to King Arthur's descendants by Sir Bors, the companion of Sir Galahad. As you may know, certain Campbell branches claim direct lineage with King Arthur.
>
> I realize that this sounds fanciful. However, this Grail has been in our family as far back as records are known. While it certainly has not bestowed eternal life upon any member of the clan, no male member in my line, from time immemorial, has failed to live to at least the age of 70. There are some clan records indicating miraculous actions that saved our men in battle. But that was long ago and I cannot confirm them.

Whatever the case, it is a treasured possession and its value in gold alone is worth several hundred pounds.

If you should be inclined to assist, please telegraph particulars as to your fee and expenses. I shall be happy to extend an advance to allow your purchase of the train fare. We have several guest rooms available to you here at Bellrose.

I hope you will be amenable to my plea. If you are unable, I would appreciate your thoughts as to other investigators who may be capable.

In all sincere hopes,

Arthur Campbell

I peered across to my friend and queried, "An interesting situation, Holmes. Who is this Ewan Gibson who recommended you?"

Holmes declined to look up from his examination of his index and merely answered, "Hmm? Gibson? Oh, just an old university colleague. I assisted him with a little problem at school and on a case a few years ago, after he joined the police force in Edinburgh.[1]

"Please enter this instruction into your notes, Doctor.

9. Investigate the sender's identity through independent means. *Burke's Peerage*, business directories, newspaper articles, library sources, government records, trusted individuals, etc."

I made the note, then asked, "And what do your files tell you about Arthur Campbell?"

---

[1] Published as *Mrs. Forrester's Complication* in *A Sherlock Holmes Alphabet of Cases, Volume Three (K-O)* by Roger Riccard (Baker Street Studios Limited, 2019). Unbeknownst to either man at this time, that case would later involve them with Mary Morstan, Watson's future wife, in Arthur Conan Doyle's *The Sign of Four*.

Holmes finally looked up and answered, "I have more than one individual by that name. However, the Baron of Bellrose does happen to be one of them.

"Campbell, Arthur Byron; Born 28th February 1821. Succeeded as 11th Baron of Bellrose on the 1st September 1858 upon death of father, Byron Bruce Campbell, aged 72. Widower, one daughter, Elise, married to Roy Lennox; twin nephews, Harold and Henry Fraser, sons of his sister, Brenda and husband, Donald Fraser. Member of the 92nd Regiment of Foot (Gordon Highlanders), served in the Crimean War and the Indian Rebellion, rising to the rank of Major. Scottish peerage. Member of Parliament 1868-1885. Residence: Bellrose Castle, Holmston, Ayrshire.

"The barony of Bellrose was created on the 20th September 1623 by King James I (King James VI of Scotland). First holder, Alexander Campbell. Achievement: Yellow boar's head on golden buckler. Motto: *Ne obliviscaris* (Forget Not). Tartan: Plaid of light green, light blue and black."

Holmes closed the book and descended into a contemplative mood. Although I had questions, I knew better than to interrupt his train of thought and held my tongue.

At last, he sat up. Returning the index to his shelves he remarked, "It poses an interesting diversion I should think, Doctor. I need to consult with some of the sources I've listed for you. Should I be inclined to travel to Ayrshire, would you be amenable to accompanying me, or do you have other plans this Christmas?"

"Nothing firm, Holmes. I should be happy to join you if I may be of assistance. It would be agreeable to spend Christmas in the land of my ancestors."

"Capital! If my enquiries merit my involvement, I shall telegraph Lord Campbell this afternoon and we can leave on the morrow."

With that he threw on his ulster, scarf and homburg. With umbrella in hand, he went out to brave the threatening weather. I looked over the list of sources he had asked me to note down. I concluded that he would likely be headed to the public records office at Somerset House and possibly to the

British Museum. I also recalled that, earlier in the year, he had introduced me to Thomas Kent, a reporter for *The Daily Telegraph*, while we were investigating the fate of Andrew Etherege. However, as I thought it out, it seemed unlikely that Kent, whose primary role was as a theatre critic with occasional reporting on criminal cases which Holmes brought to him, would have much information regarding a Scottish Lord.

I walked over to the window. The dark grey skies were threatening to let loose their moisture at any moment. The storm of the previous day had resulted in deposits of snow, which now lay, blackened by soot, in piles along the kerbs of Baker Street where it had been shovelled. Despite Christmas decorations in shop windows attempting to create a festive mood, it made for a dreary and depressing atmosphere. Yes, it would be good to be relieved of the dark days of winter in London. I found myself suddenly hopeful for the opportunity to spend Christmas in the Scottish lowlands where snow would be clean and white. Even a blizzard upon an open landscape would be preferable to the crowded and polluted capital.

Chapter Two

I decided to put my time to good use while awaiting my friend's return. As he went about researching the character of our potential client, I chose to consider the object of his investigation. I supposed this would be his next instruction:

"10. If the crime in question be a theft, learn everything possible about the missing object. Is it something which retains its value only if left intact, such as a painting, other work of art, or a document? Does it have historical significance? Could its disappearance have a deleterious effect upon the owner or the heirs, such as a missing deed or will? Can it be converted into something of more transportable value, such as a gold or silver object which could be melted down? Is its primary value as an object which can be held for ransom?"

Thus, I went through our meagre library of books to find what I could about King Arthur and the legend of the Holy Grail. I retrieved my copy of Sir Thomas Malory's *Le Morte d'Arthur* and began perusing its pages for those which were relevant to the search for the golden artefact.

I was intrigued by the fact that Lord Campbell perpetuated the Grail legend as a part of his family history. While I was well aware that the legend of King Arthur himself was historically challenging, there is, I think, an inherent need in the human psyche to believe in something greater than ourselves. While for most people, their religion and God fill that void, for many,

133

even beyond that, there still exists a need to believe in legends and heroes. We apparently want an example of someone who can prevail against the travails of life, real or imaginary, even if they have flaws, as we all do.

I found my eyes caught by certain passages as I skimmed through the pages of Malory's work. This had the unfortunate effect of distracting me from my goal as I re-read passages that were familiar to me from years ago. I lost count of the number of times I had to shake myself from reverie to continue my quest for the disposition of the Holy Grail.

Darkness was fast approaching, sped along by the heavy skies, now depositing snow upon the streets. I needed more lights to read by and took no little time in wondering how Sherlock Holmes was faring in his enquiries.

At last, I completed my investigation. I closed the heavy tome just as Mrs. Hudson knocked on the door to enquire about dinner.

"I am assuming Holmes will be here," I stated. "He did not mention any expectation of being late."

"Hmpf! Just the same, I'll turn down the heat in case he's delayed. I can always turn it up again, thanks to that new gas stove."

She returned to her kitchen. I reflected on the fact that the gas pipes we took for granted for our lighting were now allowing her to have better control over her cooking. It struck me as odd that we had these modern conveniences of science at our disposal while we were about to investigate the theft of something purported to be nearly two thousand years old.

I put the book away and went to the sideboard to fetch a preprandial drink. Just as I resumed my seat by the fire, Sherlock Holmes entered. He had left his wet outer garments and umbrella down in the hall and strode quickly to the fireplace to regain some warmth to his limbs.

I peered up at my friend as he reached for his pipe and the Persian slipper which held his tobacco. Raising my own glass I asked, "Care for some inner warmth, Holmes?"

The detective nodded, "A brandy will do nicely, thank you." He then knelt by the fire and used the tongs to pluck a coal with which to light his briar. Settling into his chair, he took a long pull. A stream of blue haze soon ascended toward the ceiling, discoloured after so much tobacco smoke over the years.

I returned from the sideboard and handed him his brandy glass. He gratefully took a healthy sip. "Ahh, that is better! Well, Watson, I trust the passing hours have not given you second thoughts regarding a journey to the Scottish coast. I have telegraphed Campbell, advising him of my need for your assistance. I've told him that we shall leave on tomorrow's train. Here is another instruction for your notes, which I passed on to His Lordship:

"11. It is imperative that police, or client be advised of the necessity to preserve the crime scene in as pristine a state as possible and that detailed observation be conducted at the soonest moment."

When I finished making note of his statement, I advised him of my own comment regarding the provenance of the stolen item in the case of a theft. He nodded in approval and replied, "You do have a gift for the turn of a phrase, Doctor. You proposed a clear and precise instruction without embellishment or romance. I am gratified that you have this capability. I only wish that you had confined yourself to it when you wrote *A Study in Scarlet*. I trust you will remember this approach to your writings, should you pursue the publication of future cases."

This compliment seemed somewhat backhanded. However, having known Holmes for some years now, I chose to concentrate upon the positive aspect of his statement and merely said, "Thank you."

"I perceive by the disturbance of the dust upon our bookshelves, that you followed through upon this instruction. What did your research reveal?"

I took a final swallow of my drink to clear my throat and replied, "Having only Malory's work to consult, the results were unsatisfactory. He does not continue the story of the Grail beyond the ascension of Galahad to heaven. His companion knights, Percival and Bors, witness this event, but the fate of the Grail is not communicated."

Holmes nodded, "I admit, I fared little better in that department. An acquaintance of mine at the British Museum indicated that Sir Bors de Ganis is the only knight to return to England from the Grail quest, but the fate of the object itself is unknown. There are several religious establishments throughout Europe who claim to possess this holy artefact. I remind you, Watson, I care nothing for legends, especially supernatural ones, as you well know. However, their existence as a matter of motive cannot be ignored. In this particular case, if the thief believes the Grail provides healing powers and eternal life, it increases our chances of finding it intact. Otherwise, with so many days gone by, it could easily be melted down and redeemed for its metallic value by now."

I replied, sardonically, "Then let us hope the thief is not quite as cynical about legends as yourself. What other information did your afternoon sojourn provide?"

"In addition to the museum, I spent some time at the Public Records Office, looking into this branch of the Campbell clan. I fleshed out a few more details which may, or may not, prove significant."

Recalling my earlier thoughts, I asked, "Did you happen to call upon that newspaper fellow, Thomas Kent?"

Holmes tilted his head to the side momentarily, then replied, "I understand your thinking, as I did mention newspapers as a source of information. However, I have journalistic sources other than Kent, who are more likely to have information regarding former members of Parliament, retired soldiers and Scottish lairds. I have spoken with one of them. I also telegraphed Gibson to get his view on the situation and expect an answer tonight."

A knock upon our door was followed by the presence of our landlady, "I saw your things in the hallway, Mr. Holmes. Dinner is warm and can be ready whenever you are."

"Your timing is impeccable, Mrs. Hudson," answered my companion. "We are ready to eat at your convenience. Also, we should prefer an early breakfast tomorrow, if not inconvenient.

We shall be leaving on the first train to Scotland and shall be out of town for a few days."

"As you wish, gentlemen. I shall take the opportunity to give these rooms a proper scrubbing in your absence. You should also be aware that I shall be spending four days with my sister, starting on Christmas Eve morning. Therefore, I shall wish you felicitations of the season now. Do try to enjoy your Christmas while you're off chasing criminals."

Chapter Three

Tuesday morning broke with fresh snowfall being ploughed off the streets as we attempted to circumvent the drifts to flag down a cab to take us to Euston station. Fortunately, the skies themselves now showed some few blue patches peeking through light grey clouds. The temperature was not quite so cold, yet chilly enough and I was glad when we were finally ensconced in our private compartment for the long trip ahead.

Holmes had advised me that we could well be riding the rails for nearly twelve hours, having to change trains once we arrived at Glasgow Central Station for the trip south along the west coast of Scotland to Ayr. Therefore, I had brought along *Le Morte d'Arthur* and a novel I had been reading, as well as the latest medical journal. For his part, Holmes bought the morning papers to help pass the time. The trip north was at least interesting in its variety of geography and weather. Once out of London, the land became a patchwork of browns and snow-covered countryside. We passed through farmlands and rolling hills as well the industrial landscapes of the northern towns and cities.

During the early part of the journey, Holmes suggested a few more instructions to be added to my narrative.

"12. Proceed to the scene of the crime with due haste and bring with you the following instruments, if possible:

A. A powerful magnifying lens.

139

B. Several small envelopes with which to gather evidence.
C. A pencil and notebook with which to make observations and sketches for future reference.
D. Matches, a small dusting brush, measuring tape, multiplex pocket knife.
E. A weapon appropriate to the situation. Leaded bludgeon, heavy-topped cane, fighting knife, etc. In extreme, or unknown situations, a small revolver is recommended. Handcuffs as well."

Arriving in Glasgow mid-afternoon as darkness was descending, we changed trains for the southbound ride to Ayr and we picked up the city's afternoon papers. Headed west out of Glasgow, we made a wide arc as the locomotive slowly changed its course southward toward Kilmarnock. After passing through Troon, the Firth of Clyde came into view, but the Isle of Arran was hidden from site by low clouds that pelted our carriage intermittently with rain.

When we pulled into Ayr Station a light snow was falling, but, unlike London, that which was already on the rooftops and roads retained its natural whiteness and gave an eerie glow in the twilight. Leaving the train, Holmes led us straight to the station telegraph office and enquired as to whether a message had arrived in his name.

There was such a message from Mrs. Hudson. Knowing that our departure might be in advance of a reply from Lord Campbell, Holmes had asked our landlady to forward any answers sent to Baker Street to the station telegraph office at Ayr. Quickly reading it he handed me the paper.

It read as follows, 'You and Watson welcome. Enquire Holmston livery upon arrival. Driver arranged'. As I was reading, Holmes asked the telegrapher directions to Holmston livery and found it was just a short walk down the street. The owner turned us over to a young fellow named Malcolm, with a bright face and eager smile, who doffed his cap and led us to an enclosed carriage hitched to a fine pair of white-stockinged, bay Clydesdales bedecked with ribbons and bells befitting the time of year.

He drove us along a road which ran parallel with the River Ayr for about two miles to where the river turned north. Just as we were coming to the change in the river's course, Bellrose Castle came into view. It was the stereotype of 13th century Scottish castles with the exception of it being triangular in shape, much like Caerlaverock Castle near Dumfries. Located on the bend of the river, it took advantage of its proximity and a moat was dredged from the river to protect the eastern and southern sides of the grounds while the river acted as a natural barrier to the north and west. Thus, in effect, Bellrose was its own island. Our carriage rattled across an old-fashioned drawbridge into a courtyard where modern touches first made their appearance with several gas lamps providing illumination.

We stepped out of the carriage, Holmes in his grey ulster and ear-flapped travelling cap, I, in my black overcoat and derby. Malcom took up our bags before we could retrieve them and led the way to the massive door under the main portico. There was a large wreath upon the door and boughs of holly with bright red berries hung over the frame.

A double tap of the ringed knocker brought a butler to the door in mere seconds, and we were ushered inside. Malcolm made the introductions, "Mr. Holmes and Dr. Watson to see His Lordship. Gentlemen, this is Aames, butler to Lord Campbell."

Aames was a stout, broad-shouldered fellow of middle height. I judged him to be roughly fifty years of age with greying hair and a moustache. His sharp blue eyes took us in quickly and a courteous smile crossed his lips as he bowed to us. He told Malcolm to leave the luggage there in the entrance hall and that he would have it attended to. Then he invited the young man to attend to the kitchen for some hot coffee before he drove back into town. To us he bid welcome. Having a footman take our hats and coats, and another servant our luggage, he asked that we follow him to meet His Lordship.

Modern conveniences did not end with the gas lamps outside. The house itself appeared to be well-heated despite its cold stone exterior. I noted heating vents strategically placed, in addition to a good-sized fireplace in many rooms. More holly boughs and other Christmas trimmings gave the interior a cheery countenance. Lord Campbell was in his library, where another fireplace roared with dancing flames. He was sitting behind a large oak-inlaid desk with exquisitely carved legs and a scallop-edged top which shone from years of polishing.

I had a picture of him in my mind, based upon the age Holmes had discovered in his index and his service in the military. However, I was pleasantly surprised by the fine figure of a man who stood ramrod straight as we entered the room. For a man who would be sixty-eight in two months, he did not look his age at all. He was taller than I, at about six feet and maintained a healthy weight. He bore a full head of iron grey hair with just a slight remnant of red, parted on the right and neatly trimmed. He was clean-shaven, wearing a smoking jacket patterned after his clan tartan, and black trousers.

When he spoke, there was a fine Scottish burr to his tone, "Mr. Holmes, Dr. Watson, I was not expecting you until much later, more likely tomorrow. You could not have received my telegram this morning and arrived this quickly."

Holmes replied, "Your case intrigues me, Lord Campbell. I confess, we left at the earliest opportunity, and I instructed our landlady to forward any telegrams to the Ayr station. Thus, we learned of your instructions."

"I like a man who takes the initiative," he smiled, sticking out his hand in greeting.

Such was his commanding presence that I nearly snapped to attention. Even so, I subconsciously stood a little taller and measured my steps, as if in march formation. Holmes, no great respecter of titles, merely strode forward and clasped the welcoming hand. When it was my turn, I found my hand in a strong grip. Green eyes gazed into mine as he asked, "You've a military air about you, Doctor. Or should I call you Captain? Where did you serve?"

Automatically I replied, "Doctor is fine, sir. I was in Afghanistan as an army surgeon with the 5th Northumberland Fusiliers and the Berkshires until the Battle of Maiwand."

"A bloody mess, that. Wounded I take it?"

"Yes, sir. Shoulder during the battle while I was tending to the wounded and my leg during the retreat."

"I thought I detected a slight limp. Cold weather aggravates it, I imagine."

"On occasion, sir. However, I can generally get by with my cane."

"Very well. Shall we sit by the fire?" Looking back to Holmes, he waved us over to a sitting area where a dark green leather sofa and four royal blue stuffed chairs were arranged in a rectangle open to the welcome blaze. Holmes and I took chairs to the left while Lord Campbell sat opposite us.

"I appreciate your quick response to my communique, gentlemen. Inspector Gibson seems to have great confidence in your powers, Mr. Holmes. He says you be more worthy than any policeman he knows and can solve cases that others refuse as impossible."

Holmes crossed his leg across his knee and folded his hands in his lap, assuming a casual air. I have seen him take this position often to show his client, or suspect, that he is not intimidated by rank or position.

"Gibson is a fine policeman in his own right, but he makes too much of my powers. They are not supernatural. However, some may consider them more than natural due to the fact so few people use the totality of the senses given to them. As I have often declared to the police and others, 'you see, but you do not observe'. Observation is what makes deduction possible, and deductions lead to conclusions."

Lord Campbell replied, "How interesting. Can you give me an example?"

Holmes tilted his head to one side, "I would prefer to examine the scene of the crime as quickly as possible, Lord Campbell. Should the thief be a member of the household, our arrival may cause him to take further steps to attempt to cover up the crime. If you will lead us to the location, I shall be happy to explain my methods as we walk."

The former army major slapped his knees with both hands and stood, "Charge right into the action. I appreciate that, Mr. Holmes. Follow me, gentlemen."

As we walked alongside our host, Holmes explained his observation process.

"You may wish to make note of this for your references, Watson:

"13. When meeting someone who may be involved in the case, no matter how peripherally, it is important to observe mannerisms, traits and physical characteristics. One must use these to ascertain their personality and character.

14. As you observe this person, it is important to notice trouser knees, shoes, shirt cuffs, elbows and collars. Take into account wear patterns and size/fit. The style and age of the clothing and how comfortable they are while wearing it.

15. Notice the hands. Note the position, size and age of any callouses or blisters. Look out for ink stains or any other discolouration. Overall, you should also note the skin complexion and the degree of exposure to sun. Be aware of scars, no matter how small. Eyes are also important. The presence or absence of spectacles or *pince nez* can indicate a degree of vanity, or the accuracy of the observations they report to you. Ears should be well-observed, as they can indicate possible relationships between parties."

Campbell interrupted, "This is all fascinating, Mr. Holmes. By your account, you must have already made several deductions since your arrival."

We were turning into the entrance to what must have once been the armoury when Holmes answered, "Allow me to give a brief demonstration. Your butler, Aames, is a proud man and former military himself. Likely he was an officer's batman at some point, though not yours. He is Scottish by birth but attended a school in England.

"He is a strict but fair leader over the household and will work side by side with them when necessary. He runs an efficient house showing excellent foresight and planning skills. He is respected and even liked by the town tradesmen. He uses reading glasses, but will not wear them during the normal course of the day. He was once a smoker, but now uses snuff."

Campbell had unlocked and was now pushing open two wide double doors when he started to make a remark about Holmes's comments, but the detective first asked, "Are these doors kept shut and locked at night?"

He replied, "We usually keep the doors closed, as there is no need to heat this room, but we do air it out once a week. I've had no occasion to lock these doors in many a year. However, since the burglary, the police have recommended that I lock them and your friend, Gibson, suggested I keep everyone out of the room until you had a chance to examine it."

My companion gazed briefly at the floor, then charged ahead, "I perceive this is where the Grail was kept."

We had reached a pedestal about four feet tall, with a glass case roughly one foot cubed. There was no lock on the case. It merely lifted off the pedestal where it was fitted into grooves which kept it from sliding if bumped. A felt in Campbell tartan covered the top of the pedestal. There was a slight indented circle where the Grail had rested upon it. On either side, low, glass-topped cases exhibited various historical items of the Campbell clan.

Lord Campbell was still digesting Holmes's findings regarding Aames and took a second to answer, "Aye, that pedestal was its display case. I must say, your assessment of Aames is amazing."

"That is my profession, Lord Campbell. Years of study and experience has made such observations and deductions second nature. It is as familiar to me as saddling and riding your horse is to you."

The floor was of flagstone with a few rugs here and there so, footmarks were highly unlikely to be found, especially after so many days. I could discern no fingerprints or smudges upon the glass cube itself, but Holmes began a closer examination with his magnifying lens. The cube was an oak-framed glass case. He checked the case and the pedestal for any markings, all the way down to the floor itself. As he did so, he asked a question.

"Did the thief put the case back upon the pedestal, or did one of your servants do so before I requested that nothing be touched?"

Campbell, who was now standing to one side with his hands clasped behind his back, replied, "T'is exactly as it was when it was found."

Holmes nodded, then began examining the tops of the counters to either side. On the left side he found marks of some type and noted, "It appears the thief set the glass case down here, removed the Grail and set it next to it, then replaced the cube. That is telling in itself. Someone thought that returning the glass could buy them time. They likely believed that someone walking through the room might take no notice of the missing Grail as long as everything else was in place and they did not look directly toward it."

"May I offer a further suggestion?" remarked His Lordship.

"By all means," replied Holmes. "The more data I have, the better."

In his pleasant baritone voice, Campbell continued, "At this time of year, we often loan the Grail out to the local church for their Christmas pageant. It is possible that someone knowing this might restore the case, so that anyone other than myself or Aames would assume that its absence was due to that situation. I do not come in here every day and the castle is large enough that Aames likely does not either."

As he was making this remark, I was surveying the room itself. Higher up on the wall where the display cases were, there hung various tapestries of historical events where the Campbell clan were involved. There was a long-faded scene of King Arthur and the Knights at the Round Table. Another of a lad pulling a sword from a stone. Although whether it was Arthur or Galahad wasn't clear. There were battle scenes of Stirling Bridge and Bannockburn, as well as the more local battle of Largs against the invading Norwegians in 1263. There was even a fanciful rendition of James VI, bestowing the baronetcy and knighthood upon Alexander Campbell.

The opposite wall was lined with suits of armour, military uniforms, shields, coats of arms and various weaponry. At one end of the room there were paintings of various Campbells down through the ages, including the most recent, Arthur Campbell himself in his finest kilted uniform. The other end featured narrow windows looking out upon the River Ayr.

There was one other entrance to the room, from the corner farthest from that which we had come. That door appeared to be bolted from the inside. Two ancient candle chandeliers hung from the ceiling; however, they were not lit. Gas lamps encircled the room every few feet and provided excellent illumination.

"Watson," said Holmes, breaking my concentration, "I see you are examining the room itself. Please note for instruction:

"16. Examine the room where the crime took place thoroughly. Include all walls, ceiling and floor. Look for secret passages, check windows and other wardrobes or anterooms. Be especially observant of any locks and their condition.

17. When examining the crime scene itself, whether theft or murder, the perpetrator may have left some indication behind. Check for footprints, fingerprints, snagged threads, fibres or pieces of cloth, smudges of mud, dirt, ink, chemicals or some such left behind. If footprints are noted, measure for size and length of stride, note the tread pattern and any unusual wear."

Finishing this dictation, Holmes went on with his examination of the room, following the steps he had just outlined. Coming to the other door he enquired, "Is this door always kept locked from this side?"

Lord Campbell replied, "Generally not. The police recommended it after their examination, in case the thief came back."

"Highly unlikely I should think," I commented.

The retired Major nodded, "I believe they just wanted to make it appear as if they were doing something. Their lack of progress was embarrassing, to say the least."

"I am sure they did their best, Lord Campbell," said Holmes as he checked the floor by the other door. "It is an unfortunate fact that today's British police force is not as thoroughly trained as they should be. This is why I am asking Watson to take note of my instructions. I am hopeful that we can create a teaching manual for them."

Looking in disgust at the floor rugs he lamented, "They also tend to blunder about like a herd of lost elephants. I count no less than four sets of footprints left by what are certainly policemen's boots. Finding the culprit's footprints in this morass will be highly unlikely.

Chapter Four

At that moment, Aames entered the room and stated, "Pardon me, My Lord, Mrs. Galway is asking what time you wish to have dinner. She does not want to interrupt your meeting."

Campbell looked to Holmes who replied, "I should be finished here in another fifteen minutes, My Lord."

"Then we shall give you and Dr. Watson some time to refresh yourselves and dress for dinner," he replied. Turning to Aames he directed, "Tell cook we shall be ready in forty-five minutes."

True to his word, Holmes had completed his task in the allotted time, and we were shown to our rooms on an upper floor. Mine had a view which looked out upon the River Ayr, currently frozen over and bordered by snowbanks. There was a half-moon showing through the broken clouds and the snowfall itself had stopped. Refreshed after a long day's travel, I changed for dinner. Then, as I had a few minutes to spare, I looked over the notes I had taken thus far. Holmes's instructions along the way were not going to be easy to weave into a narrative style and I wasn't sure if my literary agent, Doyle, or any London publisher would accept this unique way of telling a story.

I was in this contemplation when a knock came to my door. I answered. "Come in."

It was my companion, formally dressed for dinner. His fashionable appearance, however, did not match his mood. "We've work to do, Watson! This delay of several days since the time of the theft gives us not a minute to lose. I would as soon forgo this dinner in favour of continuing our investigation."

"Our host may construe that as an insult to good manners," I noted.

"Yes, but I do hope you will assist me in whatever steps I may take to move things along."

"I should be happy to conspire with you, Holmes."

He shot me a look, "Conspire. An interesting word, that. It is one of many things we must consider. For now, to keep from interrupting our dinner and extending it, please note the following for your record:

"18. When brought into a case, take special note of all the possible players in your game of wits. Include all members of the family, all the household staff, even those who only come in for specific tasks or times. Any close family friends or suitors who may have had access to the scene, however improbable. Also check with local authorities to discern if any similar crimes have occurred in the area.

19. Look into any feuds or grudges, no matter how ancient, as well as any business or property disputes.

20. Check into any work being done in the area by government workers, local tradesmen or private contractors."

After ensuring I had completed my notes, Holmes led the way down to the dining room where we arrived after His Lordship. We all remained standing for the arrival of his daughter, Elise, her husband, Roy Lennox and their son, Fergus. Once all were in place we sat. Lord Campbell at the head of the table, Roy and Elise to his left, Fergus at his right hand, then Holmes and myself beyond the boy.

Fergus was a short, skinny lad who appeared to be about ten years old but, we later learned, was actually thirteen. He exhibited the red hair of his father and the pale complexion of his mother. Elise was an attractive woman in her mid-thirties with soft, curly brown hair that surrounded her thin pale face, from which hazel eyes flitted about carelessly. Her husband, Roy Lennox, was also quite thin with a shock of red hair just beginning to show some grey, as he appeared to be entering his forties. All were well-dressed in splendid finery which bespoke of the family fortune.

After Lord Campbell had made introductions and while the first course was being served, Mr. Lennox asked the obvious question of my friend, "Mr. Holmes, how can you hope to solve this theft after so many days and succeed where the police have failed?"

"I have often succeeded where the police have failed," replied the detective. "However, the passage of time is working against us. Even after the thief is discovered, he may well have disposed of the item in a way that will make it impossible to retrieve."

"How do you mean, sir?" asked Elise Lennox, who was sitting directly across from my friend.

"It depends upon the thief's motive, madam. If they are merely out for personal gain, then they could have had it melted down strictly for its gold value. Or they could have put in motion a plan to get it into the hands of a private collector who will stash it away for what may be decades."

"What would be the point of that?" she asked innocently.

Holmes indulged her further and replied, "There are people of a certain bent of mind, who merely wish to possess what others do not have. They derive some perverse pleasure in ownership, even though no one else knows they own it."

"Really?" asked young Fergus, his eyes wide with alarm.

"I'm afraid I've known more than a few such criminals," answered Holmes. "However, we are speculating in a vacuum. I need much more detail as to the circumstances of the theft."

He turned to our host and asked, "Lord Campbell, could you please tell me exactly on which date, approximately at what time the theft took place, and who was in the house at the time?"

"A moment if you please, Mr. Holmes. Let us ask the Lord's blessing upon our food first."

The servants had finished serving the first course by this point, yet no one had deigned to touch their plate. Minding the manners of good guests, we, likewise, had refrained from eating until our host had begun. Lord Campbell's prayer was heartfelt and recalled to me my own Presbyterian youth.

Once his petitions to God were complete, each person began to eat. His Lordship turned to Holmes and made his reply.

"'Twas a week ago, the night of the ninth. Sometime between late Saturday afternoon and Sunday afternoon, when we returned from church. Pastor Reynolds had enquired of me if they might continue to have use of the Grail in the annual Christmas pageant."

I interrupted, much to Holmes's chagrin I imagined, and asked, "Excuse me Lord Campbell. It was my understanding that, traditionally, the Grail was used at the last supper and the crucifixion. What purpose would it serve at Christmas?"

His Lordship smiled at this chance to tell the story, "One of the ancient traditions is that it represents the gift of gold, given by one of the wise men to Mary at Jesus's birth. This story has her bringing it to Jerusalem during the final journey. Christ uses it at the last supper, and she retains possession. She catches drops of her son's blood in it as he is hanging on the cross. Then she turns it over to Joseph of Arimathea who has volunteered his own tomb for Christ's body."

"I see. Thank you, your Lordship."

"Fascinating as this is," said Holmes, barely hiding his scowl at my interruption. "I presume that when you returned home and looked in upon the Grail you found it missing."

"Exactly that, Mr. Holmes. One of our maids had dusted the Grail and its case on Saturday sometime after lunch. No one had occasion to go into the room after that until I found it missing the next day."

"Did you have any visitors that weekend, or were just you and the household staff in attendance?"

"Elise and her family live with me here," stated the Lord. "Roy is my estate manager. That particular weekend my sister

Brenda and her husband, Donald Fraser, were here as well as my nephew, Henry with his wife Allison. Other than that, no one."

Lennox spoke up, somewhat indignantly, when his father-in-law had finished, "Surely you don't suspect a family member would do this, Mr. Holmes?"

Holmes steepled his long fingers under his chin, "In my profession, Mr. Lennox, I must suspect everyone until I have excluded them by process of elimination. Far too often family members, or servants with many years of loyal service, have taken actions which no one would have thought possible. Tell me, was the drawbridge taken up that night?"

"No," answered the estate manager, "We keep it oiled and only raise and lower it on occasion, to ensure it is in proper working order. But since there is no particular need to keep invading Englishmen out in this day and age, (he looked poignantly at Holmes) we generally leave it down."

My friend smiled and replied, "Thank you. Fortunately, I have my good Scottish companion, Watson, here to help me mind my manners."

He took a sip of wine, and began a cursory attempt at eating. The meal went on with much lighter conversation after that. Holmes merely made a few enquiries as to the servants and their length of time with His Lordship. When the main dishes were cleared, Holmes discreetly tapped my leg, signalling that he was going to attempt to excuse us from dessert in order to continue his examination of the castle in the immediate vicinity of the theft.

However, before he could speak, Lord Campbell called his name, "Mr. Holmes, you made some remarkable deductions regarding Mr. Aames here." The butler stood stiffly at attention by his master's side as he was overseeing the serving of dessert. He looked upon his employer and then at Holmes with a puzzled expression.

Campbell smiled, "Nothing shocking, Aames, I assure you. However, I should like Mr. Holmes to explain his observations that led to his deductions about you."

My companion sighed as he placed his napkin upon the table before him. "What you are asking, Lord Campbell, is the equivalent of a magician revealing the secrets of his trade. Once explained, the mystique is gone. I cannot begin to tell you how often I have done so, only to find the person who asked the question reply, 'How absurdly simple!'"

The former Major leaned forward, forearms upon the edge of the table, "I promise to make no such statement, Mr. Holmes. The deductions you made were far too unique to be reduced to such a remark."

Holmes glanced at me and gave a slight shake of his head in resignation, "Very well. As I recall I stated he was Scottish by birth but attended school in England. This is revealed by his speech. Though he retains his Scottish burr, certain pronunciations are distinctly English, and some are unique to the higher educational institutes such as Oxford, Cambridge and the like. As to his affording such an education, I have insufficient data, but would speculate that a benefactor provided the necessary funds. Perhaps the parents of the officer to whom he was attached as batman.

"His former military service is evident by his mannerisms and the watch chain upon his waistcoat. There are not many men of his station who own a watch of this quality. However, as a batman to a military officer, it would be essential for him to possess such an instrument and it was likely given to him upon his entering that officer's service. The deduction the officer was not you was indicated by the Chinese coin and service medallion of the Second China War hung upon the chain. It indicates his service was likely in the British protectorate of Hong Kong. You, Major Campbell, according to peerage records, served in the Crimea and India.

"He treats the household staff fairly and assists as necessary was indicated by the servants' attitudes who picked up our luggage. Their smiles and countenance were out of respect, not fear. His own white gloves, though primarily pristine, had a small smudge where likely he was engaged in a task which would normally be below his station. The fact our rooms were ready indicates foresight on his part in that he could not have known what time we would arrive. The house itself is well maintained as to cleanliness. The easy camaraderie between him and our driver indicated an attitude of friendly respect and appreciation.

"There are slight indentations on either side of his nose indicating the occasional use of glasses. For a man of his age, that is likely for reading, as his eyesight seems perfectly well suited to other normal pursuits.

"While it is common for soldiers to smoke, a man in Aames's position needs to avoid the staining of his gloves, the odour of his breath and the smell of tobacco permeating his clothes. Thus, I perceive that the outline of the small box in his right waistcoat pocket is a snuff box and the few small grains of powder near it are, undoubtedly, snuff. This would assist his desire for the chemicals found in tobacco without having to indulge in the act of smoking."

Upon completion of his explanations, we had the pleasant experience of His Lordship's appreciation as he raised his wineglass. "Well done, sir! Every link of the chain proves true. Anyone who calls such a feat as 'simple' is sadly mistaken. I only hope this power is sufficient to find our thief."

Holmes returned the compliment with a sip of his own wine and replied, "As to that end, Lord Campbell, I should like to continue my observations around the house and question the servants at your convenience. Watson and I are in no need of puddings to expand our waistlines. So, if we may be excused?"

Campbell nodded, "I cannot argue with your logic, sir. You have the run of the castle. I merely ask that ye have a family member present should ye wish to examine any bedrooms. Aames will make the servants available as ye see fit."

Holmes stood and I reluctantly joined him, enviously eyeing the selection of delicious looking treats containing, among other Scottish delicacies, sweet-smelling clootie dumplings. Mrs. Lennox, noting my expression eying them said, "Not to worry, Doctor. I'll see that a portion is saved for you in the kitchen."

I returned her smile with a nod, and we excused ourselves, making our way back toward the armoury.

Chapter Five

The gas lamps were burning low when we re-entered the armoury. I started to reach for the chain to restore full illumination when Holmes stopped me. "Leave it be for a moment, Watson. I wish to observe the room as our culprit may have, if he removed the item after the household had retired."

Holmes led the way toward the pedestal as I followed. At one point, I nearly fell when I stubbed my toe upon the edge of one of the flagstones. Holmes, acting as if he expected me to do so, caught my arm and kept me upright. "A telling point, Watson. A stranger to this room may well have fallen as you nearly did with the lighting at this level. You should make another note for your instructions:

"21. If at all possible, attempt to reconstruct the crime in a manner which most closely resembles the conditions at the time of the incident. This may assist in revealing the culprit's familiarity with the site or the victim. It also may be telling as to the physical prowess of the criminal."

We finished making our way to the pedestal where Holmes examined it again. As it was directly beneath one of the wall lamps, even the low glow provided sufficient illumination to perform the necessary tasks. After a brief inspection, he requested that I turn up the gas. I retreated to the double doors of the room's main entrance and did so.

As there were display cases intermittently running down the centre of the room, one could not approach the opposite door without circumnavigating the room's perimeter. This was where Holmes had gone while I was turning up the gas. As I did so, I walked past the windows at the far end, which happened to face the river. These were several in number but narrow in breadth. Wide enough for an archer to shoot through from the inside, but not for an invader to enter, should they make it across the river. The hinged glass opened inward like a door, and I could see the light coat of dust on the sill had not been disturbed recently.

When, at last, I caught up with my friend, he was examining the floor outside the single door in the corner of the armoury. "See here, Watson. The police have made a capital mistake."

I looked upon the floor where he had waved his hand. This area was carpeted. Being a much later addition to the castle's décor, there was a wide arc corresponding to where the door brushed the carpet as it swung out into the corridor.

"The door has obliterated any footprints there might have been, Holmes," I observed, knowing that my friend saw more than I, but playing the role he expected.

"Just as the police thought," he confirmed. "Thus, they failed to take any further steps. Literally. Look here, beyond the arc."

I stepped out onto the tamped down carpet and knelt to get a better look. If I found just the right angle, I could see a trace of footprints. The fact that the carpet fibres were bent in the same direction as the path left by the carpet sweeper made their discernment almost impossible.

"I can just make out what appear to be footprints, Holmes," I remarked. "But they seem rather small. Could they not have been left by the maid who swept the carpet?"

"Possible, but unlikely," replied Holmes. "The most efficient way to use a carpet sweeper is to begin against one wall and pull toward you. As you go back and forward in this manner, you walk backwards, thus sweeping over your own footprints and any dirt your shoes leave behind. These prints had to be left after the last time this carpet was swept."

Keeping to one side, we followed the path until we arrived at the common area at the base of the back stairwell. Here numerous prints obliterated each other, and it was impossible to tell which direction was taken by our possible thief. Off to the right would have taken them toward the dining room, kitchen and the servants' quarters beyond. To the left would lead back toward the main living area, containing drawing room, library, entrance hall and great room. Of course, if the thief were a family member, they could merely return to their room upstairs.

Retracing our steps, Holmes peered intently at the floor until he found what seemed to be the clearest impression. He knelt and took his tape measure from his pocket, carefully noting all dimensions at various widths along the foot as well as the overall length. He pulled some tracing paper from his inner breast pocket and made a careful outline of the shoe print itself. I noticed that the length was a mere eight and a half inches. From my medical knowledge I realized this was approximately a woman's size four shoe which corresponds roughly to someone around five feet tall, give or take an inch or two. If this was our culprit, it was certainly not among the men of the house.

Being sceptical at the thought of one of the women being the thief, I stated, "We don't know if these are, in fact, our thief's footprints. We only know someone made them after the carpet was swept. It could have been someone who came this way to go into the armoury, found the door locked and returned to go around the other way."

"No, Watson," replied my friend. "Had that been the case, the prints would have been found on the carpet outside the door, not brushed away when the door was opened the last time by the police. We shall have to question the servants about when this sweeping occurred."

There being little more to examine in this area of the house, Holmes chose to seek out Aames and arrange for interviews of the staff. We found him eating his own dinner in the kitchen. Seeing the man *sans* coat and gloves as he ate a well-balanced meal, I could better appreciate the personality Holmes had ascribed to him. He started to stand upon our entrance, but Holmes waved him back to his seat. "Pray do not let us interrupt your meal, Mr. Aames. I merely wish to arrange some interviews with the staff. If possible, I should like to begin with the maidservants.

"Easily done, Mr. Holmes," answered the silver–haired gentleman. Turning toward the cook he said, "Mrs. Galway, would you have Mrs. Kenworth gather the housemaids for Mr. Holmes? Thank you."

The cook wiped the soapy dishwater from her hands and left the room. Turning back to us, Aames remarked, "Your deductions about me were intriguing, Mr. Holmes. You were correct in your surmise that my education was paid for by a benefactor. I was the son of servants to Sir Robert Douglas. He perceived I was a bright boy and I had grown up with his son, Clyde. When Clyde went off to Oxford, I was sent with him. He rose to the rank of captain but died while we were still in China, and I mustered out. After I returned home, Sir Robert recommended me to Lord Campbell, and I've worked my way up to my current position."

While I found this story interesting, Holmes was more concerned with the case in hand. "Thank you for your verification, Mr. Aames. However, my current concern is with your master's missing artefact."

The butler sat back in his chair in a most informal posture as he gazed upon us, almost disapprovingly. I took this as a feeling that he felt his age required as much respect from us as his station required his respect for us. Holmes took up this aspect of levelling the field, so to speak, and spoke to the man in a more confidential tone than a servant would normally command.

"As a former soldier and person of authority, do you have any thoughts on the subject? Is there anyone among the staff, for instance, who is in dire need of funds?"

Aames's Scottish burr was evident in his answer, "Nay, Mr. Holmes. All our lads and lassies came with high recommendations. The only one I don't know all that well is our newest addition, Fiona Blair. She's the parlour maid and is responsible for sweeping, dusting and so on downstairs. She started with us just before last Christmas. She's a quiet sort. Keeps to herself mostly but does good work."

Holmes nodded, "I take it she's about five feet tall, rather thin and wears Oxford shoes?"

Aames, looked upon my companion with amazement. "How do you do that, Mr. Holmes? Have you already seen her?"

"No, but I should very much like to interview her first."

Chapter Six

Aames guided us to the servants' parlour where we took seats near a pleasant fire in soft leather wingback chairs. After an early morning, a strenuous ride on the rails, the stiff carriage from town and the wooden dining chairs, this was the most comfortable I had felt all day. Even more so than the chairs in the His Lordship's office. As I sunk deeply into the well worn armchair, the effects of a full meal and long day wore on me and I could feel my eyes closing. My muscles were relaxing as I was being swallowed up by the luxury of the chair. This reverie was brief, of course, for Holmes had more instructions for me to record.

"For your notes, Watson," said he, apparently oblivious to the comfort the chairs offered.

"22. When interviewing a suspect, there are a variety of techniques that can be used, depending upon the station, personality and intelligence level of your quarry. Please refer to my monograph regarding this subject. Briefly there are three main methods with several sub-contexts for each. First you put your subject at ease. Maintain a friendly manner as if this were just routine, in order to show that you have covered all possibilities. Next treat the subject as an equal. Pretend to take them into your confidence. Ask for their advice or opinion on various aspects to see if they know more than they should. Usually the least effective and unfortunately, the one police use most often, though sometimes the situation calls for it is that you bully the suspect with an overload of facts, sometimes even ones you make up. By revealing a good deal of your hand, you may convince them you know all and their only hope of leniency is to make a clean breast of everything. It may also raise their temper and cause them to slip up during their denial, revealing some salient fact that actually leads to their guilt."

At this point, Aames arrived with a young girl in tow, whom he introduced as Fiona Blair. We had stood upon their entrance and Holmes offered his chair to the maidservant. He was obviously going with method number one in this instance.

Miss Blair was quite young, certainly not yet twenty. She was petite, roughly five feet tall and as slender as a rail. Soft brown curls extended beyond the frilled edges of her white mob cap. She had brown, doe-like eyes, a small nose and thin lips. Her overall countenance bespoke innocence.

As Holmes has so often said, however, 'Looks can be deceiving, dear fellow'. Thus, I vowed to keep an open mind and took up my pad and pencil to make notes. She had sat in the chair my friend offered, but did not relax into it, tempting as it was. She sat on the edge, back as straight as a rod and dainty hands folded neatly in her lap. In this position, I could not make note of her shoes, as her long grey dress brushed the floor around them.

Holmes, in his most charming tone, spoke up, "Thank you, Miss Blair. We shan't keep you long. I have just a few minor questions for you."

Her sweet face turned up toward the detective as she replied, "As you wish, sir."

Holmes went on to ask her about her duties on the Saturday prior to the theft; what she did and when she did it. From this he established the last time the Grail had been touched prior to the theft, and also what time she ran the carpet sweeper along the back corridor.

"Just one more thing, Miss. May I see your right shoe?"

Confused but cooperative, the girl put out her right foot beyond her dress with the toe facing up and the back of the heel dug into the rug. It was a shiny black shoe of the Oxford style. The bottom was well worn, indicating some age to it, but the leather was in good condition.

Holmes retrieved his tape measure from his pocket and knelt before her. Instinctively, she pulled her foot back and fearfully asked, "What are you doing, sir?"

She looked up to Aames, as in a plea against any untoward act this guest was attempting. The former soldier patted her shoulder and said, "'Tis all right, lass. He'll not hurt ye. I promise."

Holmes, likewise, spoke in soothing tones, "I just need to measure the bottom of your shoe, Miss Blair. I shall not touch you in any way. I merely need to compare your shoes with some footprints I found on the hall carpet."

Hesitantly, she extended her foot again, using her hands to keep her dress tightly wrapped around her ankle. Holmes took his measurements and stood. She withdrew her foot quickly beneath her dress.

Holmes wrote the numbers down on the paper where he had recorded his earlier measurements and said, "There now, all done. I have one further question of you at this time, Miss Blair. Did you return to the back hallway after you swept the carpet?

"No, sir, I did not."

"Thank you. You may return to your duties."

She rose quickly and stepped over to Aames's side, keeping a watchful eye on the detective the whole time. Aames, exhibiting a more fatherly tone, merely said, "Everything is fine, lass. Back to your work now."

She bowed her head to him, shot a bewildered look at Holmes and hurried from the room. Aames folded his hands behind his back and questioned my companion, "Must ye be doing this with all the female staff, Mr. Holmes? I would have appreciated a warning. Our ladies are all quite modest. It is a trait we insist upon when hiring them."

"I only need to check the shoes of anyone approximately her size, Mr. Aames," replied the detective. "Is there any other such person, man or woman?"

"No, she is by far the shortest person on our staff and has the daintiest feet."

Holmes nodded, "Very well, then. Perhaps we can reduce the time for these interviews if you can tell me the whereabouts of every member of the household throughout that Saturday afternoon, after she cleaned the Grail."

Aames replied, "The police already asked that question. Each member of staff had specific duties which would have kept them quite busy and nowhere near the armoury on that day. And, aye, all those duties were performed to perfection. No one had time to make a detour into the armoury and make off with the Grail. The police also searched all of our quarters and found nothing. Anything else?"

Aames had obviously taken some affront at Holmes's methods or questions and was now exhibiting a more belligerent attitude. Whether this was in response to Holmes not communicating his intentions, or at being used as a guinea pig in his demonstration of his powers, I could not discern. There was also the possibility that he was somehow involved in the theft.

"Just one more question," continued Holmes, ignoring the man's tone. "Is His Lordship's sister, or his niece, of a similar stature to Miss Blair?"

Aames reddened as he brought his hands to his side, fists balled up as he attempted to control his temper. "Miss Allison is petite as well. But I will thank ye not to accuse any member of the family in this mishap. No one would betray Lord Campbell in that fashion, and if ye persist in such a ridiculous persecution, I shall recommend that His Lordship throw ye out of his home!"

Before Holmes could reply, Aames spun on his heel and strode quickly from the room. I looked up from my chair at my friend. He stared at the retreating back of the butler until the door was brutally shut behind him. Then he pulled his pipe and tobacco pouch from his pocket and charged his briarwood as he finally settled into the chair opposite me, allowing the upholstery to adjust around his lean frame.

I looked at my friend and asked, "To paraphrase the Bard, 'Doth he protest too much', Holmes?"

In an oddly playful mood, Holmes smiled as he replied, "Methinks not, Watson. I believe he is merely protecting the household against my 'slings and arrows'. His statements alone do not eliminate any suspects, as he may be in league with someone and providing an alibi for that person. However, we shall, for the present, work along the hypothesis that he is telling the truth until we can prove otherwise."

"So where does that leave us?" I asked. "Do you question His Lordship about possible motives by his niece, or do you look harder at the chance of an outside intruder?"

"I shall have to smoke a pipe or two upon it, Watson. Tomorrow's daylight will provide me with an opportunity to examine the grounds for possible intrusion. But I must eliminate the household as well. I shall need some time to myself. I suggest you seek out that slice of dessert saved for you in the kitchen. I shall see you at breakfast."

My taste buds won out over the comfort of the chair and I arose and left Holmes to his pipe. I knew he was likely to smoke several, depending upon how the facts in his mind coalesced into some semblance of order which would ultimately reveal the culprit.

Chapter Seven

The next morning, I rose, put on slippers and dressing gown against the cold and went over to throw open the curtains to look out upon the day. The sun was too far south to be seen from my north-facing window, but the sky was a high, faded blue with scattered clouds. The snowscape from my window was pristine in its whiteness and the river a glass-like grey with drifts scattered about. Off in the distance I could see the smoke from chimneys several hundred yards away. The houses themselves were unseen behind a copse of trees, but judging by the smoke, there was a closely built number of dwellings, rather than just a single farm or estate.

Looking down, I could see Holmes standing on the snow-covered lawn, staring at the windows of the armoury which were below our rooms. I performed my ablutions, dressed and went downstairs. Knowing where the kitchen was, I popped in to see if I could obtain a cup of tea to warm myself until breakfast. Mrs. Galway was most obliging, after my compliments about her clootie dumplings the night before. She also told me Holmes had already passed through and was out in the grounds.

Preferring the warmth of the house, I drank my tea in the kitchen where a hot breakfast was being prepared. When finished, I set my cup in the sink. The cook advised me breakfast would be ready in twenty minutes and I should go and retrieve my friend. Already being outfitted in my overcoat, hat, scarf and gloves, I went out through the servants' door and made my way around to the side of the castle where I had last seen Holmes.

The world's first consulting detective was examining the ground beneath the windows. I hadn't noticed the evening before, but because the lawn sloped down to the river, the bottom of the windows were a good six feet above ground. Apparently hearing my approach, Holmes spoke without looking up. "It won't do, Watson. These windows are too high up to be entered without a ladder of sorts, even if someone were slim enough to fit through them and there is no sign of any disturbance below them. They are the only other way into that room besides the doors. The walls are not thick enough for any secret passage, and the floor is solid stone in that part of the house. Another note for your instructions, Doctor:

"23. Note the weather conditions on the day of the criminal act. They may provide a clue, or they may have obliterated crucial evidence."

We circled around the east side of the castle through a garden and came again to the courtyard and the front door. Here we found the lad, Fergus, building a snowman. He had a fairly large base already rolled into place and was working on the middle section as we approached. We surprised him, as he wasn't expecting anyone about this early. "Mr. Holmes, Doctor, what are you doing here?"

Holmes seemed lost in thought and so I answered, "A detective's work is never done, Fergus. Mr. Holmes has been examining the grounds around the house to see if anyone may have entered through a window or by some other means."

"Oh," replied the lad.

Before he could expand upon that answer, the front door opened and Aames called out, "Master Fergus, time for breakfast! Gentlemen, if you care to join the family, the meal is about to be served."

He turned upon his heel and left the door open for the boy. Fergus brushed off his gloved hands and the knees of his trousers, then made for the door. I took a step to follow, but realized my friend was still mentally somewhere else. I reached out and grabbed his elbow to pull him along. He seemed to snap out of his reverie with a wisp of a smile that was here and gone in the blink of an eye.

We brushed off the snow and removed our overcoats, then joined the family at the breakfast table. At one point, when Aames was out of the room, Holmes asked our host, "Lord Campbell, you've mentioned that the men in your family appear to have enjoyed long lives thanks to the Grail. Just how does that work?"

His Lordship set down his tea cup and replied, "It has become a tradition that everyone of this branch of the Campbell clan, starting when they are sixteen, drinks wine from the Grail every year on their birthday."

"Does that include the women as well?" asked Holmes.

"Aye, if they be in the bloodline. My sister, for example, but not her husband. Elise," he nodded at his daughter, "but not Roy. You can't marry in to the tradition. Fergus will be included when he is of age." At this he smiled at the lad.

The boy nodded and replied with a quiet, "Yes, sir."

Holmes folded his hands under his chin and announced, "If you could be so good as to provide a trap for us, I believe Watson and I could put our time to good use in the town today. I have matters to discuss with the police, and I also wish to follow up with some of the pawn shops in town."

"Certainly, Mr. Holmes," replied His Lordship. "I'll have my groom drive you in at your convenience."

Holmes held up a palm in supplication, "I would prefer that we go alone, Lord Campbell. We may have to venture into some seedier parts, and I should not wish to put any of your staff at risk, nor be distracted by worrying about their safety. Watson and I have done this sort of thing before and are quite capable working in tandem."

Lord Campbell tilted his head at the detective, frowned, but then acquiesced, "Very well. I shall have our phaeton harnessed and available for you within the hour."

He looked at Aames who would relate the instructions to the groom. Holmes posed a question, "Aames, since the night of the theft, have you noticed anything amiss in the wine cellar?"

All eyes turned upon Holmes at this apparently incongruous statement. Finally, Aames replied, "Nothing that I recall. Why do you ask, sir?"

"Just a curiosity. Whoever stole the Grail may have thought its powers only worked in conjunction with a Campbell's wine. It may provide a clue as to motive. If such were the case, then we may have hope that the theft was for the Grail's powers and not for its monetary value. Thus, we may still find it intact.

"At any rate, please thank Mrs. Galway for an excellent breakfast. I believe our journey into town shall require that we luncheon there, but we certainly expect to be back well before dark and dinner."

As we each left the table to go our separate ways, I noted that Elise went toward the kitchen, Roy reminded his son he had schoolwork to do in his room but that he could play outside after lunch. Then he went down the hallway to where we knew he had his office. His Lordship went to his study, while Aames went to deliver the message to the groom to prepare our transport.

Holmes and I ascended the stairs to our rooms. Just before I opened my door, he turned and made an unusual request of me, "Doctor, I would most appreciate it if, in addition to your revolver, you would also bring your medical bag. I'll meet you at the stables in fifteen minutes."

I cocked my head at him, questioningly, but he was already stepping inside. As I prepared for our journey, I slipped my old army Webley into my overcoat pocket and pulled my leather medical bag from the wardrobe.

I half expected to run into my friend on the way to the stables, but found I had actually beaten him there. The groom had hitched a fine pair to the Campbell's phaeton, which was just large enough for two to travel comfortably and provided some protection from precipitation, though not much from wind. Fortunately, the skies were blue with high scattered clouds. I only hoped they would remain so for the duration of our journey.

When my companion arrived, he carried an additional blanket wrapped around his left arm, "I thought we could use a little extra protection against the cold, Doctor. Would you be so kind as to drive?"

Since we were not involved in a high-speed chase through the streets of London, which Holmes knows backwards and forward, this was not all that unusual. Often he preferred not to be distracted by physical activity while he was processing the facts of a case in his mind. I set my medical bag on the floor, took up the reins, asked the groom for directions to Ayr police station and set the horses upon a trot.

We drove out to the Holmston Road. There was a clump of trees about three hundred yards south of the castle, just as the road turned west with the river. My friend bid me to pull to the side and looked carefully about.

"Your medical bag if you please, Doctor," he said. Then he unwrapped the blanket and used it to shield the fact that he was now placing the stolen Grail into the leather case.

"Holmes!" I cried in surprise. Its size was larger than I had expected and it certainly was beautiful with rubies and emeralds adorning its golden presence. I was momentarily awed by the fact we held in our hands a relic purported to have supernatural powers bestowed by God, Himself. I then lowered my voice to a whisper at his silent admonition. "Where did you find it?"

"Drive on please, Watson. I will tell you the tale as we continue our little ruse."

Chapter Eight

I whipped up the horses again and we made for town at a moderate pace, since there seemed to be no actual hurry. Holmes explained his actions while I was in my room, preparing for our journey. He began his tale by making it clear to me that I could not publish this particular case until after the death of the current Lord Campbell.

"What about all the instructions you have had me include, Holmes? This was to be your *magnum opus* for future generations."

"I am sure we will find other occasions to include my teachings, Watson. I have made a promise that I must enjoin you not to break."

"As you wish," I replied. Secretly, however, I was relieved. I had not yet determined how I was to weave his teachings into a story that publishers would feel to be appealing to the masses.

Holmes began his explanation. "You noticed my distraction when we were outside after coming upon Fergus constructing his snowman. I had come upon an idea that was highly improbable, but then, the circumstances of this theft were already *outré* to begin with.

"While it was not a certainty, the most likely explanation of the tracks upon the carpet of the back hallway was that they were left by the thief. The size indicated a person of small stature. Thus, the search among the female staff. Miss Blair is not our thief. Though her shoes are the proper size, as I observed, she is slightly duck-footed. The footprints in the hall did not turn out as her feet would. If Aames is to be believed, only His Lordship's niece, Allison, who is not a blood-relative, would be the next likely suspect.

"However, as you are well-aware, Oxford style shoes are favoured by both genders. Fergus's stature is small for his age, and thus his feet are also of a similar size to Miss Blair's. I noted this fact when I saw his footprints in the snow."

"Fergus is the thief?" I asked, incredulously. "But, why? Isn't he the next heir to the baronetcy? The Grail would be his eventually."

"It's not the Grail itself, that he craved, Watson," said my friend. "Let me repeat the story I learned while you were getting ready for our little day trip."

*****

Sherlock Holmes retrieved a blanket from his room after breakfast and walked down the hall to the bedroom of Fergus Lennox. Receiving permission to come in upon his knock, he found the lad seated at a desk by the window. A book was open and he was writing on a piece of paper by the natural sunlight that shone through when the curtains were opened.

At first, Fergus seemed confused his visitor wasn't one of the servants or his mother. Then he stood, a look of panic a thirteen year old could not hide, upon his face. "Mr. Holmes! What do you want ... sir?"

"I wish to tell you a story, Fergus. May I sit?"

The lad swallowed hard and nodded as he sat back down. Holmes sat on the edge of the bed facing the boy and began a tale which he had not even shared with Watson.

"When I was your age, I was also about your size. This was rather unfortunate, for I had an older brother who was already six feet tall. We were always rather competitive and he often drove me to temper that resulted in my fruitless attempts at physical assault upon him. Naturally, in spite of the fact that he was not athletic, he easily rendered me harmless. This, of course, made me all the more frustrated. I would have done anything to be able to best him physically.

"I believe we share that frustration. While I have noticed that you are well-coordinated, your size likely keeps you from competing as well as you would hope at school."

"It's not fair!" cried Fergus. "I can beat anybody my size at anything. But they always put me up against larger boys because of my age, and I can never win because they are all taller, heavier and stronger."

The detective looked with sympathy at the lad, then replied, "So, you thought drinking from the Grail would give you some sort of extra power due to its purported supernatural properties."

He made this statement so matter-of-factly, that Fergus took it as a known fact rather than a question and said, "Yes! If all the stories I've been told are true, then it should help me. I couldn't wait until I was sixteen. Who made that rule up anyway? I needed help now! So, I snuck down the back stairs in the middle of the night and took up the Grail. Then I went to the kitchen and poured some of the wine Mrs. Galway uses to cook with into the cup. I didn't want to be caught in the kitchen, so I rushed back up here and drank it behind closed doors. I was going to take the Grail back down with no one the wiser, but the wine made me sleepy and the next thing I knew, it was morning. There was no way to put the cup back without being seen. Then the police came and the room was always locked after that."

"Where is the Grail now?" asked Holmes.

Fergus reached down and opened the bottom drawer of his desk. He pulled out the Grail, which was wrapped in an old shirt, and handed it over to Holmes. "What will you do Mr. Holmes? You won't tell Grandfather will you?"

Holmes looked upon the artefact with interest. It was taller than he had thought it might be, though the base matched the indentation he had noted in the cloth. It was, indeed, gold with a ring of rubies and emeralds running around it. Christmas colours, to be sure. But to Holmes's mind this belied its authenticity as Christmas colours had not become traditional at the time of the crucifixion, and this was certainly not the cup of a carpenter. However, Campbell's tale of it being the original golden gift to the Christ-child might explain that. Whatever its provenance, it was the object he was paid to find, therefore he merely replied, "I will keep your secret, if I can, Master Fergus. I have a plan which I believe will satisfy everyone."

He stood and draped the blanket over the golden cup. "I am going into town with Dr. Watson. I will then bring the Grail back to your grandfather with a convincing tale so that no one will be the wiser. But I leave you with this thought. As I said, I was about your height when I was thirteen. By the time I was fourteen, I had grown five inches. I kept growing until I was as tall as I am now by the time I was twenty. So, take heart young man. Patience is a virtue and is its own reward."

*****

By the time Holmes finished his story, I was bringing our horses to a stop at the local police station. I turned to my friend and asked, "Since you already have the Grail, what are you going to tell the police?"

"Nothing, Doctor," he replied.

At my surprised look he expanded upon his answer, "Well, I may give them a few hints on how to better conduct future investigations. Primarily though, I shall introduce us to the local chief inspector and ask about the location of local pawn shops or fences where the Grail may find its way. This will coincide with the tale I am weaving for Lord Campbell."

Thus, we spent the day making discreet inquiries. We enjoyed an excellent lunch of fried steak, tomatoes, vegetables and potatoes at Tudor's Grill. Afterward, Holmes took the reins and drove us down to the Firth of Clyde.

The harbour at Ayr is not exceptionally large. However, in our favour, there were two boats heading out that day which suited Holmes's purpose. One for Belfast, and one for Oslo, Norway.

By three o'clock we were on our way back to Bellrose Castle, Holmes rehearsing with me the tale we would tell His Lordship upon our return. The weather had held, and had actually approached fifty-five degrees around two o'clock, but was now steadily dropping as the wind was picking up and night falling.

It was near gale force by the time we gained the courtyard at Bellrose and the groom rushed to open a stable door so we could pull in safely out of the weather. Fortunately, among the later renovations to the castle, an enclosed walkway had been constructed from the stables to the main apartments beside the courtyard wall. We were able to reach the living quarters in relative comfort.

This path brought us into the kitchen with the cook graciously offering us hot drinks. We thanked her, and Holmes insisted that we take them with us so we could report to His Lordship immediately, this being in keeping with the story that Holmes was about to tell.

Sweeping into Lord Campbell's library, where we had first met him, Holmes cried out, "Success, Lord Campbell! Watson, if you please?"

I opened my medical bag and produced the Grail, setting it gently upon the polished surface of the Lord's desk. He stood in amazement and snatched it up, holding it reverently to his breast for several seconds. Then raising it further, he examined it closely for any damage or missing jewels. Finally, he reached out and shook each of our hands. "Mr. Holmes, Dr. Watson, how can I thank you? I confess I was grasping at straws when I called you in on this case. You have exceeded expectations. Whatever your fee, sir, I will pay it gladly!"

Holmes cocked his head and I wondered what price he would put upon what turned out to be a fairly simple retrieval. The number he offered was far below his normal fee. In fact, it was barely enough to cover our travel and the meal we had enjoyed in town.

Lord Campbell shook his head, "No, no. Surely your time alone is worth more than that."

Holmes waved his hand and replied, "The matter turned out to be quite simple, though interesting as an exercise. I have named my fee, Lord Campbell. You may do as you see fit. Now that we have completed our task, we shall be returning to London by train tomorrow."

"But how did you find it? Where was it? Did you face any danger? I am used to receiving full reports of actions taken, sir,"

Holmes shook his head, "I am not one of your soldiers, Major. However, I shall be happy to report all, though I do not wish to repeat myself. Let us discuss it at dinner so the whole family can be satisfied."

Later that evening, all were seated around the dinner table with Aames in attendance standing to one side. Once Lord Campbell had offered the grace and the meal was served, he turned to Holmes and said, "Now, Mr. Holmes, please tell us how you were able to recover the Grail."

Holmes weaved a tale, as only he can, about how we obtained information from the police and spent the day tracking down various places where the Grail may have been sold. By his reckoning, at one pawn shop we entered just as the owner was saying 'no' to a particularly rough looking fellow. As this chap walked out in a huff, we approached the pawnbroker regarding the Grail and was told that the man who just left was trying to sell it to him. He knew stolen goods when he saw them and put the fellow off. We then, supposedly, rushed out the door and gave chase. Holmes stayed on this man's heels while he waved me to try and cut him off from across the street. When the rough turned in my direction, I had used my old rugby skills and brought him down. He dropped the bag holding the Grail. My leg though, had given out and Holmes had to help me out of the road from harm's way of the passing traffic. We saw the fellow snag a cab but had trouble finding one ourselves. It must have been a good two or three minutes that gave the thief a head start. He seemed to be heading for the docks, so we instructed our driver to do so as well. As we arrived, a small steam vessel was just pulling away. Checking with the harbour master, we found that two boats were supposed to be heading out at that time. One for Belfast and one for Oslo. We did not know for certain if our thief was on either boat. The description we were able to glean from our running observation and the pawnbroker was that of a dark, swarthy fellow of lean build and short stature.

"So, you see, My Lord," said Holmes. "While I was able to gain some interesting facts about the case, notably that he must have picked the lock on the kitchen entrance, for there were no tracks about any of the windows, it was merely old fashioned detective work that retrieved your artifact."

Lord Campbell nodded, "Well, even if it wasn't your extraordinary powers which secured the Grail, you did retrieve it for us and we are most grateful. Minister Reynolds will be as well, come Christmas this Sunday."

"Hear! Hear!" said Lennox, and the rest of the family, including young Fergus, raised their glasses to us.

"How is your leg after all that, Doctor Watson?" asked Elise, ever the concerned mother-figure.

I cleared my throat and replied, "The cold weather always has a detrimental effect upon it, Mrs. Lennox. It will be all right again in a day or two."

We stuffed ourselves that evening and again we were treated to magnificent clootie dumplings. The next morning, we packed early, but chose to breakfast with the family before catching the ten o'clock train. Before breakfast, I wandered out to the courtyard to see how Fergus was progressing with his snowman. He had nearly finished it the day before, but it still lacked arms, face, or clothing when we had returned the previous afternoon.

What I found, however, was Sherlock Holmes with the boy on a patch of snow on what would normally be grass, thus providing a softer surface. He was teaching him some unique wrestling moves and Fergus was picking them up quickly. He had just put Holmes on his backside when I walked up. "Shall I make note of this for your instruction manual, Holmes? How not to be bested by an opponent in wrestling, perhaps?"

My friend stood, frowned at me then, smiled at the lad. "I am just showing Master Fergus how to use an opponent's size and weight against him. The battle does not always go to the strongest, remember."

We said our goodbyes after breakfast and were driven to Ayr station. Once alone on the train I remarked to my friend, "You seem to have once again sacrificed truth for the greater good, Holmes."

My companion smiled, "After this experience, it is unlikely the lad will ever steal anything again. Justice is not always served by the letter of the law, Watson. Often mercy can be the greater solution."

"A most admirable attitude for the Christmas season, Holmes," I replied, pulling a flask of brandy from my coat and offering it to him saying in my best Scots burr, "*Nollaig chridheil agus bliadhna mhath ur*". He took a swig and returned it saying "Thank you for playing along with my little game, Doctor, and I wish you a merry Christmas and happy New Year as well!"

The Blue Parrot

Chapter One

On a cool Saturday autumn morning in 1906, I was lounging in front of the fire at home, casually reading a newspaper, as I waited for my wife to join me at breakfast. My study of the goings on in the metropolis of London was interrupted by the doorbell. The maid answered but was not allowed to announce our guest as he pushed past her straight to our parlour and called out in a French accent, "Are you *the* Dr. John Watson, associate of Mr. Sherlock Holmes?"

He was a rough clad fellow, in layman's garb that spoke more of the continent than England. Wild, dark, unkempt hair protruded from under his beret and he bore a thin, curled moustache. He gestured wildly with one arm as he spoke, while leaning heavily on a T-handled cane with the other.

I stood and waved the maid away as I faced this rude intruder. "I am he, what can I do for you, sir?"

"You can tell me where Holmes is!" he bellowed. "I've been to Baker Street and that old landlady of his has no clue as to his whereabouts. I need his services, monsieur. It's a matter of life or death!"

He approached me as if he were going to wring the answer from my throat. I instinctively reached for the cane beside my chair to defend myself as I replied, "Holmes no longer lives in Baker Street. I'll thank you to stop bothering Mrs. Hudson or you'll have to deal with me and the police."

Suddenly, another voice called out, "Stop right there or I'll shoot!"

This command was followed by the click of a cocking pistol and the man froze. He turned slowly with hands raised waist high and palms wide open as he dropped his walking stick. Behind him my wife had entered the room with my Webley revolver in her hand, held steady as a rock. The look on her face told the fellow she would brook no sudden action. After an uncomfortable silence that seemed to drag on interminably, he spoke again, this time with no accent at all.

"My dear, Mrs. Watson, do be kind enough not to pull the trigger. I would much prefer a lump of sugar in my tea to a lump of lead in my chest so early on a Saturday morning."

I was taken aback. The voice now was unmistakably that of Sherlock Holmes, himself. It was proven so when he pulled off the beret, long haired wig, the thin moustache and straightened to his full height.

"Darling," I said calmly, "it appears our friend is up to his old tricks."

Facing the detective, I crossed my arms and said, "Really, Holmes, have we not outgrown this little game of yours?"

"I must keep my hand in when it comes to the art of disguise, old chum," he replied as he tossed the beret, wig and moustache into an empty chair, picked up the walking stick and set it alongside. "You are my penultimate test. If I can pass muster with someone who shared my rooms for the better part of two decades and has seen many of my most characterful creations, it is the threshold to perfection. I can rest assured that I may walk about freely without recognition."

"I would think Mycroft would be your ultimate test," I said, referring to his elder brother, whose observation skills Holmes had admitted were even greater than his own.

"Exactly so, and one which I have never passed," he declared, with some chagrin. "Thus it falls to you, my dearest friend."

My wife, having set the revolver aside, broke in with a wry smile, "We were about to have breakfast. Would you care to join us and partake of some of that tea which you prefer to a bullet?"

Holmes bowed and replied, "I would be delighted, madam."

We took our seats at the breakfast table and were served with sausages, rashers of bacon and eggs. Holmes dug in with a relish which I usually attribute to his need to recharge after solving a case. Thus, I enquired about his latest activities.

"Nothing much, Watson. I was able to assist Hopkins in the capture of the Beddington jewellery robbers. You will probably read about it when you get to the rest of your morning paper."

"And what adventure brings you to seek out my husband's assistance on this fine autumn day, Mr. Holmes? Nothing too dangerous I hope?" asked my wife as she took a sip of tea.

"Darling!" I exclaimed.

"Oh, really, John. How could you not know that is why he is here?" she said, with a look that made me feel obtuse.

Holmes folded his hands across his waist, "I've always admired your perception, my dear." Turning to me, he said, "I do have an ulterior motive for my visit, Watson."

He pulled a letter from his pocket and handed it over, indicating that I should read it aloud. The attached envelope was postmarked Morocco and was oddly addressed to Erik Sigerson c/o The Diogenes Club, Piccadilly, London, England.

Dear Friend Sigerson,

I trust you remember your old friend, Ferrari. It has been a long time since you've been to Casablanca, yet I shall never forget the valuable assistance you gave to me and my family in our time of trouble. My son, Anton, is sixteen years old now! He was just a bambino piccolo when you were here. We have also been blessed with a daughter, Gabrielle, who is eleven.

I realize I expect much, but I am a desperate man, my friend. I am being troubled by rogues who threaten

---

me and my business. They operate in secrecy, so that I cannot even report anything useful to the police that would lead to their arrest. They demand protection money or say they will kill me and my family and simply take over the business themselves. They have backed up their threats with small scale actions which have damaged my business and leave me terrified as to how this might progress, or how my family might be threatened. I have since been paying it, but their methods of collection are so clever we cannot catch them in the act of picking it up.

I am hoping that someone with the skills you exhibited all those years ago can help put an end to this evil. If you can come to our aid, please reply to the French Consulate where I do business regularly. I dare not have such mail come directly to my home.

I pray you to look upon me with favour, friend Sigerson, in remembrance of our time together.

Your ever grateful host,

Val Ferrari

I looked at my friend, "Obviously this relationship dates from your years immediately after Reichenbach. This Ferrari fellow only knew you by your alias. How did you come to know him?"

Holmes leaned back in his seat, teacup in one hand, saucer in the other, eyes gazing upward with the rising steam. "It was early in 1894," he recalled. "I was returning from my time in Tibet *en route* to Paris when my ship stopped at Casablanca in Morocco. We were due to stay in port for two days and I chanced to stop into the Blue Parrot café for a meal. I was taken ill before I even left the establishment and the owner, Valentino Ferrari and his wife took me in. They made room for a cot in a spare room and called for a doctor. I was laid up for several days with a stomach ailment and missed my sailing. As it happened, several other patrons were similarly afflicted, though all the others presented symptoms after leaving the establishment.

"I was able to determine that the food had been deliberately poisoned by one of his competitors, which led to an arrest and the salvation of the café's reputation. It was a quite simple matter to an observant investigator. Ferrari makes far too much of my skills. But then, he is an emotional fellow."

I smiled at his modesty and asked, "Have you replied yet?"

"I've no intention of replying," he stated, to my surprise. Then he added, "Not in writing. Too many chances for interception. Also, while I may trust my French police sources in Paris, my travels through various European colonies have left me with the impression that corruption is too easily found when officials are far from home.

"Therefore, I shall instead reply in person. Which brings me to you, my dear fellow. If your wife and patients can spare you for perhaps a month, I should welcome your company."

We both turned to my wife, who was spreading her toast with butter. She stopped and looked at us queerly, "What? You thought I would say 'no'? As if that would deter you? I knew what I was getting into when I married you, John. I appreciate the fact that we make important decisions together, but I also know that Mr. Holmes does not take on trivial cases. This Ferrari family deserve his assistance and if he needs you, I'll not stand in his way.

"However," she voiced, in a much more commanding tone as she pointed her butter knife at the detective, "I hold you responsible for him, Mr. Holmes. You bring my husband back to me safe and unharmed. Promise?"

Holmes held his hand to his heart and replied, "My word of honour, my dear lady."

"Then have a safe trip," she replied. Looking at me, she smiled and added "Don't forget your weapon."

I smiled at her across the table. Turning to Holmes I said, "I have one patient this afternoon that I must see to. I'll make arrangements with Dr. Burnside to cover the rest of my appointments."

Holmes slapped his palm on the table in agreement and replied, "Splendid! We shall leave on the ten o'clock sailing tomorrow morning for Calais, then a train to Marseille to catch a steamer down to Morocco. I shall resurrect my Sigerson guise, but there is no need for you to be incognito. Although, if asked about *Sherlock Holmes*, I would prefer you to reply that you are not *that* Dr. Watson. Perhaps you could recall the burr of your Scottish roots and be *Dr. Watson of Edinburgh*?"

In my best recollection of my grandfather's voice I replied, "Aye, that I could do, Mr. Sigerson."

My wife looked at us like a couple of schoolboys about to play a joke and just shook her head as she returned to her meal. Holmes gulped down his tea and rose from the table. "I've preparations to make, Watson. I shall see you in the morning." Turning to my wife he added, with a grin, "Thank you for your hospitality, madam," nodding toward my revolver on the table where she had left it.

Chapter Two

I arrived at Charing Cross railway station the following morning at 7:30 precisely, carpetbag in hand. I looked all around, not sure exactly what appearance Holmes would take when he was in his Sigerson persona.

"Ready to board, Watson?" came a voice from behind me. I turned and there was a tall man with short blonde hair, moustache and neat beard. I recognized him at once from his voice, even with the Norwegian accent, but it took several seconds for me to penetrate the visual effect of his disguise.

"Sigerson, old friend!" I replied in my Scots burr as I stuck out my hand. *Sotto voce* I asked, "Was this your appearance when last in Casablanca?"

In a similar low voice he answered, "My facial hair back then was my own beard, grown out over the years of my travels. To appear more Scandinavian, I dyed my hair as you see and affected this accent. But come, it is time to board."

We made good time on the boat train to Dover, steaming through the countryside at a brisk pace. High clouds overhead had kept the temperature down and I was glad that I had packed sufficient clothing for all kinds of weather. During the journey, I was able to learn more about Ferrari from Holmes.

"Valentino Ferrari is from Genoa," stated my companion. "Travels for his father's shipping business took him to Marseille where he met Rosette, the daughter of a French restaurateur. They fell in love, but neither of their families approved. Thus, they eloped and came to Casablanca, another coastal city, where both their cultures thrive. She knew the restaurant business and he knew how to obtain the best prices from shipping companies. That led them to open the café about twenty years ago."

The ferry crossing was a little rough. Storms in the English Channel the previous night had left a choppy sea in their wake which slowed our progress. As a result, we had to rush to make our boarding of the connecting service to Paris, and then after a night in France's capital onward to Marseille where we would then catch a steamship that would take us to Casablanca *en route* to its final destination of Nouakchott in Mauritania.

Aboard ship, we found ourselves among a contingent of French police officials, assigned to Casablanca as advisors to the Moroccan police under the terms of the Algeciras Conference[1], signed earlier that year. One chap was a particularly chatty type who spoke English very well and seemed to want to practice on us. The single chevron on his sleeve indicated he was a recent recruit and a *Gardien de la paix*. (Keeper of the peace). He was of short to medium stature with a sturdy build. Thick brown hair flowed back from his pleasant round face. My impression was that he wore a thin moustache to make himself appear older, for I doubted he had seen his twentieth birthday. He introduced himself as Louis Renault and asked if we had been to Casablanca before, as he hadn't and was anxious to learn more about the place.

---

[1] The Algeciras Conference of 1906 took place in Algeciras, Spain, and lasted from the 16th January to the 7th April. The purpose of the conference was to find a solution to the First Moroccan Crisis between France and Germany from the preceding year. The trouble arose as Germany responded to France's effort to establish a protectorate over the independent state of Morocco. In fact, Germany was not trying to stop French expansion, but its goal was to enhance its own international prestige which failed badly. The result was a much closer relationship between France and Great Britain, which strengthened that relationship since both London and Paris were increasingly suspicious and distrustful of Berlin. The Sultan of Morocco retained control of a police force in the six port cities, which was to be composed entirely of Moroccan Muslims (budgeted at an average salary of a mere 1,000 pesetas a year) but now to be instructed by French and Spanish officers, who would oversee the paymaster (the *Amin*), regulate discipline, and be able to be recalled and replaced by their governments.

Holmes explained that he was an explorer who had passed through Casablanca many years before. He indicated that he had met me some time ago in Edinburgh when his ship docked in Leith, while bound to Greenland. He was taking me to Casablanca where he thought the dry climate might help a medical condition I was suffering from.

We conversed for some time until the bell sounded for lunch. Throughout the remainder of that voyage, Renault always greeted us cheerily. It seemed every time we saw him, he was chatting with other passengers, especially those whose destination was Casablanca.

I mentioned this to Holmes, "That Renault is a curious chap. I suppose it is rather smart of him to get to know the citizens over whom he will have authority. The better he knows them, the better he can serve the community."

Holmes stroked his goatee and replied, "Remember the words of Sir Francis Bacon, Doctor, 'Knowledge is power'. This fellow is adept at gaining an arsenal of knowledge which will undoubtedly assist him in his career. As it is, we shall need to be on our guard in any dealings with him."

At last after eight days upon the water we reached Casablanca. The weather was pleasant, being much closer to the equator than London, and I threw my overcoat over my suitcase as I carried it. Holmes made a suggestion which I thought prudent, remembering my army days. "Best to tie your sleeves through the handle, Watson. When last I was here pickpockets abounded."

Holmes observed how much the city had built up in the twelve years since he'd enjoyed the Ferraris hospitality. Rather than take a chance on an unknown hotel, he requested the cab driver to take us to the Blue Parrot café. "We will drop in on Signor Ferrari and seek his advice on the safest hotel for our stay. He can also inform us of any new aspects of his situation."

The streets were bustling with traffic of horse drawn carts, pedestrians and some few automobiles, such as our cab. I spotted the manmade perch with the Blue Parrot upon it, even before we could read the sign above the arched entryway. As Holmes paid off the cab driver I asked a rhetorical question, "I wonder if that is the same parrot as when you were here last? This is hardly a natural habitat for such a creature. I imagine it would be expensive to replace."

Holmes walked up to the perch and stared briefly at the blue and gold bird and said, "You see ..." The bird cocked its head and gave a low gurgle. Holmes repeated the phrase, "You see ..." This time the creature bobbed its head up and down twice and replied, "You see, but do not observe, awk!"

Holmes pulled a bit of biscuit he had secreted in a napkin in his pocket at breakfast and held it up for the bird to take. To me he said, "Blue macaws can live up to fifty years or more in captivity," he replied. "This is Felice, Italian for 'happy'. I distinctly remember her markings. The story of how she came to be in Casablanca is an interesting one, though not relevant to our case. If you are curious, Doctor, I suggest you bring it up with *Signor* Ferrari."

"I should be happy to tell it again, my friend!" came a voice from the doorway. The man making that proclamation was about forty-five years old, of medium build with olive skin, dark hair and a full moustache. He was rather tall, just under six feet by my estimate. His build was average with a bit of a pot belly. He wore a white suit, *sans* coat, though he retained his blue and gold tie which matched the parrot's colours perfectly. He marched right up to Holmes and threw his arms around my companion and gave him a kiss on each cheek.

"*Signor* Erik, I did not know you were coming." In a lower voice he asked, "Are you here in response to my letter?"

In a similar low voice, Holmes replied, "Yes, I thought surprise might better fulfil our purpose. This is my friend, Dr. Watson. He has accompanied me on some of my explorations and thought a trip to your warm climes might be a nice change from the chill of his native Scotland."

Ferrari pumped my hand vigorously and said with enthusiasm, "Any compatriot of Erik is most welcome." Looking down he saw we still had our bags. "You have not checked into your hotel? Where were you going to stay?"

Holmes answered, "With the many changes to your city over the years, I thought it best to obtain your recommendation. Is there a safe place close by?"

Without a second thought our client piped up, "The Hotel Napolitano should be perfect for you and the Doctor. It is merely two streets down that way and around the corner to the right. But first you must come inside and refresh yourselves. I will send Anton to make your reservations."

We stepped into the cool atmosphere of the café. It took a moment for my eyes to adjust, after being out in the bright sunlight. When they did, I saw an expansive dining room with a bar and a kitchen at one end, and stage at the other. The stage held several seats with music stands to one side, which were unoccupied at the moment. The café itself was not crowded at this time of day, being a good hour before luncheon. Ferrari led us to the end of the room near the kitchen. He opened the kitchen door and called out, "Rosette, Anton, Gabrielle! Come see who is here!"

A tall woman just a few inches shorter than her husband led the way, wiping her hands on her apron. Unlike her husband, she was stout and pale with light brown hair and spoke with an accent more French than Italian. "What is it, Vito? We must get the food ready for the noon meal." Then she saw Holmes and cried out, "*Monsieur* Erik! *Mon Dieu!*" She strode over and subjected Holmes to another hug and more kisses. Holmes introduced me and she curtsied politely, then turned to the children who had followed her from the kitchen. "Gabrielle, Anton, this is *Monsieur* Erik Sigerson, who helped your papa when we almost lost the cafe years ago."

Ferrari added, gesturing to me, "and this is his friend, Dr. Watson."

Anton strode forward and held out his hand in greeting. He was large for sixteen. As tall as his father already, yet stout and pale like his mother. His English was perfect and we later learned that he also spoke his fathers' Italian and his mothers' French fluently, as well as the local Arabic dialect. Gabrielle, with the universal shyness of all eleven year old girls, approached us slowly. She took more after her father with her olive skin, long dark hair and brown eyes. One could see she would grow into a real beauty. She also curtsied and said 'hello'. Holmes and I both bowed in our most gentlemanly manner, which brought a smile to her face as she retreated to her mother's side.

Ferrari said to his son, "Anton, go over to the Napolitano. Speak to *Signor* Martino and tell him I would like him to arrange two adjoining rooms for *Signor* Sigerson and Dr. Watson."

"On my way, Papa. Gentlemen, if you will excuse me?" He bowed courteously to us and strode out the door to run his errand. His father waved us to seats at a table far from the rest of the light crowd as he requested his wife to bring food and wine. She and her daughter returned to the kitchen. We sat and Holmes asked, "Have there been any further developments in your situation, Valentino?"

The café owner looked about to ensure we weren't overheard, then replied, "There have been new demands, Signor Erik. I do not understand them, but I am compelled to comply."

"What makes these demands unusual?" asked Holmes.

"They are orders to expand my menus and change my entertainers. These extortionists say they want me to be more successful."

I spoke up and commented, "Perhaps they believe the more successful you are, the more money they can extort."

Ferrari shook his head in frustration, "My café has been built on my reputation for quality food and pleasant entertainment. We have been successful for years. There's no reason to change."

Holmes asked, "Does your menu still consist of Italian and French food?"

Ferrari nodded, "Yes, the tourists are comfortable with our cuisine. Yet, in their latest demand, these *criminali* want me to add traditional dishes of English, and Spanish food. All because of the new status after the Algeciras Conference, which is bringing in more foreigners than ever before."

Holmes nodded and continued his enquiry, "What changes in entertainment have they suggested? Any particular performer or group?"

Our host shook his head again, "No, no one in particular. They simply want me to change from our traditional Italian and French musicians to include Spanish and English acts as well. They are insisting that we become more *cosmopolita*, so as to attract all the variety of new tourists pouring into the city."

"Did they use that word, *cosmopolita*?"

Ferrari held his open palm to his chest, "No, Signor Erik. That is my own. All of their demands have been written in English."

"Interesting. Do you have the messages they sent?"

"Sì. I will get them for you." He left just as Rosette and Gabrielle brought two steaming plates of spaghetti with garlic covered bread and wine.

"I remember how you enjoyed my spaghetti when you were here before, *Signor* Erik. *Bon appétit*, gentlemen. There is plenty if you want more," she said with an infectious smile.

I broke off some bread and began swirling the aromatic pasta around my fork. Holmes merely took a sip of wine and said "I recommend moderation, Doctor. It is a bit spicier than what you are used to at Rivano's in London. He tends to use milder ingredients in his sauce, due to the tastes of the English palate."

Following this caution, I reduced the size of the bite I was about to take. It was indeed spicier. Not so much as the Indian dishes I had been exposed to in my army days, but zesty all the same. I followed it with a sip of wine and was glad I had bicarbonate of soda in my medical bag.

Ferrari soon returned and gave Holmes a handful of typewritten sheets. My companion gazed intently at them, using his magnifying lens. As he did so, Anton returned and advised us that a doorman from the Napolitano was waiting outside with a cart to take our luggage to the hotel. Noting the papers, he asked his father something in Italian, to which Ferrari replied, "Do not be rude, my son. *Signor* Erik was of extreme help the last time someone tried to take over our business. I've asked for his assistance again. I trust him as a *fratello*. You will do anything he asks while he is here, so we may get to the bottom of this madness."

"As you say, Papa," he nodded. To us he bowed and added, "At your service, gentlemen."

"Thank you, Anton," replied Holmes. "Ferrari, I should like to take these with me to examine more closely."

"Anything you need."

"May we also take our food with us? I should not wish to insult Rosette, but I would like to settle into our rooms and get started on this problem quickly."

"Of course! Thank you, Erik!"

"Excellent! We shall return this afternoon."

Chapter Three

We settled quickly into our rooms. Once unpacked, I knocked on the adjoining door and walked in at Holmes's invitation. I noted he had set our spaghetti on a small table and he indicated I should go ahead and eat while it was still warm. He had spread the letters out on the bed in order by the dates Ferrari had written on them. Each was neatly typed, so there would be no handwriting to analyse. That in itself, meant something to my friend.

"There are two primary reasons to type such messages, Watson. Either to disguise the person's handwriting, which implies that Ferrari may have been able to recognize it, or that the writer has some condition which makes handwriting difficult or impossible."

I nodded in agreement as I continued to eat and poured myself more wine from the bottle Ferrari had sent along. "I would think the former is more likely. Although, I suppose you can ask Ferrari if he knows of any such person."

Holmes nodded and continued, "I also note that the requests seem to broaden as they move forward in time. This extortionist has become more confident from his successes and begins to suggest changes to the operations of the business. Also note the difference in the sums he demands. They do not remain the same, nor do they continually increase, as is common with this type of crime. He asks for smaller amounts of cash when he requests a change in the business that will require expenditure."

"What changes has he asked for?" I enquired.

"The first was to replace the coal burning stoves in the kitchen with gas ovens. That demand appeared in the third letter, after the first two were merely for cash. Then, the cash demands reduced for a time, apparently in response to the expense Ferrari incurred to put in the new ovens.

"The next improvement was to put the musicians on tiered levels instead of having them flat on the stage. Apparently, an effort to improve the sound quality of the entertainment."

I finished off my garlic covered bread and took a sip of the excellent Merlot before replying. "It appears Ferrari's extortionist has the man's success at heart. One could almost look upon it as having a paid consultant. Albeit an enforced one."

"Which begs the question, Doctor. Who benefits from this arrangement?"

"Certainly the extortionist," I observed. "He's getting money through threats and obviously the more successful Ferrari becomes, the greater this person can raise their demands."

"What have I said in the past about obvious facts, Watson?" countered my companion.

I searched my memory and recalled, "That there is nothing more deceptive than an obvious fact."

"Precisely," answered Holmes. "We need to take a closer look at all the players in this game. There is more data to gather before we draw any definite conclusions. First, we must determine the source of these letters."

He handed me his magnifying lens and the first letter, "Tell me what you see, Doctor."

I read through the demand and it seemed straightforward enough. The money was to be paid in paper currency and placed in an envelope to be delivered by the boy, Anton. He was to walk along a specific street until confronted, then turn the money over. There was the usual demand for no police or any tricks, or the boy would be the first to suffer. Since Holmes had handed me his lens, it seemed apparent that I was to study the document itself, rather than just read it. The paper was a clean, white, quarto sized sheet. The typing was neatly done with no spelling errors. I looked at specific letters to see if there were any distinguishing characteristics. A few of them appeared smudgy, while the rest were clean and crisp. I noted these to Holmes and he nodded, approvingly.

"Anything else?" he queried.

I took another look and noticed the watermark, "This paper seems to have been manufactured in Italy. The name on the watermark appears to be Italian. Could he have an enemy from his home country who has come to Casablanca for some type of revenge? Or, perhaps another Italian business rival?"

Holmes shook his head, "Not Italian, Watson, Latin, which could mean anywhere in Europe. But there is a telling clue in the salutation. Look closely."

I leaned in as close as possible to the document with the lens and noticed that there appeared to be scrape marks above the letter 'n' in *Signor* Ferrari. Almost as if someone attempted to peel away a layer of paper. I reported my finding to Holmes.

"Precisely. I believe the person who typed this letter was unfamiliar with the keyboard and didn't realize his error until it appeared on the page. He then used a pen knife or razor to attempt to scrape away the telltale mark."

"What mark?" I asked.

"I would contend that our extortionist was using a Spanish typewriter. While it has all the normal English letters, it also has a separate key for the letter 'n' with a tilde above it for typing words like *señor*. He used the correct key later on for the rest of the 'n's but he was afraid to let that one be noticed and likely didn't have time to retype the letter. Another telling fact."

"What do you conclude from this, Holmes?" I asked.

"We shall have to determine what businesses have Spanish typewriters. It will most likely be one where the person was not a regular employee, but was borrowing the typewriter surreptitiously and had limited time to use it. It may also mean that he is a Spaniard and typed that character out of habit."

I nodded and asked, "Just how do we go about that? With all the recent immigration since the Algeciras Conference there must be dozens of new Spanish businesses, not to mention those that have been here for decades."

"I believe that we shall start with the Spanish consulate."

"There is a consular office here? I know only of the Spanish embassy in Rabat."

"Correct," affirmed Holmes. "However, with the population of Casablanca being the second largest in all Morocco, they have installed a consular office here as well.

"First, however, we shall return these dishes and silverware to the Blue Parrot and question Ferrari and his son further. I need to see just how this person or persons were able to avoid capture."

Chapter Four

Not long afterwards, we were back at the Blue Parrot. Holmes had chosen to return at a time when it was more likely that the lunch crowd had dwindled so our client and his family would not be too busy to answer our questions.

We settled again near the kitchen, far from the few remaining patrons. Ferrari and his son sat with us and Holmes peppered them with questions. I could barely keep up my note-taking whenever the father spoke. Occasionally, he would slip into his native tongue and when he had to repeat himself in English, it allowed me to catch up. Anton, on the other hand, was very deliberate in his speech. He took his time with his answers, so that he might give all the detail he could remember.

"I walked down the street, as they demanded. It was dark at that time of night and the streetlamps in the area are far apart. I was just passing an alley when someone stepped out of the shadows and gave the code phrase."

"Can you describe him or her?" queried the detective.

Anton raised his eyebrows, "It never occurred to me that it might be a woman, although the voice was of a high pitch. I still believe it was a man. He was dressed all in black with a black fedora pulled low and a scarf covering up most of his face. He was a short fellow, less than five and a half feet tall, I should think. He had a small gun in his hand, so I was not inclined to argue. He demanded the envelope and I handed it over. He warned me not to follow and ran back down the alley, turning to the right when he got to the far end. As I am not athletic," he continued, looking down at his stout physique, "I did not pursue."

"Very likely a reason they chose you," noted Holmes. "I should like to visit the scenes of all these drop offs at your convenience."

"Certainly. I have a meeting with my tutor this evening, but I can be free up until seven o'clock."

"That will be a good start, thank you," replied my friend.

We spent the next forty-five minutes going over the various scenarios where money was delivered. The places all varied, they were all at night and they all provided a convenient escape route with multiple options in case of pursuit. The person had no discernible accent, just the high-pitched voice. Other than being short, he was of average build and seemed well coordinated as he ran. Anton had no knowledge of guns. He could only tell us that the weapon was a revolver.

As we still had some daylight left to us, Holmes requested that Anton and his father take us to the places where money was delivered. Ferrari informed his *maître d'* to take charge while he was gone. This man, whose name was Vito, was a short, balding fellow of average build with a handlebar moustache and a distinct Italian accent. He bowed and replied *"Assolutamente, signor"* and returned to his duties.

Once outside, Holmes insisted that we visit the destinations in the order in which they occurred. Ferrari hailed a cab and gave directions to the driver. As we rode, Holmes asked our client, "How many employees do you have?"

Ferrari counted them off on his fingers, "The family, of course, then Vito, who has been with me for three years. I have two bartenders, Aramis and Gilberto. Aramis was here when you last visited. He is a cousin of Rosette. Gilberto came to us about a year ago, when old Carlos retired. He only works nights as he also has a day job at the Spanish consulate as a courier. We have two other cooks besides Rosette and Gabrielle. There are two waiters and three waitresses. Oh, yes, there are also three assistant waiters and the cleaning staff, which is the three Manetti sisters."

Holmes nodded, while I was impressed at the size of the operation and certain that Holmes had noted the Spanish consulate connection. The detective then asked, "Have you ever had any problems with any of them, or has anyone complained about their pay?"

Ferrari shook his head, "Never a complaint. I treat my employees very well."

I noted at that statement that Anton slightly shifted in his seat, bowed his head and pursed his lips briefly. They were all subtle movements and his father did not notice, but I'm sure Holmes did, though he chose not to enquire at that time.

Ferrari went on, "Gilberto, the bartender, has twice asked me for an advance on his pay, in regards to some medical bills for his wife."

"Did you advance him the money?" asked Holmes.

"That favour is usually reserved only for my most long term and trusted employees, *Signor* Erik. However, I did take pity on him, for I have met his wife and she is a frail little thing. I insisted, however, on paying the doctor directly, just to be safe."

"A wise precaution," stated my friend.

We arrived at the first drop off point, the alley where the thief took to his heels. It had been several weeks, so Holmes did not expect to find any physical evidence. He primarily wanted to examine why this location might have been chosen. This would gain him some insight into the extortionist's mind.

He turned to Anton, "Where were you when you heard his voice?"

Anton took a stance on the pavement, "Right about here."

"And where was he standing?"

"From where you are, about two steps back and over next to the wall."

Holmes took up the indicated spot. "So, he was here when he spoke to you. Did he have the gun pointed at you, or just in his hand?"

"He was holding it at his right hip, pointed at me."

Holmes nodded, "Walk through the motions of what happened."

"He called out my name and said "Come here". Anton started walking toward Holmes and then stopped, "When I got to this point, he told me to stop and put the envelope on an old crate that was there against the wall. Then he made me take two steps backward. He picked up the envelope, peeked inside and said 'Very good. Now stand there until I'm out of sight. If you try to follow me I will shoot'. He turned and ran down to that end of the alley and turned to the right."

Holmes examined the area where the perpetrator stood. He noted a side door to the establishment next to the alley nearby. He then walked out to the street, looking up and down at the various businesses and streetlamp locations. Satisfied, he then led us down the alley to the far end and turned right to see what lay in that direction. It was another alley, a bit broader, where many of the businesses had their loading doors or rear entrances. A half dozen possibilities presented themselves as to where the man had gone, or he could have even run down that alley to another turning. As long as he maintained a fair distance, there were a myriad of ways to elude capture. Again, a sound reason for insisting upon the bulky Anton as the carrier.

Holmes waved us back to the waiting cab to proceed to the next destination. As we walked, he asked another question, "You say he looked into the envelope to ensure that the money was there. Was the envelope sealed? Did he tear it open?"

The teenager replied, "It was not sealed, Mr. Sigerson. He merely lifted the flap and took a quick look. He did not take time to count it."

Holmes acknowledged this answer with a mere hum and we moved on to repeat the same routine at all the other destinations. Each one was chosen for its multiple escape routes. Some were the vestibules of hotels or shops, where Anton was called in off the street and the same person made him go back outside while he slipped out one of many possible exits. One was a spot under a balcony where the culprit lowered a basket on a rope for the envelope. A little money slipped to the manager revealed that that room was supposed to be unoccupied and no one recalled any person leaving through the reception at the time in question. To be thorough, Holmes suggested a look at the roof, where evidence suggested someone had crossed over to an adjacent rooftop, though pinning down an exact time frame was impossible.

By this time, it was dusk and we returned to the Blue Parrot so that Anton could eat before going to his lesson. Ferrari insisted that we join them for dinner. As we were eating, or rather, as I was eating while Holmes smoked and drank coffee, I asked the young man what subjects he was being tutored in.

"I am studying Spanish, Doctor. I have a desire to increase my language skills to include all those spoken in our fair city."

Chapter Five

Holmes's eyebrows raised at that remark and he enquired, "A noble ambition, young man. Where do you study?"

"A friend of mine works at the Spanish consulate. We meet at the city library and trade lessons. He teaches me Spanish and I teach him French."

"How convenient," replied Holmes. "What does this fellow do at the consulate?"

Anton cocked his head and replied curiously, "He's just a clerk. He's a bit older than I, but not much. We met in the marketplace. We were at adjoining booths haggling over prices with merchants who chose not to understand what we were saying in order to frustrate us into paying their high prices. As we each overheard what was going on, we came to each other's rescue by translating for one another."

"Most fortuitous," stated the detective. "I have some business with the consulate, perhaps I shall run into him. What is his name?"

The rotund teenager dabbed at his mouth with his napkin and replied. "Pablo. Pablo Ugarte. But he works in a little back office processing paperwork. I doubt that you would have a chance to see him."

Holmes raised his wineglass toward the youth, "Paperwork processing is exactly what I need. In my line of work, I often need permission from government officials to enter certain areas for exploration, especially when I'm working with archaeologists. There is a British expedition scheduled for early next year. I thought I would visit the Spanish and French consulates while I am here now, to see what papers will be necessary under this new ruling conglomerate of nations. What does this Ugarte look like?"

Anton stood to leave for his appointment and replied, "He is a short fellow, perhaps five foot three inches and maybe one hundred and thirty pounds. He has black hair cut very short and is clean shaven. His face is very round with brown eyes that have a sort of sleepy look to them."

He then chortled, "He has a bit of a wheezy, nasal voice, but altogether he can be a charming fellow. Now, if you'll excuse me, I don't wish to be late. Shall I tell him you'll be coming by the consulate?"

"Yes, that would be splendid," said Holmes. "It's always good to have an inside connection when doing business."

"But, he's just a clerk, *Monsieur* Sigerson. He has little influence."

"Ah, you never know, Anton. Just as if you wish to know the intimate secrets of a household you ask the servants, so, too, with most businesses, including government. You can often learn more from the staff members than the directors and officers. Have a good lesson."

The lad left us, as did his father to attend to his patrons now that the dinner hour was filling the café. I presumed Holmes would wish to go back to the hotel to smoke a few pipes over the information he had gathered today. I was thus surprised when he merely sat back and lit up a cigar as he shifted his chair for a better view of the small stage where the musicians were about to begin the entertainment.

The leader of this little band announced from the stage that they were going to play a series of songs from a popular American Broadway musical, *Little Johnny Jones*[1].

He turned to his troupe and began a series of lively tunes comprised of ballads, ditties and rousing cadences. For a group

---

[1] George M. Cohan's first Broadway musical from 1904 about the American jockey Tod Sloan in England, produced several popular songs such as: *Give My Regards to Broadway* and *Yankee Doodle Boy*.

of a mere eight musicians, they performed extraordinarily well, even though the café was filled with the usual bustling noises of meals being served, tables being cleared and multitudes of conversations taking place.

I thoroughly enjoyed them. Holmes, however, was busily scanning the room. At one point, he got up and took a long circuitous route around the entire café, pausing on occasion to take a longer look at certain personages. He also observed closely the band from the side of the stage, applauding them as an admirer to allay suspicion of the fact that he was studying them.

He returned to the table and sparingly ate some bread and cheese while finishing off a second glass of wine. When the performers took a break, he suggested we make our *adieus* to Ferrari and return to the hotel. When we parted ways for our separate rooms, he informed me that he would be going back out for an hour or so and that he would see me in the morning at eight o'clock. I asked if he could use my assistance but he declined and replied, "Merely a little reconnoitring, Watson. I feel an urge to visit the library."

Chapter Six

The next morning, I was in the hotel restaurant, enjoying a cup of coffee and debating whether to order breakfast, as I did not know what Holmes's plans might be. He arrived at precisely eight o'clock and sat with me, motioning for a waiter. "Order heartily, Doctor," he advised. "I do not know where our travels might take us. There is no guarantee as to when our next meal might be."

During our repast, my companion informed me of his nocturnal trip to the local library. "I went as myself, Watson, so as not to be recognized by young Anton. I found an excuse to research several volumes on shelves near the table where he and Ugarte were exchanging language phrases. I could not overhear everything said, but the gist of the conversation appeared to be what we were told. I managed to wait until they left and heard Ferrari's son tell Ugarte to expect a visit from me. The little Spaniard seemed puzzled but told him he would do what he could, though he hoped I would not expect too much from a man in his position."

"So, all seems legitimate," I commented. "What were you expecting?"

"Just examining all possibilities," he replied. "As you may have noted from Anton's description, Ugarte bears a striking resemblance to the person collecting the extortion money from Ferrari. Their behaviour last night would appear to refute that notion, for now."

"For now?"

"Watson, you know I loathe to eliminate suspects too soon. But Ugarte has moved a little farther down the list."

Once fortified, we set out upon our day. We first visited the French consulate on the Boulevard Rachidi, where Holmes sent a telegram off to his brother. While there, we happened to run into our fellow traveller, the *Gardien*, Renault. He greeted us most enthusiastically and asked if he might speak to us in private.

The three of us stepped into a small anteroom whereupon the policeman closed the door and bade us to sit down with him. Holmes, wary of the sly look upon the young man's face, spoke first. "How may we help you, *Monsieur* Renault?"

The fellow waved his hand as if brushing away a fly as he shook his head, "No, no, *Monsieur*, you misunderstand. It is I who wish to assist you, *Mr. Sherlock Holmes.*"

Holmes held the fellow's gaze, whereas I started, being not so practiced at concealing my emotions without advanced preparation. Renault turned to me and continued, "and Doctor John Watson, not of Edinburgh, but of London, by way of Afghanistan in her Majesty's service."

Holmes still refused to react, whereas I blurted out, "How …" until Holmes held up his hand to forestall any further outburst. "What is it you wish, sir?" the detective asked, without his Norwegian accent.

"Do not misunderstand me, gentlemen. I only wish to help you with whatever case has brought you to Casablanca. Of course, if my assistance proves worthy, I would be pleased of any commendation you might mention to my superiors. Imagine having the recommendation of the great Sherlock Holmes on my record!"

"Is that all?" asked Holmes, suspiciously.

Renault placed his right hand upon his heart, the white glove in sharp contrast to the deep blue uniform. "Upon my word of honour, *Monsieur*. I am merely a civil servant anxious to do his duty and rise through the ranks to an appropriate station where I can administer justice proficiently.

"As to your unspoken question, Dr. Watson," he said, turning to me. "In my quest to master the English language I've read many British books and magazines. One of which contained your story of *The Empty House* and the revelation of your friend's *nom de guerre* of Sigerson."

Returning to my companion he concluded, with a smile and a twinkle in his eyes, "As you might say, Mr. Holmes, the deduction was elementary."

Holmes mulled this over, finally nodded and replied, "You may possibly be of assistance to us, Renault. Being a newcomer to Casablanca, you are unknown, thus you could easily blend in with tourists. Have you any experience with undercover work?"

"Only what they taught us in our training. I should be happy to learn whatever you wish to teach me."

Holmes said, "I shall keep you apprised. I believe we may have need of your services soon to surreptitiously follow someone. The situation is currently delicate and I must wait for the next action of our culprit before putting a plan into place. I presume I may reach you here if needed?"

"*Oui, Monsieur* Holmes. What is the nature of your case?"

"An ongoing scheme of extortion. This is why I must wait for the next demand."

"How intriguing!" said the young man, rubbing his hands together, "I shall be ready, whenever you call."

Holmes held up a finger, "Not a word to anyone, Renault. If it becomes known that our victim has asked for outside assistance, the consequences could be disastrous. Also, when you receive word from me, you must come in civilian clothes. The presence of official police in the area will defeat our purpose."

"As you wish, Mr. Holmes. I am yours to command."

We left the consulate and walked on toward the Spanish consulate, which was close by, just across a large park. As we did so, I questioned my friend on his bringing Renault into the case.

"At some point, Watson, we are likely to need official police to make an arrest. Better that we have someone of whom we have some knowledge."

"But are you sure you can trust this fellow?"

"No. We cannot yet classify him as a friend or foe until he proves himself. But he knows who we are. It is better to play along with his proposal for now. We shall practice a saying I learned in the Orient. 'Keep your friends close and your enemies closer'."

Arriving at the Spanish consulate, Holmes walked up to the reception desk and enquired in a rather halting fashion, "Pardon me, umm, *dónde esta' Señor Ugarte, por favor?*"

The young man at the desk smiled and replied, "You may speak English, *Señor. Señor* Ugarte's office is down that way, turn right and it will be the fourth door on the left."

"Thank you," replied Holmes, back to his Norwegian accent. As we walked, I questioned him quietly, "I thought your Spanish was better than that, Holmes?"

"It is, Doctor. However, I have now established that I have little knowledge of it and it may lead someone to believe they can speak it within our earshot without worrying about whether we can understand it."

I gave a little sniff of acknowledgement and we were soon at Ugarte's door. It stood wide open, revealing the little man at his desk with piles of papers before him. Holmes introduced us as Sigerson and Watson, friends of the Ferrari family and the clerk bid us to sit down.

It was a small room, but it did have a window opposite the door which at least made the atmosphere slightly less oppressive. There were no paintings on the walls, merely a calendar behind his chair and rather worn filing cabinets in one corner. The walls were a dingy cream colour and in need of paint. The visitor chairs were small, wooden affairs with no cushions. His own chair was merely a slightly larger version of those in which we were seated, but with arms to rest his elbows upon. Being short in stature, the edge of the desk was just below his breastbone. Working at that level had caused his shoulders to hunch upward as he leaned over his paperwork.

Our visit seemed to be a welcome respite and he sat back somewhat in relief of what I, as a medical professional, was assured was an aching back. He spoke to us in that unusual voice which young Ferrari had described.

216

"Yes, gentlemen. Anton told me you would be calling. How may I help you?"

Holmes spoke up, "I have a group of archaeologists in Great Britain that wish to explore the region of Lakhyayta to the south. With the implementation of the Algeciras Conference, I understand there are new protocols in place to gain permission for foreigners to conduct such expeditions. Is there some paperwork which I may obtain in order to start that process?"

Ugarte sighed, an odd sound coming from that nasal voice. Then replied, "There is much paperwork involved in such instances. There are also many fees as well as restrictions on what can be taken out of Morocco and what price will be exacted. But, as you are friends of Ferrari, I will collect nothing today. You may bring back the geological disruption fee of one thousand pesetas when you return the completed paperwork. When your expedition arrives, you will be assessed and need to pay an additional fee per person."

I was outraged at this obvious attempt at bribery but held my tongue. Holmes replied that he would inform his expedition partners and asked if he could take the paperwork to be filled out. Ugarte went to a filing cabinet and pulled several sheets of paper out to hand to my companion. As Holmes looked at the paperwork, he noted one document that required approval from the French consulate. He held it up and asked, "I will be visiting the French consulate later. May I borrow your typewriter and complete this form now?"

Ugarte hesitated, but the chance to get out of his chair and stretch his body for a little while was a welcome respite, so he offered his seat to Holmes and the detective slowly typed out the necessary information on the form. When complete he stood, shook the clerk's hand and told him that we would be back when we had the approval and funds from our expedition sponsors.

"It's been a pleasure, *Señor* Sigerson. I hope to see you soon."

Chapter Seven

I thought that would be the end of our visit to the Spanish consulate, but as we made our way to the exit who should we run into but Ferrari's night-time bartender, Gilberto, just returning from one of his courier runs. He seemed shorter, seeing him out from behind the bar, which I suppose is natural. One is usually looking up at the bartender when seated on a barstool. He was a wiry fellow in his mid-twenties with short curly hair and a moustache. He spotted us immediately and cried out, "Dr. Watson! *Señor* Sigerson! What brings you here? Is everything all right at the Café?"

Holmes assured the fellow we were here on business and repeated the same story he had told Ugarte. Gilberto shook his head, "How much did he try to charge you?"

Holmes, acting naive, voiced the amount, along with the fact that Ugarte did not demand any payment today.

"*El bandito!*" declared the courier. "That fee is twice the normal amount and there is no *per person* charge. The Moroccan government does require payment for artefacts taken out of country, and that goes through their officials, not ours."

"*Grácias,*" answered Holmes. By the way, do you have access to a typewriter? I should like to type out a message to my expedition sponsors in London."

"*Sí,* come with me. There is one in a common area for all to use."

He led us to a table outside the post room where a typewriter sat with reams of paper and a stack of envelopes. It was against a wall but no one sat nearby who could see what was being typed. Holmes sat down and I engaged Gilberto in conversation so he could not observe what the detective was typing. When finished, Holmes thanked the gentleman.

"I can post that from here, if you wish?" volunteered Gilberto.

Holmes waved the envelope he had placed the paper in and replied, "Thank you, Gilberto. However, I have some other documents that need to go with this back at my hotel. Your kindness is much appreciated though."

"Any *compadre* of Ferrari is an *amigo* of mine," he replied, shaking our hands as he returned to his work in the post room.

Once back out on the street I turned to Holmes, "That was fortuitous. Now you have samples of two possible sources of the extortionist's demands."

"Yes, that saves me the time that my other plan would have required. Let us return to our hotel to compare these samples and see what we can conclude."

Meticulously Holmes compared the new typing samples with the original notes received by our client. He verified the watermark on the paper and examined each single letter and punctuation mark with his lens, attempting to find some unique characteristic that could be traced back to one typewriter or the other. He made several notes along the way. Finally, he set down his pencil and magnifying glass and leaned back in his chair. He had a contemplative look on his face, which told me something didn't set right with him. He got up and walked to the window, drawing his pipe and tobacco from his pocket. As he lit his old clay, he peered out into the street. I felt I had been patient long enough.

"Well, which one is it, Holmes?"

"I have somewhat of a quandary, old friend. On the one hand we have a loyal employee who has been forthcoming about his money troubles and been treated more than fairly by Ferrari. On the other, there is Ugarte, who has formed a symbiotic relationship with young Anton. Overriding all of that, what is the motive for either of these men to demand improvements to the café's operation?"

I nodded, "I see your point. But if I had to choose, I would say Ugarte's our man. He is dishonest and fits the general physical description Anton gave us. He could have disguised his voice, especially if it was muffled by a scarf. He keeps the money for himself, but does his friend a favour by ordering improvements to his father's business. If Gilberto is our man, he must have an accomplice who met with Anton since many of those exchanges were at night when Gilberto was tending bar."

"I'm afraid our suspects have not completely narrowed, my friend. While I am certain now that it was Ugarte's typewriter that was used, it is easily accessible, since his office door has no lock. Any person with access to the building could have slipped into the man's office and typed those notes."

"But, Ugarte also fits the description Anton gave us," I commented.

"To a certain extent, except for the voice," replied Holmes. "Ugarte's is very distinctive and it is hard to believe that Anton would not recognize his friend."

"So, what do we do now?"

"I need a private discussion with Ferrari."

That evening, we returned to The Blue Parrot and met with our client. Holmes explained that we had narrowed our suspects, but that there could be accomplices involved. He did not mention who his suspects were, for fear that Ferrari may inadvertently change his attitude toward them and make them suspicious. Holmes explained his plan to the restaurateur, emphasizing that no one else should be told, not even a family member who might let it slip. Ferrari agreed and we set things in motion.

During dinner, Holmes announced that he had received news from Norway that his mother was gravely ill and he would be returning home. He did not know when he might be able to come back to help his friend. Rosette was most sympathetic and I was sorry Holmes had to put her through such emotions, but this lie was necessary to our plan.

We departed the Napolitano the next day. Three days later, Ferrari received another demand.

Chapter Eight

The Vista Del Mar hotel was quite pleasant and offered an excellent view of the beaches west of Casablanca's main harbour. The sea air was invigorating and a pleasant change from that of the central city. We were lunching out on the terrace when a young man in a white wool suit arrived. He recognized us immediately and came over to our table.

"Mr. Holmes, Dr. Watson, a pleasure to see you gentlemen. I have the message you were expecting from *Signor* Ferrari." He handed over a sealed envelope, which Holmes immediately tore open as he bid the fellow to sit down. He read through it quickly and commented, "Excellent! We now have an opportunity to spring our trap. Can you be available for some covert work tonight, Monsieur Renault?"

"I am at your service, sir. What do you require?"

"Just you in clothes which do not stand out on the streets after dark. Do not bring any other officers with you. If an arrest is to be made, you will be able to take full credit. However, I must advise you that there may be no arrest, depending on what we discover and the mood of the victim. In any case, I will advise your superiors of your valuable assistance."

"Thank you, Mr. Holmes," replied the *Gardien* with a smile. "Where and when do you need me?"

Holmes gave the fellow instructions and he agreed to meet us accordingly.

After he left, I commented to Holmes, "Are you sure you can trust him, Holmes?"

"Absolutely not!" he replied to my surprise. "To quote the Bard, 'he has a lean and hungry look'. However, we know he was not involved in this extortion scheme, since he is a new arrival. He is also an ambitious sort who will take any advantage he can. The fact that he knows who we are works in our favour. Thanks to your chronicling of our cases, I have gained a reputation of sorts as someone not to be crossed. He is young and smart enough to know not to make an enemy of me. At least, not this early in his career. If he can, instead, make me an ally, it will be to his great advantage."

*****

That evening Anton Ferrari stepped out as before, instructions in hand and an envelope of cash in his pocket. Unbeknownst to him, he was being expertly followed by Holmes in a black Moroccan *tadjellabit* with the hood pulled up to hide his features, which were now his own rather than Sigerson's. Blending into the shadows, he was never detected by the young man who lumbered his stout frame along the route he had been ordered to take.

Also in disguise, I stayed ahead of Anton, slipping into establishments where he might be confronted, until such time as he passed by. I then would leapfrog over the next such location by crossing the street and passing him. Fortunately, his usual slow gait made this method feasible. Renault would cover the buildings I skipped, then he, too, would go ahead of me and settle into one further along the way.

We kept this pattern up for some time. After about three quarters of a mile, I was in the reception of a hotel which had a dining room adjacent. To my surprise, Anton walked in. I had seen no one signal him, yet he came in without hesitation and walked straight into the restaurant. I surreptitiously moved to a greater vantage point and took note of his actions. He had sat down and was soon joined by a young woman. She appeared to be in her late teens but was attempting to appear more mature with her hairstyle and makeup. She was dressed in a fine emerald green evening gown with a cut which emphasized a full-figure. Her dark hair and tanned complexion suggested she was Italian and were in sharp contrast to a beautiful white smile, pearl necklace and pearl earrings. Overall, she was a very attractive young lady.

I slipped out to the street and signalled Holmes. As he came from the alley across the way, Renault also caught up, *en route* to his next surveillance post. I pointed out our young friend. The detective and *Gardien* each took a clandestine look. Holmes indicated that we should retreat out to the street where we could speak freely without being overheard.

"This was the one option I feared most," declared the detective. "Apparently, the extortionist is Anton himself."

"Extraordinary! You really had Anton among your suspects?" I exclaimed.

"Everything the extortionist asked for benefits Anton as the son and heir," replied Holmes. "Had it just been for the money, the net casts wide. But the demands for business improvements smack of one who cares about the welfare of the family. Anton gets cash for himself to spend on his appetites and the business prospers."

"Why wouldn't he just make these suggestions to his father directly?" I asked.

"He may have made some small suggestions in the past that were shunned by his father, coming from one so young with no experience. I've no doubt the young lady has also aroused his desires to succeed."

"Shall I arrest him?" asked Renault, eagerly.

Holmes looked at the young officer sternly, "Not all crime is black and white, *Monsieur* Renault. You will learn this as your career progresses. In this case, I doubt the father will actually press charges. I am sure he will wish to settle the matter within the family. Putting the young man in prison will do more harm than good. May I suggest, among your reading material, you should add *Les Misérables* by Victor Hugo. It is an excellent example of how a policeman can be consumed by expecting perfection and strict interpretation of the law. You do not wish to become an Inspector Javert. You must learn when to temper legalism with forgiveness."

"So, what do we do now?" I asked.

Holmes pulled back his hood and thought a moment. At last, he pulled the *tadjellabit* off over his head, revealing a black suit underneath. Even now, in European dress, he was not likely to be recognized by Anton, since he was clean shaven and his hair was its usual jet black.

He said to me, "Watson, go to the hotel and change back into your normal attire. Then proceed to The Blue Parrot and await for me there. Say nothing to Ferrari until I arrive. Just report that I am still following his son. I shall keep an eye on our young friend for the remainder of the evening."

Turning to our companion he declared, "*Monsieur* Renault, thank you for your assistance. You may take the rest of the evening off. I shall deliver a recommendation to your superiors before I leave Casablanca. Good luck with your career, young man."

He put out his hand and Renault shook it firmly, "Thank you for the opportunity, Mr. Holmes. Should you ever need my assistance again, I shall gladly be at your service."

I caught a cab to the Vista Del Mar and changed into my normal attire. As I returned to The Blue Parrot, I wondered what I should say to *Signor* Ferrari. He would surely wonder why Holmes had sent me back. Walking through the door into the café and wending my way through the late evening crowd to the bar, I finally decided that I would merely report that the situation called for us to back off, for fear of being spotted and that Holmes alone was continuing the surveillance.

In the meantime, Holmes was taking decisive action, which he later reported to me.

The detective observed Anton and the young woman as they ate. When the bill came, Anton pulled out the extortion payoff envelope from his inner breast pocket, took out some cash and handed it to the waiter. That confirmed what had appeared obvious and as they stood up, Holmes walked over to their table.

"Excuse me, miss. Mr. Ferrari and I have some business to discuss. I'm afraid he will not be available for the rest of the evening."

Anton glared at the detective, "Who are you, sir? How dare you interrupt us?"

Reverting to his Norwegian accent, Holmes replied, "You know me best as *Signor* Sigerson and you know why we need to talk."

The young Ferrari was taken aback. Then he leaned closer to Holmes and said, "You are not Sigerson! Leave me alone!"

He started to brush past, but Holmes grabbed his upper arm and whispered in his ear in his normal voice, "I *am* occasionally Erik Sigerson, but at the moment I am Sherlock Holmes, a British detective. We must decide how to explain your extorting of your father. I have sent the police away so that you and I can speak privately. If you insist, I can bring back the *Gardien* who was very eager to arrest you."

Anton realized he was trapped and turned to his companion, "I am sorry, my dear. It appears my presence is needed elsewhere. I shall be in touch."

He kissed her hand, she curtsied and batted her eyes at him, in a very coquettish fashion, which made Anton's interest in her quite obvious. Then, she walked away and Holmes bade Anton to sit down. A waiter came by and Holmes ordered two coffees.

As they waited for their beverages, Anton asked, "Does my father know you are not who you appear to be?"

"Not yet," replied Holmes, "I shall reveal my true identity when I return to the café tonight. I have two questions for you first. Does Ugarte know you used his typewriter to advance this scheme of yours? Was he ever involved, or did you just use his description as one being easy to remember?"

The youth folded his beefy hands across his ample belly and replied, "Ugarte allowed me to borrow his typewriter from time to time, but he did not know my true purpose, nor did he ever see the documents. He was not involved in this plan at all. I used his basic description as you said, it was easy to remember a real person. I also had him in mind as a contingency plan, should I ever need to use a second person to maintain this little fiction. But that is all."

Holmes nodded his acceptance of that statement and continued, "The last question is, what shall we tell your father about you? If you care to explain yourself, perhaps I can help."

Knowing he was caught with nothing to lose, Anton confided the reasons for his actions to Holmes. "My father is a decent employer and treats his workers well. However, over the past year he has delegated more and more tasks to me. As a good son I felt obligated to comply, of course. But, as time wore on I came to realize he was taking advantage of our relationship. Yes, being a family member has its rewards in free room and board. He has also paid for my education and my basic needs. However, lately I have been doing the work that he used to pay others to do. I would prefer not to use the knowledge I've gained to go to work for one of his competitors. I have seen what they are doing and if he does not keep up with the trends, his business will fall farther behind.

"Of course, he ignored my initial suggestions regarding change. That, and the fact that he has never even thought of paying me wages, resulted in this plan of mine. The money amounts were never excessive. I have access to the accounting ledgers and know what he can afford. At some point in the future, when he has absorbed the changes and realized their value, I will tell him all."

The coffee arrived and the young Ferrari took his up and drank. Holmes leaned back and looked him over. Myriad thoughts swirling through his mind as to options that lay before him.

Finally, he stated, "I cannot assist you in deceiving your father, Anton. However, I believe I have a plan."

He outlined his idea to Anton. The young man was sceptical, but saw that he had no choice. Within the hour they walked into The Blue Parrot together.

Chapter Nine

After I had answered Ferrari's questions about our mission, he left me at the bar to attend to his patrons. The café was crowded with people anxious to eat, drink and be entertained. As it was getting well into the evening, I decided to order something to eat while awaiting Holmes's arrival. I took a small table near the kitchen and was soon eating a beef tagine with assorted vegetables accompanied by a glass of red wine.

I was nearly finished when Holmes walked through the door with Anton in tow. I swallowed the last of my wine and walked over to join him. I arrived at the same time as Valentino Ferrari. Holmes held up his hand at the Italian's barrage of questions and suggested that we go into the kitchen to bring Rosette into the conversation.

There was a table off to one side where the kitchen staff could take their meals in relative privacy and we all sat around it. Holmes then began his tale. "First of all, my friend, although I was traveling as Sigerson when last you saw me, my real name is Sherlock Holmes. I am a consulting detective from London."

"I have heard of Sherlock Holmes," recalled Ferrari. "But, I thought he died many years ago. Something about a waterfall."

"To quote the American author, Mark Twain, 'the rumours of my death have been greatly exaggerated'. I escaped Moriarty's trap, but to avoid his gang I adopted the identity of

Sigerson and travelled throughout Europe, Africa and Asia. After returning to London when it was safe, I asked Dr. Watson here to refrain from writing any more stories about me until four years ago. It was only three years ago that the story finally came out about my escape and return to London.

"But enough of that. The man extorting you is in custody. The French police are ready to press charges."

Ferrari slapped his hand on the table and exclaimed, "*Bene! Bravo Signore!* Who was he? What was his motive for all these changes he demanded?"

"I'll get to that in a moment," answered my friend. "First, I have some questions for you. I am sure the French police would want to know these answers so as to determine the exact charges to impart."

"*Certamente!* What would you like to know?"

"May I see your accounting ledger?"

Ferrari shrugged his shoulders and raised his hands, palms upward, "If you wish. *Un momento.*"

The café owner stepped into a back office. While he was gone, Anton instinctively reached for his mother's hand. She tilted her head at him curiously. Then, her countenance suddenly changed. Her mother's intuition made her realize that her son may be in trouble, though she couldn't understand how.

Ferrari returned, sat back down and handed Holmes the ledger. Looking over my friend's shoulder I could see that the entries were written in Italian, mostly in Ferrari's hand, though some exhibiting the more graceful writing of his wife. Fortunately, numbers are numbers throughout Europe and I could see a distinct pattern over time. This appeared to be what Holmes was looking for.

"I see that your business has undergone significant increases in income over the last few months," said the detective.

"It is a good thing!" declared Ferrari. "Look at how my expenses have increased. I have had to buy a greater variety of food, pay for multiple entertainers, hire more staff who were multilingual, the list goes on!"

"Agreed," replied Holmes. "I would point out though, that your profit margins are greater than ever. Even after paying this fellow what is really a nominal amount, all things considered."

"*È un criminale!*" he cried. "He set a fire and threatened to do more!"

"As I understand it, the fire was in a metal barrel ten feet away from the building and in plain sight of the back windows, where it could easily be spotted. In fact, it was Anton who noticed the fire, was it not?"

"Yes, he was taking the rubbish out."

"Rather a menial task for someone who knows three languages and is learning a fourth," noted Holmes.

"He is young, and he needs to learn all the aspects of the business if he is to take it over someday."

"Not so young as all that," countered my companion. "Many young men his age are already working at their first jobs, saving money for their own home and marriage."

Ferrari answered in agitation, "Who would hire him without the knowledge I am giving him? What need has he of money, when I provide his room and board? Marriage and a home are years away. There will be time enough for that! What has any of this to do with the man you have in custody? Where do I go to file the charges?"

During this diatribe I noticed Anton's grip tighten on his mother's hand, to the point she had to place her other hand upon his to calm him. But it was too late.

The boy raised his considerable bulk out of his chair, shaking off his mother's grip and ignoring her plea, "*Non, ne pas!*"

He leaned forward across the table, knuckles grinding into the red and white chequered tablecloth. His father stared up in confusion at this reaction by his son and started to speak, "Anton! What ..."

"Be quiet, father! For once in your life, you are going to sit there and listen to *me!*"

I could see by the look on Holmes's face that this was not the direction he had planned this conversation to take. His own muscles tensed as he shifted on his chair into a position where he could rise to prevent a physical attack. The lad's emotions were running high. His face was now red with barely controlled rage and his eyes stared daggers at his father.

"*I* am the one in Mr. Holmes's custody. It was *I* who set the fire! It was *I* who demanded money and then demanded the improvements that are making you richer by the day! You have never appreciated my ideas, nor my talents. I have two other establishments willing to hire me right now as a business manager or purchasing agent."

Ferrari leaned back, startled by these revelations. Before he could respond, Anton went on. "I had planned on revealing all of this to you soon, so that you might realize what you had right under your own roof. But, Mr. Holmes managed to follow me tonight and accelerated my agenda. Now, to listen to you belittling me in front of mother and these men, I see that you are as blind as ever. You can't even acknowledge the profits I've made for you. Well, you can find yourself a new errand boy, old man. I'll not stay where I am not respected."

He turned to go as his mother grabbed his sleeve. He stopped momentarily and looked at her as he patted her hand, "I am sorry, *Maman*. I will keep in touch." He walked on. His father stood and bellowed, "Anton, come back here at once!"

The boy kept walking, waving his hand above his head in a dismissive fashion and refusing to look back. Ferrari started after him but Rosette stood and blocked his path.

"No, you will not confront him now! Not like this. You are both too angry and stubborn to speak to each other now. One of you will do something that cannot be forgiven. You will give him time and if you are lucky, *maybe* he will come back to you,"

"He needs to learn respect! He cannot ..."

"So do you!" she said, in a tone I would never have expected from her.

"Always *le tout Savior*," she said, then turned to us. "Thinks he knows everything this one. His own son, he doesn't know. Nearly seventeen years under this roof and he does not understand him at all!"

She turned on her heel and stormed back to the kitchen, leaving him speechless and embarrassed. He sank back into his chair, his head falling forward into his hand with his eyes closed. After several seconds he leaned back and let his hand fall to the table.

"What is happening here? *Sono tutti pazzi?* First you tell me you are not Erik Sigerson, but Sherlock Holmes. My son disrespects me and walks out. My wife, my little Rosette, speaks to me as she never has before. What am I to think? What am I to do?"

Holmes responded, "I sympathize, Valentino. It must be disconcerting to have so much change come upon you so quickly. I am afraid my counsel in family matters is extremely limited, having never headed up one myself."

Then my friend, my companion, my comrade in arms, turned to me and dropped the question in my lap. "Watson," he said, affably, "you are much more experienced in the matters concerning marital bliss and the female mind. Perhaps you have an opinion for this situation?"

I started at this sudden request for my opinion. Usually on a case, Holmes only seeks my medical advice, or tests out ideas on me to see what the common man might think. I cleared my throat, folded my hands upon the table, tilted my head to one side in thought and willed my mind to race for the right thing to say.

At last, I spoke, "*Signor* Ferrari, I can only speak to you from my experience in my culture. I do not know what the expectations are of an Italian, or should I say, a French-Italian, household. However, I have been married twice. Both times to very intelligent and formidable women. In my case, these were women whose opinions I respected and often sought out. I was still the head of the household, but my marriages were more a partnership than a patriarchy. I have found it much easier to work together on things than to try and take everything on myself. Why should I bear the total burdens of life when I have a helpmate as my wife? Perhaps this could be of use to you?"

Ferrari shook his head, "This is not how we do things in *Italia*, Doctor. My father, my father's father, all my ancestors, ruled their households. Their word was law and no one was allowed to argue!"

"But you are not your father's son," chimed in Holmes.

The café owner bristled and turned red at this apparent attack on his birthright, but Holmes held up his hand. "Hear me out, Ferrari. You, yourself, told me the story of how you defied your father in order to marry Rosette. The two of you came here to start a new life without his help or his blessing, nor that of her father, either. You *both* made that decision, for she was under no obligation to turn her back on her home just because you asked.

"Now your son, who may have his mother's looks, but certainly gained most of his spirit and stubbornness from you, has defied you. Just as you defied your own father for what you believed to be right, so he has followed in your footsteps."

This revelation took Ferrari aback. The tension went out of his countenance. He leaned forward, elbows on the table and rubbed his forehead and temples with both hands. Finally, he dropped one hand on the table and said, "So, what do I do?"

Holmes leaned back and held his lapels in both hands, "For now, nothing. Your wife is right. You must let both your tempers cool. If he is, in fact, walking out, I am certain I can find him and let you know where to reach him. But only when you are able to speak to him man to man, for he is no longer the errand boy you had created."

"Thank you, *Signor* Holmes. I must find Rosette. Please, go and have something to eat in the café and I will find you later."

He walked back to the kitchen and we saw him and Rosette talking on the far side of the room as we made our way back out to the dining area. Rather than eat, however, Holmes suggested that we try and track down Anton's whereabouts. Gilberto, the barman, informed us that he saw Anton leave with a suitcase and his overcoat draped over his arm.

Holmes was able to track down the girl Anton had been with by talking to workers at the restaurant where they ate dinner. Over the next two days he was able to follow her to Anton, and in turn to his new domicile. We also found that he had started working for another establishment. Not a direct competitor of his father's, but a firm who would benefit from his purchasing connections and multi-lingual capabilities.

Three days after the confrontation, we were able to inform Ferrari and his wife where they could reach their son. We boarded our ship back to France and, exactly a month from when Holmes had requested my assistance, we were back in Queen Anne Street, where I was greeted with open arms by my wife.

I had insisted upon Holmes coming home with me, as it was nearly dinner time. I had telegraphed ahead and the table was set for three. After a warm and affectionate welcome from my sweet lady, she turned and walked up to Holmes. She grabbed on to his coat lapels to pull him closer as she raised up on her toes to plant a kiss on his cheek.

"Thank you for keeping your promise, *Sherlock.*"

Straightening back up, Holmes brushed the spot on his cheek with his finger and replied. "It would never do for an English gentleman not to keep a promise to so gracious a lady, my dear. I just hope our friend Ferrari learns the lesson of a happy household from the example that you and Watson have set."

Fun Fact To Accompany This Story

Sydney Greenstreet, who would play the grown up Ferrari in the 1942 movie *Casablanca*, had his acting debut in a 1902 English stage production of *Sherlock Holmes*.

The Gray Elegy

Chapter One

By the turn of the twentieth century, the detective Sherlock Holmes had become a household name in London and, I daresay, over most of the English-speaking world. It was in the summer of 1900 when a particularly interesting case, regarding a famous piece of English literature, came to our lodgings at 221B Baker Street.

It started with a telegram delivered early one morning while Holmes and I were still breakfasting. Shortly after the ringing of the front doorbell, an act which, much like the recent experiments of Pavlov's dog, struck my companion in such a manner as to bring all his senses to full attention, our landlady, Mrs. Hudson, escorted a telegram delivery boy up the stairs to our rooms.

With a soft knock she opened the door. In our two decades under her roof, she had changed little. A bit stouter and whiter of hair, but still soft-spoken and polite as always. She enquired in her Scot's-tinged accent, "Begging your pardon, Mr. Holmes, there's a telegram for you and the boy has been given strict orders to place it directly into your hands and no other. It sounds important, or I would not have interrupted your breakfast."

Holmes dabbed his thin lips with his napkin and set it down next to his plate as he replied, "By all means, Mrs. Hudson, let the lad in."

She stepped aside allowing a skinny youth in a sharp post office uniform to pass her by as she pointed to my roommate, "There is Mr. Holmes, young man."

The boy crossed the room rapidly toward my companion and held out the white form. Holmes took it, unfolded it with some haste and read through it quickly. His expression indicated a keen level of interest in its contents. He fished a coin out of his pocket and flipped it to the lad, who caught it deftly, smiled in appreciation at the denomination and gave Holmes a knuckle salute with a 'Thank you, sir.'

"I shall be preparing a reply shortly," responded Holmes. "Come back in thirty minutes."

"Yes, sir!" the boy answered and walked out, giving a nod of thanks to Mrs. Hudson on the way. As she closed the door, she said, "I'll let the lad straight up when he returns, Mr. Holmes."

Holmes was too absorbed in thought for a reply. Therefore, I interceded for his lack of manners and thanked her for her diligence. Turning to my companion, I asked, "What is so important that it required the message to be delivered directly into your hand, Holmes?"

He handed the form over to me then reached for one of his index books, apparently to review his information regarding our potential client. I read through the message and found it rather cryptic. It said:

HOLMES STOP DOCUMENT OF GREAT LITERARY SIGNIFICANCE MISSING STOP REQUEST YOUR ASSISTANCE IN RECOVERY STOP DISCRETION PARAMOUNT STOP PLEASE ADVISE SOONEST WHEN YOU CAN COME STOP WATSON WELCOME STOP WILLIAM CHESTERFIELD DIRECTOR V AND A STOP

I looked over at my companion, who now had his index containing the letter 'C' on his lap. I offered, "Surely you know who Professor Sir William is, Holmes? He's a prominent scholar and historian. Especially when it comes to English and Scottish literature."

Declining to look toward me, Holmes began perusing a specific page as he replied, "Indeed, Watson, I am well aware of him by reputation. However, I wish to glean a fuller picture of the man before I meet him in person. Ah, here we are, 'Chesterfield, William Royce, Professor, Kt, OBE. Former Lieutenant, Royal Navy. Born 1848 to Captain Charles Chesterfield, Royal Navy and Susanna *née* Royce of Brighton, East Sussex. Attended Eton, Brasenose Oxford, Dartmouth. Served in Third Anglo-Burmese War. Mentioned in dispatches and recognized for gallantry at River Fleet at the Battle of Minhla. Discharged after a bout of Typhoid fever left him incapacitated for a month. Returned to continue studies in English literature at Brasenose. Awarded professorship. Acknowledged as the premier Shakespearean scholar and expert on English literature of the last millennium. Knighted 1898 and appointed Director and Chairman of the Board of Trustees, Victoria and Albert Museum in 1899. Married 1880 to Catherine *née* Carlyle of Abingdon. One daughter, Victoria Susanna, born 1883. Resides Pelham Crescent, Chelsea'."

He returned the volume to its place on his shelves and walked to the writing desk to compose a reply. "I presume you wish to be involved, Doctor. Especially after being recognized in Chesterfield's request. Are you available this afternoon?"

"My patient load is light, as you know," I replied sincerely. "I am free the rest of today and can move appointments tomorrow if necessary"

My companion completed his message and we awaited the return of the telegram boy. He said to me, holding up the form, "I've advised Professor Chesterfield that we shall be available any time today at his convenience."

I nodded then suggested, "Why don't you step down to the corner and telephone him, Holmes? Surely there must be an instrument at the museum."

He pointed to the telegram I still held and shook his head, "He is insistent upon discretion, Watson. He would not wish some telephone operator or any other persons on the party line to eavesdrop upon our conversation and discover his secret. No, I am afraid we shall have to rely on the telegram services."

Still anxious to be involved with the investigation and whatever adventure it might bring, I further suggested, "Why not just go down there right now? It's less than three miles and we could save the waiting."

Holmes seemed to ponder that, for I that knew he was also like a hound straining at the leash to take up a new case. He leaned over the form once again and seemed to add one more sentence. As he did so, the messenger boy returned. Holmes handed him the reply, neatly folded and sealed, along with some coins. "There's more than enough money there to pay for a telegram, lad. However, I wish you to deliver this message yourself into the hands of Professor William Chesterfield at the Victoria and Albert Museum. Here is something for your trouble. Be off with you now, double quick!"

The lad smiled broadly, said 'Thank you, sir!" and was gone like a shot. I stepped over to the window which looked down upon Baker Street and watched the lad as he cycled away in the general direction of South Kensington.

In the meantime, Holmes had retreated to his bedroom. It was a little over five minutes later when a familiar figure emerged. A muscular fellow, certainly more so than Holmes's normal physique, stood before me. A thick full moustache of dark brown adorned his upper lip. The face was full and a straw boater added to the effect of a wide forehead. A double-breasted suit, apparently padded, added to the larger size he now portrayed.

"What do you think, Watson? Will it do for attending the V&A incognito?

I gazed him up and down for a few moments then replied, "Hardly incognito, but certainly not recognizable as yourself. From more than a few feet away I should presume you to be my literary agent, Conan Doyle."

"Then I have succeeded," Holmes intoned with gratification. "Very few people outside Doyle's inner circle are aware that he is in South Africa writing about the Boer War. Even if someone knew he had gone there, it has been several months, so he could have easily returned, though you and I know better. Therefore, what could be more natural than such a man of letters visiting the museum where so many of the nation's great literary masterpieces lie. It should certainly gain me an audience with Professor Chesterfield in private.

"In the meantime, you should wait here for his reply, then join us at the hour he names, which I will presume to be before noon, for the urgent tone of his message would hardly be compatible with anything later. Of course, you, going by yourself without me should also allay suspicion, being a somewhat famous author yourself. Your presence along with your literary agent would hardly be questioned."

I nodded in agreement and remarked, "You are assuming then, the museum, or Professor Chesterfield in particular, are being watched?"

"I am assuming nothing, Watson. Merely taking the precaution of being discreet as per Chesterfield's request. I shall be off now and likely I will see you later this morning." Putting his hand on the doorknob to leave, he suddenly stopped and glanced back at me with one last comment. "Assuming nothing, but preparing for anything, I should like you to slip your Webley into your pocket before you leave."

Chapter Two

With that statement, he was out of the door. I went to the window and watched him amble down Baker Street with a spring in his step, imitating Doyle who was a few years younger than either of us. After letting a couple of cabs go by, he finally flagged one down and was southward bound.

I retrieved my old army revolver, ensuring that it was clean and loaded, I set it down where I would remember to pick it up on my way out. Then I sat at the writing desk where I put my mind to work on some documents I needed to complete as I awaited the next telegram, or my friend's return.

Meantime, as Holmes would later relate to me, the cab ride to the V&A was a short one and Holmes entered the museum through one of the oak doors under the high arched façade, confident in his role. Inside he found a member of staff, introduced himself with a Scottish-accented voice as Doyle, and asked to be taken to the Director's office. The young man bowed in revered deference to the man he considered to be the great author and led the way through a hall filled with various statuary. They turned into a side wing and Holmes was led to an upstairs room. He was turned over to a secretary in an outer reception area and she was advised that, 'Dr. Doyle would like to see Professor Chesterfield'.

The young lady, properly impressed, asked *Dr. Doyle* to have a seat while she informed the Professor of his presence

It was but a few seconds when she returned and informed her guest that he could enter.

Once behind closed doors, Holmes was asked to take a seat across the great walnut desk from Chesterfield, who stared with curiosity upon his visitor. The Director was a large gentleman of perhaps six feet and with an athletic build as befits a soldier, though years in academia had begun to expand his girth and he now wore eyeglasses for reading. He had retained his military-style moustache which had turned completely grey as opposed to his hair which was still a light brown and full, worn in an almost leonine fashion. His voice was a commanding baritone, even when engaged in normal conversation.

"I only just got your note, sir and I must say, your impersonation of Dr. Doyle is spot on. Were it not for your grey eyes I would be prepared to swear that you were him."

Holmes, now using his own voice, replied, "I thought a visit from a well-known author would be more in keeping with your request for discretion than a visit from the detective, Sherlock Holmes. If you care to reply to my note, Watson is waiting at Baker Street and can join us as you please."

He called out to his secretary, dictated a short invitation and told her to have one of the staff run it over, rather than sending it as a telegram. That task completed, he turned back to Holmes. "Shall I outline the details for you now, or would you rather wait for your friend?"

"Oh, by all means, commence with your tale, Professor. I can fill Watson in later," said Holmes, crossing his leg over his knee and folding his hands into his lap. "I perceive this event occurred some time during the night and came to your attention only this morning. You abhor the thought of publicity at this time, thus your message to me instead of the police. Now what was this document, where was it kept, and when was the last time it was seen?'"

The former officer set both hands flat upon the edge of his desk and enquired, "How did you know that I hadn't thought the situation over for a day or two before contacting you? Yes, it happened during the night."

The detective tilted his head and replied, "We are well into the morning, sir and yet you have not changed the calendar on your desk over to today's date. In all other respects you are a methodical man and a creature of habit, as indicated by certain items, patterns of wear and stains about the room. Therefore, something upset your routine almost immediately you arrived this morning. Your decision to enquire of me was made without hesitation. Now please, answer my questions."

The Professor cleared his throat and commenced his report, "I arrived at my normal time this morning, that is to say, seven-fifteen. I do not usually take the most direct route through the building to my office. I prefer to vary my way, in an effort to enjoy the works on display, check on their condition and make sure that nothing is amiss. Care, security and pleasure combined. I have so little time during the day and I rarely have the luxury to enjoy the fruits of my labours. Today, I happened to pass through a room where many famous documents are on display. It was then that I noticed one was missing."

"What drew your attention to that particular document?" enquired Holmes.

"We are planning to make a special exhibit out of it next year when we celebrate the sesquicentennial of its first publication. I naturally noted its display case as I was walking by and was stunned to see it empty!"

"Obviously not Shakespearean then," commented the detective. "What is this piece of literature which has caused you such distress by its disappearance?"

Chesterfield took a deep breath and, with gravity to his voice, replied, *"Elegy Written in a Country Churchyard* by Thomas Gray. The document we have on display is believed to be the original hand-written, first completed draft."

Holmes's eyebrows knitted closer together. He shifted in his chair and reversed the crossing of his legs. At last, he replied, "I beg your pardon, Professor Chesterfield. The knowledge I have collected over the years of my career has mostly to do with crime and its history. What literary facts I've stored in my brain are left over from my university days, or those documents dealing with the law or the annals of criminality. Remind me about this work and why it is important."

The Professor was taken aback at the detective's statement of ignorance. His pale eyebrows rose and his brow furrowed as he replied in a surprised tone, "Why, Mr. Holmes, Thomas Gray was once the Poet Laureate. While he was not a prolific writer, his works are among the most revered of his time. The *Elegy Written in a Country Churchyard* is considered a classic work of literature on the subject of life and death. Sections of it are still often quoted at funerals to this very day."

"I've not attended a funeral in many years, Professor," said Holmes. When he did not expound upon the point, Chesterfield let it drop and continued his report.

Clearing his throat, the Director said, "Naturally I was taken aback. I consulted immediately with our head of manuscripts, Professor Henry Blanchard, to see if he had removed it for some reason and had yet to place a movement label in the display case and was going to report that fact to me when I arrived. But he was just as shocked as I and joined me in re-examining the case and the area around it. Noting no sort of clue as to what had happened, our first thought was the night staff and cleaners. We caught the head watchman just as he was changing shifts and questioned him thoroughly. No one, other than the cleaning staff, had entered during the night. He assured us that the doors and windows were all secure when he came on duty. He also affirmed that they were still this way when the day staff arrived."

Holmes reached his hand toward Chesterfield in supplication and requested, "I should like to examine the display case and the room where this manuscript was kept, Professor, if you would be so kind as to continue your narrative as we walk."

The Director nodded and rose from his seat, leading the way out of his office, through several corridors and galleries. Upon arrival at their destination, their footsteps echoed from the tiled floor in the deserted chamber, as it had been closed to the public temporarily. Many impressive items were kept under glass for public viewing. Its most prominent feature was a bronze statue of Samuel Johnson. Yet, despite being surrounded by some of the most revered documents in British history, Holmes went straight to the one empty display case in the room.

Stopping about ten feet away, the detective crouched down to obtain a viewing angle of the floor. Daylight streaming in from high arched skylights lit the room well and was supplemented by numerous electrical fixtures. Holmes moved to various positions for observation, but for the most part the tiles were clean and shiny, having been mopped during the night. There were a few scuff marks about the rectangular pedestal which drew the detective's attention. He manoeuvred closer, then removed a pocket tape to measure something which Chesterfield could not see, but was clearly a footprint to Holmes's trained eye. Moving a little to one side, he measured another and also took some longer measurements. Still crouched by the pedestal, he asked his client, "Professor Blanchard is at least six inches shorter than yourself and uses a cane with a rubber tip so as not to slip on these tiled floors?"

Chesterfield hesitated a beat in surprise, then replied in the affirmative, "Yes. How did you know?"

"The advantage of a freshly mopped floor allowed me to discern both of your footprints, faint as they be. His are much smaller and of a shorter stride than your own. The rubber tip of his cane left its own markings as well."

Holmes stood to his full height and continued, "The disadvantage of a freshly mopped floor, of course, is the wiping away of all other footprints. There are none besides those of you and your colleague."

At this particular moment, I arrived, having urged my cab driver to make all haste to the museum from Baker Street as soon as Professor Chesterfield's reply had been delivered. In answer to Holmes's remark I countered, "Tell us, *Dr. Doyle,* had the floor not been mopped last evening, how would you have discerned which footprints belonged to your culprit?"

Holmes's smile flashed beneath the Doylean moustache he wore, then he replied, "As your fellow lodger, Holmes might observe, it would depend upon the positioning of the footmarks. If we had been able to find a set that stood roughly perpendicular to the display rather than facing it, it may have indicated someone drawing his right foot back as his body turned when he opened the display case door to remove the document."

I nodded my satisfaction at his answer, then shook Chesterfield's hand in greeting. "Thank you for the invitation, Professor. I should like to be of any service I may to the museum."

"Your presence is always welcome, Doctor. The popularity of your own works, I believe over time, may very well land you a place here someday."

Holmes cleared his throat rather coarsely. I had no doubt it was to hide an ejaculation of his opinion which would not have been in good taste. Attempting to recover, he said aloud, "Let us take a closer look at this display itself."

Stepping up to the front he took his lens from his pocket and began an examination. The pedestal upon which the case sat appeared to be of marble. A rectangular obelisk, about three feet tall and perhaps eighteen inches square. Atop it was a display case with a solid oak bottom and back, and oak-framed glass sides and top. Inside was a slanted stand upon which the document had sat at an angle conducive to viewing. There was a brass locking mechanism on the left-hand side. It was this which drew the detective's immediate attention as he bent to gain a magnified look at its keyhole.

He was silent in his examination, though even through his disguise I, who knew him so well, could see the pursing of his lips, and the narrowing of his eyes which, to me, indicated a swirl of brain activity as he appeared to be cataloging his observations for later reference where he could coalesce them into a theory regarding the crime. His gaze seemed to shift from the lock to the corner of the frame and he asked a question.

"Professor, did you, or anyone else, open this case for any reason after your discovery?"

Our client, exhibiting the habits of his military days by standing as if at rest on parade, replied, "No, sir. It was obviously gone. If it had somehow slipped off its stand it would still be quite visible through the glass. There was no need to open it."

Holmes nodded and stood to look upon the Director, "That is well. Tell me, in addition to being shorter than yourself, does Professor Blanchard have unusually small hands?"

Chesterfield squinted in thought, took his right hand from behind his back, contemplated it a moment, then held it out toward us and replied, "I'm not sure what you would consider 'small'. I obviously have rather large hands myself. It has even been remarked so to me, so I believe that they may be above average in size. Whenever I've shaken hands with Blanchard, I quite envelop his hand. I am not sure if that is due to my own being large, or if his are indeed small for his size. They do seem rather slim, much like that of a woman's. But then, he is a slender fellow himself. Why do you ask?"

Instead of answering the question, Holmes asked one of his own, "Do you have a key for this display case with you, and if so could you unlock it please?"

Chesterfield gave a slight frown at not receiving the answer to his question, but dutifully reached into his pocket and pulled forth a ring upon which was several keys. He quickly sorted through them, selected the proper one, unlocked the lid and opened it wide.

Holmes bent over with his lens and examined around the interior, especially near the lock. As he was doing so, I heard footsteps behind us. As I turned, a voice called out, "William! What goes on here? Who are these gentlemen? I thought we were keeping this quiet."

Chapter Three

Chesterfield spoke up, "It's quite all right, Henry. Come, let me introduce you."

The diminutive Professor shuffled over on his cane. Holmes was quite right. This aging fellow of a receding white hairline could not have been more than five feet five or six at most. Bifocals were perched upon his beak-like nose and he looked us up and down like a bobbing bird, as if trying to bring us into focus. Before any of us uttered another word, he suddenly put out his hand toward my friend, "Dr. Doyle! My word, sir. Forgive me for not recognizing you immediately."

Holmes, reviving his Scottish-accented impersonation of my literary agent, took the man's hand gently and bowed. "Good morning, Professor Blanchard. Allow me to introduce my colleague, Dr. John Watson."

"Eh? Watson, you say?" He turned and shook my hand as well, looking up at my face as if trying to place me."

"Yes, sir. John Watson. Dr. Doyle and I work together."

"Oh? Are you also an ophthalmologist? I've been meaning to see someone about my prescription." He tapped the side of his glasses. "I do believe there is something wrong with these. I can read well enough but distant objects appear to be out of focus lately."

Chesterfield broke into the conversation and said gently, "Henry, Dr. Doyle and Dr. Watson are here to look into the matter of the missing *Elegy*. They are attempting to use the methods of their friend, Sherlock Holmes, to see if they can shed any light upon the case."

Blanchard gave a start as he looked at his colleague, "Sherlock Holmes? That fellow from *The Strand Magazine* stories? What good would those impossible fictions do in a case like this? No, William, we need a real detective. Someone well-known yet discreet. Perhaps we should not trust this to anyone in England. That's it! We should send to Paris for Bertillon[1]. He's the man we need. Scientific methods and all that. You should wire him straight away, William!"

The excited passion of the elderly Professor put him to shaking and I believed him to be in danger of fainting if not worse. Blanchard and I gently led him to a bench and sat him down. I pulled my hipflask from my pocket and urged him to take a swig from it. As he took a tentative sip I said, "You shouldn't excite yourself so, Professor. It's not good for your constitution. Why don't you sit for a minute and then return to your office? We can see to any communications needed for Monsieur Bertillon."

The man looked upon me, almost without recognition, then down at the flask in his hands. He took another swallow and handed it back, "Thank you, Doctor ..."

"Watson, sir. You are quite welcome. Let me walk you back to your office and get you settled."

He started to hand the flask back to me, but Holmes intercepted it. "I'll take care of this, Doctor. You'll need both hands to assure his safe return."

I nodded and helped Blanchard to his feet. While we were gone, Holmes continued his examination of the display case. Long ago he had established the habit of retrieving fingerprints whenever he could, even though it was not until 1901 that they

---

[1] Alphonse Bertillon was a French police officer and biometrics researcher who applied the anthropological technique of anthropometry to law enforcement. From 1880 he became chief of criminal identification in Paris. The system he introduced in 1882 incorporated a series of refined bodily measurements, physical description and photographs, and later fingerprints as well. In *The Hound of the Baskervilles* Holmes is described as being the second highest expert in Europe next to Bertillon, since 'to the man of precised, scientific mind the work of *Monsieur* Bertillon must always appeal strongly'.

would be admissible in court. He had developed a chemical powder which he now brushed lightly upon the surface of objects in question, then transferred the markings left behind to transparent tape and thence onto a microscopic slide. He now repeated this procedure along one side and along the top of the glass case. When Chesterfield questioned how he came to look there, Holmes explained. "When you opened this case, you merely put in your key, turned it and pulled the door open using the key still in the lock. In other instances, a person opening such a case might place their left hand upon the side or the top as they opened the door with their right."

"I see," replied the former officer. "But it seems I read recently, Scotland Yard was still petitioning the courts for the ability to use fingerprints as evidence. What use would they be?"

Holmes murmured as he concentrated on his work, "Legally, none, but from an investigative standpoint they can be invaluable in the identification or elimination of suspects for us to consider."

Holmes finished and placed the evidence into an envelope which went into his inner breast pocket. Then asked our client, "What were the dimensions and condition of the document?"

"It was written in ink upon good quality paper," answered Chesterfield. "Foolscap folio, around eight by thirteen inches and consisting of six pages. It was not bound and appears to have been folded into quarters at some point. It was in surprisingly good condition as it was not brittle, though it was a little worn around the edges."

It was at this point that I returned to rejoin the conversation and spoke to our client, "Professor Blanchard seems to be exhibiting early signs of dementia. Have you noticed how long this has been going on?"

Chesterfield took a deep breath and let it out slowly, as if reluctant to speak. At last, he looked about to make sure we couldn't be overheard by anyone near the room entrances and replied, *sotto voce*, "He *has* been having trouble with his memory lately. It began to manifest itself earlier this year, shortly after his wife passed away."

Holmes, who at first seemed impatient with my seemingly non-case related question, now tilted his head and asked, "Just what were these *manifestations?*"

Our client continued, "Exceedingly more forgetful. He would miss meetings, he would be found walking around with an artefact he was supposed to be putting into a display but getting lost on the way. Other times he would be seen sitting at his desk, just staring at nothing. Often, he would issue orders or make statements and then repeat himself a few minutes later, as if he had never said them before."

I shook my head, "Has he been seen by a doctor? Has the board of trustees taken any action in his regard?"

Chesterfield held out a hand in supplication, "You must understand, gentleman, Professor Blanchard is a senior member of the trustees. He is practically an institution himself. The board was willing to look the other way in deference to his years of service and, I must admit, each of us have covered for him in one way or another. He has one more exhibition he is in charge of, which will open this autumn. We had planned to carry him through that, then convince him to retire."

"But no one has suggested a medical examination?" I asked.

"We just assumed it to be a combination of age and depression, Doctor. He is nearly seventy years old and was married to his wife for well over forty years."

That statement reminded me of my own depression at the loss of my Mary, seven years previously. The first year thereafter I was inconsolable. Had not Holmes returned to life the following spring I very likely would have sunk further into alcoholism. Knowing this depth of feeling I had at that time, I could only imagine what Blanchard was going through. It must have felt like half of him was missing after all those years together.

My thoughts had taken me into my own distracted silence which was eventually broken by my friend, "Watson, I believe you recently mentioned sometimes such symptoms could be the result of physical aberrations. Narrowing of arteries, tumours, that sort of thing?"

His question shook me from my reverie and I replied, "Yes, that certainly is a possibility. If I may, Professor Chesterfield, I would like to suggest that the board makes some excuse to require him to obtain a physical examination. Perhaps a policy requiring all trustees to have an annual physical examination. A medical examination for key members of staff. Something that seems like he is not being singled out would be less threatening and may reveal a treatable condition."

Chesterfield nodded, "Thank you, Doctor. I shall suggest it to the other trustees and see what we can do. We have several medical specialists among our patrons. Perhaps we can make a discreet arrangement with one of them."

Holmes, eager to get back to the case, remarked, "I should like to speak with the head nightwatchman and cleaner if you would be so good as to provide their names and addresses."

Our client nodded, "Certainly, I'll have my secretary write them down for you. Is there anything else you wish to examine?"

"I shall spend a while circumnavigating the building to verify that none of the exterior doors or windows have been tampered with. We will stop by your office before we leave. If there are any further developments, please come and find me."

Professor Chesterfield wished us well and returned to his office. Holmes bade me follow him and we stepped outside to begin examining windows and doors. Looking both ways from the entrance I remarked, "By Jove! There must be well over a hundred ground floor windows alone! This could take days!"

My companion raised his hand up near his chin as if to halt my protest and replied, "The singular advantage to living in such a city as London is the soot and grime which coats everything. We merely have to walk along the exterior and observe if there has been any disturbance which might indicate someone passing through a window. It would be impossible for anyone to enter without leaving some trace."

Mollified by this explanation, I followed along with Holmes, careful to address him as *Doyle* whenever we spoke. It took us nearly half an hour to walk the outer perimeter with some occasional stops for closer examination. As we did so, Holmes had me make note of the location of all exterior doors, so we could re-examine them from the inside if necessary. None of the windows indicated anyone entering. All the doors were securely locked and showed no sign of being forced. Holmes examined each lock and deduced that there were no signs of any being picked. But that did not eliminate anyone with a key, or a clever twirler who was an expert at leaving no trace.

He remarked to me after checking one such door, "One of the erroneous conditions you and many other authors seem to foist upon the public is that it is easy to tell when a lock has been picked by scratches left around the keyhole. Observe, Watson."

He reached into an inner pocket, withdrew a small toolkit, selected the proper instrument, and proceeded to pick the lock of the door before us, which fortunately was not in a public area of the building.

"Note how the lock picks are inserted into the hole? There is no reason for them to come in contact with the outside of the mechanism or leave any scratches. Only certain types of older locks requiring a skeleton key may result in such traces. Unless the culprit is extremely clumsy or nervous, a picked lock would have to be taken apart to see if it has been tampered with inside the keyhole."

"But I've seen you point out scratches indicating picked locks before," I replied, somewhat miffed he would accuse me of misleading my readers.

"Yes, I have. However, those were cases where the work was done by less than an expert, or someone who was suffering physical difficulties due to nerves, or the influence of drink. I recall one case where the scratches were not left by the lock picks, but by a ring the thief was wearing on his left hand."

As he finished that statement, the lock clicked, and he was able to open the door. It was the entrance into one of the many storage rooms where supplies were delivered. He held his arms wide to keep me from entering and knelt by the threshold. Pointing to the floor he observed, "Note the dust, Watson. No one has come in here for several days."

We completed our investigation of doors and windows and reported to Chesterfield's office where Holmes intended to collect the names and addresses he had requested.

The Director's secretary said we could go right in, and we found Professor Chesterfield reading over the list. Noting our presence, he indicated that I should close the door, then invited us to sit.

"I have something to report, gentlemen and it is rather delicate."

Chapter Four

We sat at attention, eager to hear what had developed in the short time we'd been outside. Chesterfield folded his hands under his chin, looking rather grave. At last, he spoke, "I stopped by Professor Blanchard's office as I was returning here. He was seated at his desk, but staring at the wall and did not appear focused upon any particular object. I asked him if he was all right. He slowly turned toward me and said 'Rose must have the *Elegy*. It must be read at her memorial'."

The Director let his hands drop to the desk, "I should explain, gentleman, that Rose was his wife. But she died last year and, as I recall, a portion of Gray's *Elegy* was read from a book by the vicar at her memorial service. We certainly did not need to take the original manuscript from its case to do that. It is easily available to the public in numerous books. I am afraid he may have forgotten that memory and might possibly be our thief."

Holmes leaned forward. "It is a possibility we should investigate, yet I still should like the names and addresses of the head watchman and cleaners. No stone unturned, sir. In the meantime, it is nearly lunchtime. Do you believe you could convince Blanchard to accompany you to some restaurant and keep him away from his office for at least forty-five minutes?"

"It is not uncommon for us to do so, Mr. Holmes. I believe it can be arranged."

He then reached for the paper he had been reading and handed it to my friend. "And here is the information you requested. I believe Carnigan, the watchman, usually goes home to breakfast then bed until late afternoon. I cannot say the same of the cleaning staff."

Holmes asked, "Have these people been with you long?"

"Carnigan is a former police officer, in his fifties. Been with us about four years I believe. A widower. Lives by himself and has a grown son in the navy and a married daughter. The cleaning staff are from a family business by the name of Jepson. Three brothers, their wives, and several sons and daughters. I've only ever spoken to the eldest brother, Tom. Seems like a decent chap and a hard worker. They've been with us many years. Well before I joined the Museum."

Holmes gave the paper a glance before placing it into his inner breast pocket. Addressing Professor Chesterfield again he added, "I shall follow up with these persons this afternoon. Could you discreetly ensure Professor Blanchard's office is unlocked when you take him to lunch? It will save me precious minutes which may prove invaluable. Does he also have a secretary?"

"He does, but she takes a lunch hour from noon to one o'clock. You should not be disturbed."

"Excellent! Then we shall have a look around while you are gone. One other question for you. Was the Professor still here when you left last night?"

Chesterfield thought for a moment, then replied, "Yes, I'm fairly certain he was. His secretary was gone but I noticed a light on behind the window of his door." Holmes nodded and I could see by the blink of his eyes that he had filed that information in his mind.

Several minutes later, we discreetly watched Chesterfield and Blanchard leave for lunch. Once they were out of sight, we slipped into the Professor's office, closing the door behind us. For someone whose memory seemed to be slipping away, his desk was surprisingly neat. The large walnut surface was highly polished with a beautiful grain pattern. The only things on it were a silver framed photograph of a much younger

Blanchard and an attractive woman, whom I presumed to be his wife. This sat on the right side of the desk. On the left were an inbox with very few papers, a small calendar, an ink bottle and a pen in a silver holder. A blotter took up the centre of the desk, and there was a document upon it which the Professor must have been reading when the Director called upon him for lunch. Holmes glanced at it briefly without picking it up. Judging it to be irrelevant, he asked me to assist in checking the contents of the drawers. These were not quite so neat. Apparently, Blanchard had taken to shoving whatever was on his desk into a drawer at the end of the day. We each took a side of the desk and went through the drawers. There was no sign of the *Elegy*, but I did observe some documents which had deadlines attached to them. I made a mental note to tell Professor Chesterfield of these later so that he could follow up.

This task took very little time and we then began to check the two bookcases in the room, neither of which were locked. Then Holmes had me look behind the paintings for either documents or a safe, while he picked the lock on Blanchard's briefcase. Finding nothing, we took a final look under the rugs and seat cushions of the chairs. Holmes came away satisfied that the *Elegy* was not in that room.

As we walked back to Chesterfield's office, where Holmes intended to leave a note, I asked, "I supposed Blanchard could have taken the *Elegy* home in his briefcase last night. What do you think, Holmes?"

"I observed enough to know that if Blanchard were in complete control of his faculties, he could have easily orchestrated this theft. Do you believe his condition is intermittent at this point, Doctor, or that is he in a continuous state of dementia?"

I shook my head slowly, "From what little I've gathered in our conversations with Professor Chesterfield and from what I've observed, I would say this has been an oncoming condition. It may have been the result of the physical stimuli which accompanies anyone who has suffered the death of a loved one. Such a shock releases chemicals into the bloodstream which may have exacerbated some physical defect and caused the speeding up of an already existing condition or awakened a dormant one. It is one of the reasons an elderly person so often dies soon after losing their spouse. Or it may truly be psychological. Freud and his colleagues are just scratching the surface when it comes to human emotions and responses. As time has passed since his wife's death and he has come to realize more and more just how alone he is in the world, his mind may be withdrawing into an alternate reality which is not quite so terrifying as the truth."

I looked at my companion, as we had come to Chesterfield's office and Holmes was scribbling out a note, which he left folded on the desk. "I hate to say it, Holmes, but stealing the *Elegy* could have been Blanchard's subconscious mind, making him take an action which would force him to accept his wife's death. A defence mechanism of sorts."

Holmes took me by the arm and led me out of the museum, "Watson, my friend, you are indeed a conductor of light. I do not know how I would get on without you and the specialized knowledge you are able to impart as a medical man. You may very well have hit upon the proper solution."

I took no small pride in this praise from my friend. However, after two decades of companionship, I knew enough to be patient.

As a cab pulled up to take us back to Baker Street, he continued, "The only objection I can see in your reasoning is that Professor Blanchard is left-handed. It is not a fatal flaw to your conclusion, but it is enough to make him an improbable, though still not impossible suspect."

I thought back. As usual, I had 'seen but not observed' as Holmes's mantra goes. I realized the placement of objects upon his desk, the way he wore his watch chain, the hand he used to drink from my flask, the finger he used to point at his glasses when complaining about his prescription all indicated a left-handed person.

As we rattled along the streets, I turned to my friend and enquired, "You are sure then that the culprit is right-handed?"

Holmes was leaning forward in thought, his chin resting upon the hand atop his walking cane. "It is highly likely. Our thief, not knowing how successful he was at picking the lock, or what amount of force he would need to open the display case door, held his left hand on the top and left side as he opened the door with his right. By itself it is not conclusive, but it represents a high probability."

Chapter Five

Once back at our quarters, Holmes quickly removed his Doyle disguise and was soon the tall, lean figure of the well-dressed detective. Mrs. Hudson prepared lunch for us, which I dug into heartily. Holmes, as was his wont, refused to partake, lest the act of digestion should interfere with his cognitive powers as he puzzled through the facts he had at hand. His first order of business was to check the fingerprints he had taken with those of Professor Blanchard, which were still on my hip flask.

It took mere minutes. He soon rose from his microscope and handed my flask back to me. "As I suspected, not a match, Watson. The prints from the display case were badly smudged, but enough was visible for comparison."

He sat by the fire, drawing upon his black clay pipe. The plumes of smoke curling toward the ceiling. His eyes were closed, yet one could almost imagine his mind's eye sifting over multiple permutations. He had finished a second pipe by the time he spoke to me again. Finally, he arose from his chair and called to me as I was at the writing desk, transcribing my notes of the case thus far. Holmes had only recently given me permission to attempt another publication of one of his adventures after several years of silence. I hoped it would be the start of a new series.

"Watson! Your hat and coat if you will. I believe it prudent to start with the cleaners. A better chance to find some of them awake I think, than our night watchman whom we've been told sleeps until late afternoon."

I slipped back into my coat, donned my derby and, though not asked, put my Webley into my pocket again. We found a cab easily enough and proceeded across the river into Lambeth to the address of the eldest brother in charge of the cleaning service.

Answering the knock on the door of a three-storey tenement was a young lass of perhaps fourteen. She had long, brown hair, woven in braids down either side of her thin face to the top of her bodice. She looked shyly up at the tall figure of Sherlock Holmes and enquired, "Yes, sir? What can we do for you?"

Holmes, in that way he has of putting women of whatever age at ease, doffed his top hat and replied, "Good afternoon, miss. I am Sherlock Holmes, and this is my colleague, Dr. Watson. The Victoria and Albert Museum has asked us to look into a small matter. Is your father awake? I need to speak with him."

She gave little reaction to his statement and merely said, "If you'll wait here, gents, I'll go and see."

She closed the door gently and we could hear the murmur of voices, but were unable to make out the words. Soon a set of heavier footsteps approached the door and it was opened to reveal a tall, stout woman of middle age with brown curls mostly stuck up under a maid's bonnet and a look upon her face that indicated more curiosity than fear at our arrival.

She looked us up and down and decided my companion was in charge of this visit, "You say you're from the Museum, Mr. Holmes? My husband is asleep. He generally stays awake when the night's work is done and sleeps late afternoon and evening until it's time to go in again. Is there anything I can help you with?"

She made no move to invite us in, though I believe it was out of concern of too much noise of conversation which might wake her husband, than any lack of manners upon her part. Holmes merely leaned against the railing and commenced his questions.

"Thank you, Mrs. Jepson, I shall be brief. Do you recall the room with the statue of Samuel Johnson?"

She bit her lip hesitantly and I chose to step in to the conversation, "It's the bronze statue of a chubby fellow with long hair and glasses, standing and holding a book in front of him with the other hand raised and a finger pointing up."

She brightened at my description, for it was obvious to me she either couldn't or hadn't read the plaque at its base. "Oh! Yes, sir. I know that room well. Me and my Donny dust and mop it every night."

Holmes smiled, appearing delighted at her answer, "Capital, Mrs. Jepson. You are exactly the person I need! Last night, do you recall if there was any disturbance to the document which is in the case on the pedestal about fifteen feet in front of that statue? Perhaps the case was slightly askew or the door to it was ajar?"

She thought a bit, her eyes rising upward, searching her memory, "No, Mr. Holmes. I can't say that anything struck me as odd about it. We're very particular about checking such things on our shift. There's lots of precious things to look after and we take pride in our work."

"I presume Donny is one of your sons. Does he do the mopping after you've dusted?

She looked at Holmes as if he were daft, "Well, of course! I can't very well walk about on wet floors to do me dustin' now, can I?"

Holmes had the good sense to look chagrined, as well he should, I may add. Then he asked, "May I speak with him?"

She sighed and said, "Wait here. I'll fetch him."

Again, we found the door closed in our faces. Fortunately, the day was not exceptionally hot and there was a small overhang to protect us from the elements. While we were alone I questioned my companion, "Holmes, surely you must realize that dusting needs to be done before mopping. How could you ask such a question?"

He glanced at the door then turned to me, "Of course, Watson! However, I have found it useful to feign ignorance over such trivial matters in order to lull suspects into a false sense of superiority. That often results in their giving away more information than they intend, as they are less likely to be on guard. Ah, I hear multiple footsteps. She must be bringing the lad back."

The door opened again to reveal a strapping boy of perhaps twelve years of age with long brown hair falling into his eyes. He had a cocky look about him as he placed his hands high up upon his braces, much like a lecturer might upon his lapels. I saw it as an attempt to make himself appear older. His mother stood behind him, but allowed him to speak for himself.

"Yes, sir what did you need to know?" he said, politely and without fear.

"Yes, Donny, my name is Sherlock Holmes, and this is my colleague, Dr. Watson. The Victoria and Albert Museum has asked us to look into a slight disturbance of one of the exhibits in a room your mother tells me you mopped last night."

He yawned and tilted his head to the left, looked down with a slight frown and asked, "Which room would that be, sir? I mopped several."

"It's the room with the bronze statue of Samuel Johnson, the chubby fellow with the long hair holding a book. There is a document in a glass case on a pedestal about fifteen feet in front of that statue. We just wish to enquire if you saw anything unusual about that case last night. Was it opened or was the case moved in any way?"

The lad pursed his lips, shaking his head as he looked up to his right, as if searching his mind's eye. Then he replied, "No, sir. Didn't notice anything odd about it. I'm very careful mopping around the base of those pedestals, so's they don't get knocked about you know."

Holmes gazed down upon the lad, but the boy held his ground. Finally, the detective asked, "Did either of you see anyone about the Museum last night other than yourselves or the night watchmen?"

Before Donny could answer, his mother spoke up, "I saw the old professor there. Still working at his desk at half past nine he was."

Holmes nodded looking more pointedly at the boy, "Anyone else?"

Donny had given his mother an odd look, but now answered quickly and confidently, "No, sir. Just Professor Blanchard, like mum says."

Holmes nodded, "Well, that's fine then." He reached into his pocket and handed the boy a shilling and his card and said, "Be sure to keep a sharp eye out when you go back to work tonight. If you see anything unusual, you send me word at that address."

Donny looked hesitantly at the card and the coin. He rubbed his eyes, then looked again. It seemed he could read it, but there was a strange look upon his face as he replied, "All right, Mr. Holmes. Thank you."

Mrs. Jepson smiled at Holmes's kindness to her son, then nodded and closed the door. As we stepped back out upon the pavement, Holmes waved his cane at an oncoming cab. As we boarded, he gave the driver the address for the watchman's home. We settled into our seats and he leaned back with eyes closed. I knew not to interrupt his thoughts and turned my gaze upon the passing scenery. The warmth of the summer day had driven the fog off early. Though it was not oppressively hot, the temperature added a certain pungency to the aromas typical of London's streets. Whether they be fresh-baked bread as we passed a bakery, or the smell of a tannery from a quarter of a mile away.

Suddenly my companion spoke, "What did you make of our young mopping boy, Watson?"

I looked upon my friend, whose eyes remained closed, tilted my head and replied, "He seems a bright lad. I believe he's smarter than he let on, and that he has at least some reading ability. There was something about his eyes though, when he answered your questions. Almost as if he were trying too hard to be convincing."

Holmes turned his gaze upon me and exclaimed, "Excellent, Watson! Yes, I am quite certain he can read and he has imagination, for he was able to lie rather convincingly."

"You are sure he lied?" I questioned.

"You noticed it yourself, Doctor. But did not realize what you were seeing. Throughout my career I have made a study of bodily reactions when people speak. A tilt of the head, a shifting of the eyes, twitches of cheeks, lips and eyebrows, the colouring of the face. There are any number of telltale signs which exhibit emotion. Among other things, he looked up and to the right before he answered about the *Elegy*. While it is not foolproof, it is often a sign that the person is searching the creative portion of his mind to come up with a convincing lie. In this case, however, I believe it is more of an omission of truth, rather than an actual lie. For the most part that boy was telling the truth. But he also knows something he's not telling. Did you notice the look he gave his mother when she interrupted? I believe if she had not blurted out the fact that Professor Blanchard was still there at half-past nine, young Donny would not have volunteered that information."

"So, what does that mean, Holmes?"

He shrugged his shoulders and replied, "For now it is a fact to be stored for retrieval when needed. I also believe it may require reconnaissance." Suddenly he tapped the roof and gave the driver an address for a short detour.

This new route took us to a street near St. John's Gardens and Holmes kept an eye out of the cab window. Suddenly he ordered the driver to stop. He got out, indicating I should wait. I moved across the seat where I could observe where he was going and saw him approach two young boys. I smiled inwardly. Holmes was engaging the Baker Street Irregulars, that ragamuffin gang of street urchins who often worked for him in observing and trailing suspects since no one ever took note of them.

He returned to the cab and we again set out for Carnigan's home. "There," he exhaled, "Oscar and Frank shall keep an eye on Donny for the remainder of the day and evening until he goes to work. If he does anything unusual, they will note it and report."

After several minutes we stopped at the watchman's address. By now it was near four o'clock. As Holmes rang the bell, I looked up and down the street and noted, "Rather nice diggings for a retired police officer."

Holmes nodded, "Excellent observation, Watson. Should things take a turn his way, we may have to look into Carnigan's family and finances."

Before he could continue, the door opened, revealing a bald gentleman with a fringe of grey circling his round head. He was clean-shaven, in fact his face appeared to still be wet from a fresh pass of his razor. His eyes were blue, and still a little drowsy. He was in shirtsleeves and braces. His gaze was still that of a wary police officer as he took us both in with an up and down glance.

When he spoke it was with a grumbly bass voice, "Yes? May I help you? Wait, aren't you Sherlock Holmes?"

Holmes bowed his head. (His ego always appreciated recognition, whether he would admit it or not). "Indeed, Mr. Carnigan, and this is my colleague, Dr. Watson."

The fellow put his hand out to shake each of ours and invited us in. We dismissed our cab and followed him. He had us take seats on a settee in the parlour and asked if we would care for something to drink.

"Thank you, no," said my companion. "We just have a few questions about the incident at the museum last night."

He nodded his head eagerly, "I'll be happy to help, if I can. I remember being on duty at the scene where you were investigating a jewel theft. Oh, that must have been fifteen years ago now. A workman like task you made of that, sir. Found just the clues you needed when we had missed them. I became a better Bobby because of you. Rose to the rank of sergeant."

Holmes chose the flattery route of questioning and even I could observe this man had a simple and honest face. He gave straightforward answers to each of Holmes's questions, which included detail most witnesses would not observe.

Near the end of this conversation, Holmes enquired, "We've been told Professor Blanchard left sometime after nine-thirty. Do you know exactly when he departed?"

"Yes sir, it was ten o'clock on the spot. The clock was striking when he left."

"Was he carrying anything other than his briefcase?"

"No, sir. I remember I opened the door for him because he had his briefcase and his cane in his right hand while he was holding his overcoat tight around his throat with his left."

Holmes pondered that for a moment, "Was he in the habit of wearing his overcoat on warm summer nights?"

"Oh, yes sir. I believe it was due to his age, sir. Always complaining about the cold, even if was a mild night. You may have noted that the museum is kept quite cool. They say it helps maintain the integrity of the exhibits. I can tolerate it just fine, but the Professor always seemed to feel a chill."

"Just one more question, Mr. Carnigan," said the detective. "When the cleaners left, did they appear to have anything unusual in their equipment? Something in which they might be able to hide a document?"

The former bobby replied, "Nothing unusual. But they do use a cart in which they empty the rubbish bins and then take it around to a larger bin around the back where they deposit it ready for collection by the authorities. They do that last thing, bringing the cart back and putting it in their storage room just before they leave for the night. All their cleaning tackle is kept in that storage room. They carry nothing in or out of the building."

"Were any of them acting strange, especially the twelve year old, Donny?"

Carnigan bowed his head and shook it slowly, "I'm afraid I don't know any of the young ones' names. Just the three adult brothers. But all seemed normal. They trudged out as usual, tired from a long night's work."

We stood to go and I complimented the man on his lovely home. He smiled wistfully and I was afraid that I had stirred up an unpleasant memory. "Thank you, Doctor, he finally choked out. "My wife's doing, naturally. She inherited the house from an uncle who had no children. I'm afraid I haven't kept it up to her expectations. I've closed off a couple of rooms which I have no call to use now she's gone. Yet I still have to have a maid come in weekly, just to keep up with the dusting and cleaning."

"I am sorry for your loss, sir."

"Thank you, Dr. Watson. If you need anything else gentleman, I will be back on duty at six o'clock tonight."

Holmes replied, "Thank you, Mr. Carnigan. You have been most helpful. Good day."

Chapter Six

Returning to Baker Street, we settled down for tea. Rather, I should say, I took up some tea and biscuits faithfully provided by Mrs. Hudson. Holmes took to cogitating in his chair before the fireplace with his old black clay pipe puffing away like a steam engine. Not half an hour passed before an envelope arrived with his name printed in block capitals by a double nib pen. Holmes briefly examined the envelope, then tore it open, and after a quick scan he stood and cried, "Watson, we must return to the museum immediately."

Once again, I donned my hat and coat, my revolver still in its pocket. He handed me the latest message. It was from Professor Chesterfield:

> Ransom note received. Need advice and assistance. Come at once. Payment due tonight!

We rushed out into Baker Street and, just as he was hailing a cab, the young boy, Frank, arrived and handed him a note. "From Oscar, sir. He's still keeping an eye on the boy."

Holmes unfolded the paper and cried, "Ha! It all begins to come together, Watson. Donny was seen entering a post office shortly after we left him. Tell me Frank, did you actually see him send a telegram?"

The boy bowed his head, "No, sir. There was a bit of a crowd coming out as a fire engine was rolling past and everyone wanted a look. By the time we fought through he was at the counter collecting some mail."

"Very well," said Holmes with some disappointment. "You an Oscar keep an eye on him until he and his family go to work. Afterward you may pick up some supper for yourselves." He handed the lad several coins to pay for two decent meals and we boarded our cab.

I asked him as we drove, "Do you think Donny was tasked with sending the ransom note?"

"It would be rather foolhardy, but I must see this message first before drawing any conclusions."

This time Holmes made no effort to disguise his identity and we went straight to Chesterfield's office, bypassing his secretary who stood as if she was going to announce us. I closed the door as Holmes approached the Director's desk, then followed him to sit across from the distressed man.

Professor Chesterfield handed over the telegram and said, "This arrived about four o'clock."

Holmes took the form from him as I expressed my thoughts, "They really did send a telegram? Don't they realize we can trace its origins?"

Holmes held up a hand for silence as he read through the message. Then he handed it to me. "Cleverly worded, Doctor. The telegraph operator would have no reason to suspect foul play."

I pondered his answer as I took the telegram. It read:

V AND A TRUSTEES STOP ITEM YOU DESIRE FOR SALE STOP 1000 POUNDS STOP DELIVER TO INNER CIRCLE REGENT'S PARK STOP CHESTER ROAD STOP 9 PM STOP BLANCHARD TO DELIVER ALONE OR NO DEAL STOP

"I see what you mean, Holmes," I said. "Nothing that would indicate a criminal act taking place, nor to raise suspicion by the telegrapher."

Holmes, elbows on the arms of his chair, steepled his long fingers beneath his chin and proclaimed, "Interesting that they should choose the Professor for delivery. Is he aware of this demand?"

"Yes, and that distresses me, Mr. Holmes," said our client. "You've seen his mental condition. We can keep an eye on him here at the museum. But for a task of this magnitude? I'm afraid for his health. The strain could be too much. The fact they want no one to accompany or follow him is too risky. He says he is willing, but how can we possibly comply?"

Holmes looked at me. The silent communication clear after so many years working together. He then turned back to the Director and said, "I believe we can overcome that objection, Professor. Is the museum able to come up with the amount?"

He was surprised at Holmes's answer, but a nod from the detective seemed to pacify him and he replied "Yes, I've made a discreet request of one of our benefactors. Once he was assured Sherlock Holmes was on the case, he was willing to loan us the funds. They will be delivered by six o'clock this evening. He has great faith in your ability to solve the matter and return his money, Mr. Holmes."

Holmes bowed his head, "I am gratified by your benefactor's faith. Let me explain what we must do to keep the professor safe."

*****

Thus, it was at eight forty-five that evening, the money and its courier were seated at a bench near the junction of Chester Road and the Inner Circle. Holmes and I had scouted the location earlier and he was very curious about the spot chosen for a ransom drop.

"Our thief is either a very poor planner or there is something amiss, Watson. He insists that Blanchard comes alone, yet there is a multitude of hiding places among the shrubbery and hedges for the police to hide and spring a trap. The roads are lined with hedges, forcing him to leave in one of only four directions, all of which could easily be blocked. It's all wrong, Watson!"

I gazed about at all the features he had mentioned and was in total agreement. I said to him, "What could be the object of their plan then, if the exchange is not? Do you suppose they expect to kidnap the Professor and use him as a shield in their getaway should we have reneged on the deal and brought the police with us?"

He shook his head, "That would hardly be efficient, Watson. There are certainly easier ways to kidnap the Professor if that be their object. I must smoke a pipe or two upon this."

He sat upon a nearby bench, the sun was setting and by my watch, the money should already be at the museum ready to be brought to the exchange. In order not to disturb him, I sat on a bench across the road and smoked a cigar of my own. Casually watching couples and families leave the park as dusk approached. Lamp lighters plied their trade and soon a long, curved row of balls of light with their spotlights on the path took up where daylight had left off.

At last, Holmes stood and said to me, "Watson, I only see two alternatives and I cannot be in two places at once. You shall have to be my eyes in one while I observe the other."

Chapter Seven

"There is a strange dichotomy to this case, Watson. The theft was cleverly conceived and brilliantly carried out, yet this whole ransom business smacks of rank amateurs."

I replied to him, "Perhaps the Jepsons were only hired to do the job by the person who had planned the theft, and now they have double-crossed him. They are attempting to get the value of the ransom, rather than whatever their fee was for the theft."

My companion tapped his thin lips with a long index finger, his thumb tucked under his chin, "You have certainly coincided with my deductions when you say *they*, Doctor. I am convinced this was not a one-man operation, yet the involvement of the Jepsons is not a forgone conclusion. Although the reasons for involving a second party are unclear ..."

He suddenly stopped talking. Had he not been wearing gloves I am sure he would have snapped his fingers as he exclaimed, "Of course!"

As was his irritating habit, he declined to explain, but merely led me back to the museum where plans were made. Chesterfield would escort Blanchard to the meeting place and leave him there just before nine o'clock. They were to meet after the drop at St. John's Lodge, a hundred yards away. If the Professor had not shown up by ten minutes after the hour, Blanchard would return for him. For the sake of guarding the money and the Professor, Holmes had additionally enlisted Carnigan's aid.

However, there was no mention of Holmes's or Carnigan's roles. If he had known, Blanchard would most likely have argued against their involvement on account of their presence possibly scaring off the thief.

Thus, Blanchard assumed his role and was quite willing to do so, despite Holmes's offer to go in his place in disguise.

"No, sir!" he exclaimed. "They are expecting me and by George they're going to get me! I assure you, gentlemen, I will not turn over any money until the *Elegy* is in my hands!"

It was a bold and brave statement, but when delivered with a raised fist that quivered uncontrollably, its underlying promise was suspect. Still, the Professor was allowed to pursue his mission, none the wiser of Holmes's plan.

At ten minutes to nine, Chesterfield escorted the old man to the bench closest to the junction and waited with him until just before the hour. He then left him alone as per the thief's instructions.

The Professor was bundled up quite warmly. His stooped shoulders were covered by a shawl in addition to his overcoat. The white fringe of his hair stuck out from under his fedora and, as he held his cane in front of him, it shook with that condition so common in older gentlemen. The thief had not specified denominations for the ransom money, therefore he merely carried an envelope in his inner breast pocket containing mixed notes. He was under one of the gas lamps, but still presented a vulnerable target to any mugger, let alone the expected criminal. This was the primary reason Holmes had chosen Carnigan to assist.

Meanwhile, per Holmes remark in the park, I was guarding another location which Holmes had determined to be a possible place of action this night.

Events unfolded that evening which, even the great detective admitted, were not such that could have been predicted with any certainty. Suffice to say, shortly after nine-thirty, Chesterfield returned to the museum, supporting an injured Blanchard. The old scholar had his overcoat removed and was laid upon a couch in his office, one that had been provided months before, as he had occasion to need a nap now and then. Carnigan was sent to relieve me, so that I might see to the man's injuries. I arrived at his office to find a head wound above the Professor's right eye. As is common with head wounds, this one was bleeding profusely, though, thankfully, it was not deep and would require no stitches. I was more concerned about the other bump on his head, however, and applied cold compresses in an attempt to keep the swelling down.

As I administered to the fellow, Holmes strode in looking quite grave. Once I had wrapped the compress in place and returned the Professor to a supine position, I stood and took my companion aside. I whispered accusingly, "Holmes, how could you have let this happen? Where were you and Carnigan? The man might have been killed!"

He raised his hand to silence me momentarily and asked Chesterfield to keep an eye on my patient. Then he drew me out of the office to explain. "I assure you, Watson, no death could have taken place. Though I admit I failed to predict this action."

I was still fraught with anger and demanded, "If it was unpredictable, how can you be certain there would be no death?"

"Because our thief did not do that to him," he stated blandly.

Before I could respond to that outrageous statement, he was walking off, bidding me to follow silently. We soon came across Carnigan, who had taken up the hiding place I had been in, where, for some reason known only to Holmes, I had been tasked with keeping an eye on the room with the now empty display case. Holmes dismissed Carnigan, telling him to walk his rounds and behave as he normally did while on duty each night.

I started to speak and he raised his hand again, "Whisper, if you must, Watson. I am expecting company and they may arrive anytime between now and dawn."

Keeping my voice low, I queried, "What company? Are you expecting the Jepsons, or whoever the thief is, to steal something else now that he's got away with the first theft? That would be madness!"

Holmes gave that sardonic smile of his and replied quietly, "Indeed it would. Yet, what I now suspect I am sure will appear to be equally as mad to you, Doctor."

"And what is that, Holmes?" I asked in as demanding a tone as a whisper would allow.

"Be patient, old friend. And when you see it occur, please do not act unless I do."

And so we waited in the darkness of our hiding place.

Chapter Eight

We could occasionally hear the cleaners in other areas of the building and once we noted the distinctive click of Carnigan's heels on the stone floor as he passed near us. At about eleven o'clock Mrs. Jepson came into the gallery where the theft had taken place.

Holmes kept a discreet eye on her as she went about her business. Afterward she left to go on to another room and Donny came in with his mop and two buckets. One for soapy water, the other for the rinse. He mopped in an odd pattern, then I realized, he was leaving his final section as a clear pathway from the *Elegy* pedestal to the exit.

When that section was all that was left to do, the lad set his mop into a bucket, looked around and reached inside his shirt. Holmes placed his hand upon my shoulder as a reminder not to act. The boy pulled out some papers from inside his shirt, then reached into his pocket and retrieved a key. He opened the case, setting his left hand atop the glass while pulling open the lid with his right. Carefully he set the papers back upon the stand and closed the lid, quickly wiping his handprint with his sleeve.

From there he finished his mopping along the path to the exit and went about his business. I couldn't believe my companion had continued to hold me back. "Holmes, what are we doing? We had him caught red-handed."

"Caught doing what, Watson? Returning a stolen item? That could be grounds for a reward, not an arrest."

"Oh, come now, Holmes. He had the key! He's obviously the thief!"

"Or, he found the document, stole it and the duplicate key back from the original thief and returned it secretly because he did not wish to implicate the culprit."

I shook my head, "Surely you intend to question him to find the truth?"

"If necessary, Doctor. For now I suggest you return to your patient and check him for a concussion. I wish to contemplate this scene a little more."

Arriving back at Blanchard's office, I found him still groggy on the sofa. I checked his eyes for dilation and reaction and agreed with Holmes's suggestion. I turned to Chesterfield and said "We should get him to hospital. At his age this injury needs careful observation."

Holmes arrived just then and stepped in to help me get Blanchard to his feet while Chesterfield went out in to the street to hail a cab. My companion held the gentleman up while I reached for his overcoat and helped him into it.

I accompanied Blanchard, but Holmes chose to remain behind, stating he needed to discuss the next steps of the case with the Director. It was a good two hours before I returned to Baker Street, well into the wee hours. Holmes was still up, smoking his long-stemmed churchwarden peacefully before the fire, a whisky and soda by his side.

He greeted me with a confident air, "Draw yourself some refreshment, Watson. Then take a seat and tell me about your patient."

I removed my hat and coat, poured a brandy for myself and fell, somewhat exhausted by this hour, on to the settee opposite my friend. "Blanchard's age and medical conditions are working against him. He is being carefully watched and I shall return to his bedside first thing in the morning. Now, Holmes, tell me all and leave out no detail, no matter how trivial!"

He smiled at my phrasing the demand he so often uses upon his clients and handed over the cigar box to me. "Smoke on one of those, Watson. This may take a while."

Thus ensconced with a fine cigar in my left hand, an excellent whisky in my right and the comfort of the overstuffed settee supporting my tired frame, I settled in with all attention upon my friend. Holmes looked toward the fire for a few moments, as if determining best how to begin his report. At last, he blew a significant puff of smoke ceiling-ward, pointed the stem of his pipe at me and began his remarks.

"First of all, Doctor, I must tell you I shall need your medical diagnosis to confirm the suppositions I have been led to by my observations and deductions. They shall be critical as to determining motive in this most bizarre of circumstances."

Removing the cigar from my mouth, I replied, "I should think the motive obvious, Holmes. £1,000 is no mean sum. I presume some members of the Jepson family took it from the Professor. His overcoat pocket was empty on his return from Regent's Park. Why did he not receive the *Elegy* in return at that time? Why this elaborate charade? They nearly killed that old gentleman in the process. That was outrageous! Why did you not confront them at the Museum?"

In reply Holmes reached into his coat pocket, withdrew an envelope and passed it across to me. I opened it with great curiosity and was amazed at the contents, "The ransom! How did you get it back, Holmes? Did you confront Donny after all? Did you have the Jepsons arrested after I took the Professor to the hospital?"

He slowly shook his head as another puff of smoke emanated from his pipe. "I have yet to make up my mind as to how to handle this most difficult case, Watson. I can assure you, the Jepsons did not make the ransom demand, nor did they injure Blanchard."

I shook my head in confusion. I was tired and thought perhaps I had misunderstood my friend. "But we saw Donny return the document! Did you not get this ransom back from him, or his father, perhaps?"

"No, my dear Doctor. While you were reaching for the Professor's overcoat, I was reaching into his rear hip pocket. That is where I retrieved that envelope."

I looked down at the envelope in my hand, dumbfounded. The notes caused it to bulge significantly with temptation. Then I looked upon my friend in bewilderment. He set his pipe aside and took up his own whisky for a sip. Several moments passed as I awaited his explanation.

Finally, he contemplated his glass briefly, set it down and turned his gaze back to me, "What I am about to tell you, Watson, I desire to keep between us for now. No one else knows what happened save I. Yet, as I said, motive is still a conjecture and I intend to search the Blanchards's house tomorrow morning to see if an answer may be found there."

I had started to reach for my notebook, but Holmes's admonition stayed my hand. I merely set the envelope next to my whisky on the table and took up my cigar instead of my pencil.

"When we arranged our positions at the park, Chesterfield was at the Lodge, awaiting the Professor's return. I had stationed Carnigan at the junction some eighty yards to the west where there was ample cover among the bushes and trees, though he did not have a direct line of sight to the Professor. I, myself, took up a spot at the southeast corner of the intersection of Chester Road and the Inner Circle. As you no doubt recall, the hedges along there are a good six feet in height and impenetrable, though I was able to make a discreet hole to see through. At that particular point, there is a tree which grows close enough to the hedge that it has a low branch overhanging it above the pavement which parallels Chester Road. My intention was such, that I would leap for this branch and use it to swing over the hedge at the opportune moment. If the culprits took off to the west, my police whistle would alert Carnigan, who could apprehend them, or detain them long enough for me to arrive and assist in their capture. If they were not coming his way, he would rush to join me in pursuing them to the east.

"The Professor was diagonally across the road from me on a bench. He was not aware of our presence. As you recall he had been adamant about following the ransom instructions to the letter. Chesterfield stayed with him until just before the exchange was to take place, then left him alone.

"It was at that time when the most extraordinary event took place, Watson. I admit I was expecting something unusual, but I did not anticipate so violent an action to be taken."

"For God's sake, Holmes," I interjected. "How could you not expect the possibility of violence when dealing with criminals expecting so great a sum of money?"

Holmes took up his pipe again and relit it, before answering. This being an annoying habit of his when seeking a pause for dramatic effect. This time it indicated that a surprising answer would be forthcoming. I thought back to his previous statement and added, "What did you mean before, when you said the thief did not cause Blanchard's injury?"

My fellow lodger threw his spent match into the fire, took a puff of smoke and replied, "The Professor inflicted that injury upon himself, Doctor."

"What?" I cried. "Whatever for?" I asked.

He pointed his pipe stem at me again and said, "That is what we must ascertain before we expose this situation to anyone else. All I can tell you is that, once Chesterfield was well out of sight, Blanchard moved the envelope from his coat pocket to his back trouser pocket. Then, apparently in an effort to make it appear that he put up a struggle, he struck himself in the forehead with the heavy knob of his cane. I can only presume he underestimated the effect of this blow, as it caused him to fall sideways where his head hit the metal armrest of the bench and then to the ground. It was fortunate there was soil beneath the bench, for if it had been concrete another blow may have been fatal.

"Naturally, I swung over the hedge and rushed to his side. Some instinct within prevented me from blowing upon my whistle immediately. Instead, I checked his pulse, and laid him flat upon his back, for he was unconscious from the blows he had received. I made up my mind not to reveal all I knew yet. I then blew upon my whistle which brought both Carnigan and Chesterfield to my aid. I explained that two men had arrived at nine o'clock, immediately overpowered the Professor and took the money. I tripped one up as they ran back to Chester Road to the east, but he scrambled to his feet again and the sound of the Professor's groan drew me back to his side as I feared for his health."

I leaned forward, elbows on my knees and head thrust forward, as if being closer to Holmes would help me better understand what he was saying. "Do you mean to tell me, that doddering old man planned this scheme all along for the money? Why wouldn't he just pocket the cash and hand over the *Elegy* as if the exchange had taken place?"

Holmes met my gaze, "This is where I need your medical opinion, Doctor. Was this a result of his increasing dementia, or was that, too, an act to cover his crime? Did he enlist the boy's assistance in order to frame him if something went wrong, or was it merely a precautionary act upon his part, so he wouldn't be caught with the document himself?"

Holmes stood and walked over to the writing desk, opened a drawer, took up a large envelope and brought it back to our sitting area. This he also handed over to me, saying, "Open it with care, Watson."

I did so and removed a folded document of some age. It was the *Elegy*! "Holmes!" I cried. "Why did you remove it once it had been returned? Chesterfield will be frantic!"

He was leaning forward in his chair now, lips pursed, elbows on knees, his palms held in front of his chin, rubbing up and down as if he were rolling a ball between them. "I am attempting to avoid a scandal, old friend. To do so requires me to have the option of having both the manuscript and the ransom in my possession. I retrieved that," he pointed at the paper in my hand, "when you left to attend to Blanchard, and as soon as the boy had left the room. Only you and I know of these envelopes. I have not brought Chesterfield into my confidence as yet. I did admonish him, however, to say nothing to the benefactor who lent the money other than that I was in pursuit and was confident of its return."

"What will you do now?" I asked.

He leaned back, rubbing the bridge of his nose with thumb and forefinger as his head tilted up. "Now I must determine whether Blanchard is demented or devious. Then I shall know what course to take."

Chapter Nine

Next morning, with much less sleep than I would have preferred, I arose with the intention of a quick bite of breakfast and plans to be off to the hospital. I found Holmes sitting at the dining table, a steaming cup of tea before him and a plate of buttered toast at the ready. The sight was unusual for two reasons. One, he rarely partook of meals during a case and two, he was again wearing his Doyle disguise.

"Ah, Watson! I was afraid your late night would cause you to miss breakfast."

I sat down, poured myself some tea, selected a thick slice of toast and slathered some butter upon it. While doing so, I questioned Holmes, "I presumed you would have been off to the Professor's house by now. Why are you dressed as Doyle again?"

"With Blanchard in hospital, there is nothing at his home which shall not be there later today. I have decided to accompany you and see if it might be possible to discreetly question the fellow. I believe he shall be more likely to be frank with his friend, the author, rather than me, the detective."

I took a bite of the toast, a sip of tea and then commented, "I am surprised you did not wake me an hour ago. You are usually so anxious for answers."

He snorted, "Ha! I know my Watson. Insufficient sleep makes him a dull fellow and I need you at your best if we are to make a correct diagnosis. I also know hospital policy and early visitors are unlikely to gain admission. However," he now cried as he checked his watch, "the hour is now sufficient for us to depart and gain the earliest opportunity to see this venerable fellow. Finish your breakfast, Watson. I shall summon a cab."

He threw on his overcoat against the morning chill and was bounding down the stairs before I knew it. I grabbed my things and was out the door about thirty seconds after him. When I reached the pavement, a hansom was just pulling over at his beckoning and we were aboard and southbound in less than ten minutes after I had entered our sitting room.

The hospital wards were bustling with activity. We made our way to the part of the hospital reserved for the more seriously ill where there was deathly quiet. There were no trolleys rolling along the corridors, and the only sounds were hushed conversations and the occasional squeak of the rubber-soled shoes of the nurses.

Due to his condition, Professor Blanchard had been placed in a private room. Holmes and I entered quietly. The gentleman was asleep. Holmes walked over to one side of the bed where he could observe him more closely.

I motioned to my companion, indicating we should step out into the hall. Once there I spoke softly, "Holmes, it does not appear you will be able to question him for quite some time."

Just then, Dr. Anstruther, a colleague and neighbour of mine, who so often took on my patients when I was called away on one of Holmes's cases, came up to us. "Good morning, Watson." He took a second glance at my companion and Holmes broke the confusion. "Good morning, Anstruther. It is I, Sherlock Holmes. We've come to see about Professor Blanchard."

"Ah, Mr. Holmes. I am afraid his injuries are quite serious. He has become comatose and his prognosis for recovery is not favourable. His age and existing health conditions are working against him. I should be much surprised if he lasts a week."

With this bitter news we left the hospital and returned to Baker Street, where Holmes reverted to his normal appearance.

Mrs. Hudson was kind enough to prepare fresh tea and toast so that I might complete my breakfast as he did so.

Once he emerged from his rooms again, I asked, "Will you still go to his home?"

My fellow lodger poured himself some tea and replied, "Given this new development, I have fairly made up my mind what tale to tell Chesterfield when we return his money and document, Watson. But to satisfy my own curiosity, I should still like to delve into the Professor's life to ascertain what he was thinking.

"I shall also be obliged to call upon young Donny again later this afternoon. I believe his part to be completely innocent, but I shall also need to assure his cooperation if my plans are to succeed."

At Blanchard's home Holmes found the Professor's diary, whilst I was reviewing his account books. I found he had spent a considerable sum on his wife's funeral and crypt and his cash reserves were dangerously low. Should he lose his position and salary from the museum his future would have been bleak indeed. I reported this fact to Holmes, as he was absorbed in the entries written since his wife's death.

He replied to my announcement, "You have found motive, indeed, Watson. I believe I have found the reason. See here. What is the first thing that strikes you about these last few pages?"

I took the book from him and skimmed over the entries for that year. "The handwriting is wildly inconsistent, Holmes. It hardly seems it could have been written by the same person. Wait, Holmes, listen to this. It's from ... two weeks ago.

So, they mean to turn me out do they? Ungrateful fools all! I'll name my price before they do. £1,000 pounds should suffice. They'll get it back in the end. But I'll have the use of it until my end. Should it run out, I shall do the deed myself. I cannot bear this life without my Rose, but I must have the means to be with her in eternity. Yes, £1,000, should do.'

"Holmes, this is practically an admission."

"Indeed," he replied. "I believe this is proof his dementia was quite real. Not only the handwriting, but many of his statements indicate an unbalanced mind. As you note, he had both good and bad days, but worsening as time progressed. If you note the last two weeks after he wrote that, he mentions 'a plan'. I believe this to be his scheme to steal the *Elegy*. He also refers to his last will and testament later on in such a way as if it would make amends for his actions."

I said to my friend, "There is no will among his other important papers. But there is correspondence with his solicitor." I picked up another paper I had noted and read aloud, "A Dennis Kranepool. Here's the address."

Armed with that information, we set off and arrived at Kranepool's office within a quarter of an hour. We had to wait several minutes while he finished a meeting with another client, but were soon shown in to a modest office with simple furnishings except for the massive bookshelves lined with legal volumes.

Introductions made, I informed Kranepool of the Professor's medical condition. He was saddened, but not surprised, by the news. "I've been afraid of this ever since Rose died," he said. "Of course, he needed to change his will, so we have been in contact more often recently. Though he was still of sound mind I had to assist him frequently during our discussion as to the disposal of his estate. Even though it is quite simple."

"Simple how?" Enquired Holmes.

Kranepool did not even have to refer to the document, "Once his funeral arrangements and debts are paid, the entire estate is to be sold off and the proceeds given to the Victoria and Albert Museum."

"And this has been finalised?" added my companion.

"Yes, Mr. Holmes. It was signed last month."

The detective nodded, "Well, that settles it then. Watson, I believe we have another appointment. Thank you, Mr. Kranepool, you have been most helpful."

"May I ask, Mr. Holmes, does your interest mean there was foul play involved leading to his current condition?"

Holmes shook his head, "No, Mr. Kranepool. It was quite accidental, I assure you. Thank you."

With that, we were off again. Returning once more to Baker Street I found I had a note from one of my bedridden patients requesting my presence. Holmes waved me off and stated he would not need me in his questioning of the Professor's accomplice. Thus, it was late afternoon, after I had seen my patient and stopped by the hospital again, before I returned. I had our rooms to myself, as Holmes was still out. Thus, I poured a whisky and settled down with the *Elegy* to read for myself, as it had been years since I had done so.

The beauty and poignancy of the poem brought tears to my eyes and thoughts of my sweet departed Mary. When finished, I topped up my glass. As I was doing so, Holmes arrived in a satisfied mood. He threw off his outer garments, and took a whisky for himself, and we both took to our usual seats before the fireplace.

He handed over a piece of paper saying, "That was given to me by our young friend. It answers the last of our questions."

It read as follows:

To Whom It May Concern,

Let it be known that Donald Jepson was paid by me to help in an experiment to test the security measures in place at the Victoria and Albert Museum.

I gave him a key and instructions to see if he could remove Thomas Gray's Elegy document from the building without being caught. He was also given a sealed telegram to be sent. He was not aware of its

---

> contents nor is he a participant in the actions
> described therein.
>
> He is innocent of any crime and is a fine young man,
> whom I trust with this experiment. He is not to be
> punished in any way, as he was acting upon my orders.
>
> Henry Blanchard
> Trustee V&A Museum

I handed the note back saying, "Extraordinary. And Donny had no clue as to the contents of the telegram?"

"None whatsoever. He was given a sealed note and told to take it to the post office the day after the theft without opening it. He was also instructed to return the document the next night, without telling anyone."

I took a sip of my drink and said, "So, Blanchard made up this charade, and he would never actually have possession of the *Elegy*, thus remaining untainted by the crime."

"Yes, Watson. It was actually quite brilliant. I also stopped by the funeral directors who had arranged his wife's burial. He had purchased a crypt large enough for both he and his wife to lay in coffins side by side. It was rather expensive and he had recently paid in advance for his own entombment. It appears he just wanted to ensure he had enough funds to maintain a dignified lifestyle until that day came. Which he suspected would be sooner, rather than later."

"Very likely sooner," I replied soberly. "I stopped by the hospital after seeing my patient and Blanchard is sinking fast. He could well be gone by tomorrow."

Holmes bowed his head, staring into his drink, "Perhaps for the best," he said softly. "Only pain remained for him in this life. His Rose awaits him in the next."

I nodded sadly, finished my whisky and asked, "What will you report to Chesterfield?"

"I wish to discuss that with you, my dear fellow. I have sent word to the Professor and requested that he come by here after the museum closes tonight.

*****

Thus it was at seven-thirty that evening, Mrs. Hudson announced the arrival of Professor Chesterfield. She offered refreshment, but he politely declined and merely took the seat offered by Holmes.

He could not contain himself and immediately asked, "Have you got it, Holmes?"

"I have," said Holmes placidly, after a brief moment to draw out the suspense. "I should like to ask you a question however."

The next several minutes were spent discussing the bravery and reward for the actions of Professor Blanchard in this endeavour.

Once all details were agreed to, Holmes handed over the *Elegy*. The historian carefully opened and examined it. "Yes!" he cried. "It is intact and undamaged. Thank you, gentlemen!" He slipped the document into his briefcase and said, "I will take this back immediately tonight. I had a locksmith in today to change the lock as a precaution. Did you catch the thief, Mr. Holmes?"

"I am afraid he escaped beyond my purview, Professor. However, I did also retrieve this." He handed over the envelope with the ransom money.

Chesterfield took it and said, "However did you manage to get both?"

Holmes looked at me and said, "As Watson will tell you, I have resolved recently to be less forthcoming with my methods. I prefer my clients to be happy and amazed."

Holmes stood, effectively ending the interview, to Chesterfield's surprise. He also rose and placed the money into his inner breast pocket. "I shall return this tonight as well. Our benefactor will be glad to know his trust was justified."

As he walked toward the door, Holmes made one last comment, "You shall receive my bill for services rendered and nothing more. Good evening!"

Holmes went over to the mantel and stuffed his pipe, saying "Do be good enough to ring up Mrs. Hudson for dinner, Watson. I am famished!"

Appendix

Elegy Written in a Country Churchyard
Thomas Gray

The curfew tolls the knell of parting day,
The lowing herd wind slowly o'er the lea,
The plowman homeward plods his weary way,
And leaves the world to darkness and to me.

Now fades the glimm'ring landscape on the sight,
And all the air a solemn stillness holds,
Save where the beetle wheels his droning flight,
And drowsy tinklings lull the distant folds;

Save that from yonder ivy-mantled tow'r
The moping owl does to the moon complain
Of such, as wand'ring near her secret bow'r,
Molest her ancient solitary reign.

Beneath those rugged elms, that yew-tree's shade,
Where heaves the turf in many a mould'ring heap,
Each in his narrow cell for ever laid,
The rude forefathers of the hamlet sleep.

The breezy call of incense-breathing Morn,
The swallow twitt'ring from the straw-built shed,
The cock's shrill clarion, or the echoing horn,
No more shall rouse them from their lowly bed.

For them no more the blazing hearth shall burn,
Or busy housewife ply her evening care:
No children run to lisp their sire's return,
Or climb his knees the envied kiss to share.

Oft did the harvest to their sickle yield,
Their furrow oft the stubborn glebe has broke;
How jocund did they drive their team afield!
How bow'd the woods beneath their sturdy stroke!

Let not Ambition mock their useful toil,
Their homely joys, and destiny obscure;
Nor Grandeur hear with a disdainful smile
The short and simple annals of the poor.

The boast of heraldry, the pomp of pow'r,
And all that beauty, all that wealth e'er gave,
Awaits alike th' inevitable hour.
The paths of glory lead but to the grave.

Nor you, ye proud, impute to these the fault,
If Mem'ry o'er their tomb no trophies raise,
Where thro' the long-drawn aisle and fretted vault
The pealing anthem swells the note of praise.

Can storied urn or animated bust
Back to its mansion call the fleeting breath?
Can Honour's voice provoke the silent dust,
Or Flatt'ry soothe the dull cold ear of Death?

Perhaps in this neglected spot is laid
Some heart once pregnant with celestial fire;
Hands, that the rod of empire might have sway'd,
Or wak'd to ecstasy the living lyre.

But Knowledge to their eyes her ample page
Rich with the spoils of time did ne'er unroll;
Chill Penury repress'd their noble rage,
And froze the genial current of the soul.

Full many a gem of purest ray serene,
The dark unfathom'd caves of ocean bear:
Full many a flow'r is born to blush unseen,
And waste its sweetness on the desert air.

Some village-Hampden, that with dauntless breast
The little tyrant of his fields withstood;
Some mute inglorious Milton here may rest,
Some Cromwell guiltless of his country's blood.

Th' applause of list'ning senates to command,
The threats of pain and ruin to despise,
To scatter plenty o'er a smiling land,
And read their hist'ry in a nation's eyes,

Their lot forbade: nor circumscrib'd alone
Their growing virtues, but their crimes confin'd;
Forbade to wade through slaughter to a throne,
And shut the gates of mercy on mankind,

The struggling pangs of conscious truth to hide,
To quench the blushes of ingenuous shame,
Or heap the shrine of Luxury and Pride
With incense kindled at the Muse's flame.

Far from the madding crowd's ignoble strife,
Their sober wishes never learn'd to stray;
Along the cool sequester'd vale of life
They kept the noiseless tenor of their way.

Yet ev'n these bones from insult to protect,
Some frail memorial still erected nigh,
With uncouth rhymes and shapeless sculpture deck'd,
Implores the passing tribute of a sigh.

Their name, their years, spelt by th' unletter'd muse,
The place of fame and elegy supply:
And many a holy text around she strews,
That teach the rustic moralist to die.

For who to dumb Forgetfulness a prey,
This pleasing anxious being e'er resign'd,
Left the warm precincts of the cheerful day,
Nor cast one longing, ling'ring look behind?

On some fond breast the parting soul relies,
Some pious drops the closing eye requires;
Ev'n from the tomb the voice of Nature cries,
Ev'n in our ashes live their wonted fires.

For thee, who mindful of th' unhonour'd Dead
Dost in these lines their artless tale relate;
If chance, by lonely contemplation led,
Some kindred spirit shall inquire thy fate,

Haply some hoary-headed swain may say,
"Oft have we seen him at the peep of dawn
Brushing with hasty steps the dews away
To meet the sun upon the upland lawn.

"There at the foot of yonder nodding beech
That wreathes its old fantastic roots so high,
His listless length at noontide would he stretch,
And pore upon the brook that babbles by.

"Hard by yon wood, now smiling as in scorn,
Mutt'ring his wayward fancies he would rove,
Now drooping, woeful wan, like one forlorn,
Or craz'd with care, or cross'd in hopeless love.

"One morn I miss'd him on the custom'd hill,
Along the heath and near his fav'rite tree;
Another came; nor yet beside the rill,
Nor up the lawn, nor at the wood was he;

"The next with dirges due in sad array
Slow thro' the church-way path we saw him borne.
Approach and read (for thou canst read) the lay,
Grav'd on the stone beneath yon aged thorn."

The Epitaph

*Here rests his head upon the lap of Earth
A youth to Fortune and to Fame unknown.
Fair Science frown'd not on his humble birth,
And Melancholy mark'd him for her own.*

*Large was his bounty, and his soul sincere,
Heav'n did a recompense as largely send:
He gave to Mis'ry all he had, a tear,
He gain'd from Heav'n ('twas all he wish'd) a friend.*

*No farther seek his merits to disclose,
Or draw his frailties from their dread abode,
(There they alike in trembling hope repose)
The bosom of his Father and his God.*

COMING SOON

The Colourful Cases of Sherlock Holmes (Volume 2)

The Black Beast of The Hurlers Stones
The legend of a huge black cat threatens an archaeological dig on Bodmin Moor

The Crisis of Count de Vermilion
A French Count seeks Holmes's help against a blackmailer

The Blue Mystery at Windsor
A blue stain is the only evidence left behind when a lady-in-waiting to the Queen goes missing

The Pawnbroker's Apprentice and the Priceless Painting
Wiggins goes to work for Jabez Wilson and discovers a new case for Holmes

How Green the Valet
A dead valet exhibits a strange green hue to his skin – could his employer also be in danger?